TOXIC TIE

CW00750668

KEITH COUSINS

This book is a work of fiction. Any similarities to People, Places or Events is purely coincidental.

Thank you to my wonderful Wife Suzanne who had to put up with me throughout this whole process. Her input, time and again, proved to be invaluable.

Thanks also to me close friends, Phil Humphries and Tracy Fowler.

They know why

PROLOGUE

1979

The gusting North sea wind howled over the beach, ploughing up channels of sand that ran with rivers of the incoming tide. A gritty cloud of blown debris swirled in eddies, picking up long discarded ice cream sticks and greasy chip wrappers. The rain swept in on a shower of freezing needles, forming a screen of almost invisible wetness that seeped into everything. Black, threatening clouds, dense with freezing precipitation, advanced like Panzer battalions on to the sandy ramparts of the beach stretching into the distance.

Off in the distance to the North the misshapen, broken, rusted and partly dissected shape of the pier rose ghostly from the frothing white caps. For the best part of a century until the night of the 11th of January the year before when it succumbed to high spring tides and a North sea gale. The far end of the Pier, containing the Theatre and

Victorian shelters, had sheared away leaving a gaping chasm to be consumed and was now separated from the rest by the battering sea. The rusted and slime coated legs now groaned and screeched with the wind. Tired, bent and flaking painted signs creaked and moaned, offering tea, coffee, ice cream and other long forgotten Summer delights, their stalls on the landward anchored remains now shuttered, empty and desolate.

The rundown and tired seaside town on the English North East coast struggled against the late Autumn gloom to be something else but failed miserably. Its famous Jolly Farmer posters with their merry 'Skegness Is So Bracing' slogan seemed lost and out of place among the paint flaked drabbery. It's hay days long gone, it no longer shone as a magnet for holidaying families. Its Victorian splendour was now grime streaked and squalid. The draw of cheap flights to the Costas had taken the once bustling crowds to guaranteed sunshine, cheap booze and offered something it no longer had. Even in summer it failed to shine.

He eased the bike through the sandy morass that covered the car park. The putrid and gritty slurry stuck to the tyres and the bike snaked and slid as they searched for purchase amongst the gravel. Picking his way through the rutted and loose surface he aimed the machine at the kerb and killed the engine. The little 250 engine pinged as the heat dried the wet, slimy deposits caked to the cooling fins. The once shiny forks and gleaming petrol tank, that he spent so much time cleaning, now dripped with a dirty slick of grime. His waxed cotton jacket was sodden and ran with rivulets of rain water, clinging to his arms and chest like a straightjacket. Despite the addition of two other layers of woolly pully and now damp rugby shirt he had felt no protection from the biting Lincolnshire wind. After two hours of battling the driving rain, his jeans hugged his legs and the seemingly endless cold had driven all feeling from his numbed fingers. His eyes ached from the constant straining into the gloom through the grunge splattered visor that had spent more time up than down, and the tired remnants of the night shift he had completed that morning had left them feeling raw and grainy.

Guiding the small and fairly light machine into a parking space by paddling with both feet in the frothing puddles at the kerb edge he flicked down the prop stand and dismounted. Gripping the edge of the seat he eased the bike onto its main stand, taking in the tired, run down and generally grotty surroundings of the once proud jewel of the Lincolnshire coast. He fumbled the key, in two hands, between numbed thumbs, his fingers had long lost any useful feeling, into the steering lock on the handlebars and engaged the bolt. He was not sure who would be about in this filthy, grotty weather to try and steal it, but it was his pride and joy and he always made sure it was fully secured when left anywhere. Fumbling his raw fingers under his chin he battled with the strap to remove his crash helmet and stripped the soaked and misshapen gloves from his frozen hands, wetter on the inside than on the outside. Pushing the helmet and gloves into the bike's storage box perched high on its rack at the back he turned, hunched against the icy cold wind, to look back towards the nearby building at the end of the car park.

The only others around were a couple of hardy day trippers fighting upturned umbrellas as they trudged hopefully towards the town away in the distance. In the dank Winter afternoon it seemed unable to shake off the gathering funereal feel that threatened to envelope it. The weak street lights were already fighting to lift the afternoon murk, mini sand storms eddied across the worn and barren grass at the side of the promenade. The pitch and putt and crazy golf courses looked lost and forlorn in the middle of a marshy quagmire that had once been a manicured lawn.

He made his way slowly to the low building at the edge of the beach that housed the public toilets and, tucked on the end like a compromised late addition, a small café with steamed up windows. Even in Summer, he remembered, it offered nothing in the way of appeal and now in its Winter misery it looked hopeless and unwelcoming. Luckily, the toilets were open. He made his way through the open half of the metal mesh door, the other half still secured to the solid concrete doorpost with an industrial sized padlock. The inside smelled of urine and vomit and the floor was awash with water that was pouring from a cracked cistern pipe. Squinting through the flickering light provided by the one muck smeared strip light he made his way to the sink and was amazed to find it turned when he gripped it between his frigid hands. Surprisingly, as he propelled his tortured fingers to turn the tap, the water was almost hot as he ran his frozen hands under the brown, sandy ooze that dribbled from the rusted taps. His fingers at first tingled and then throbbed as the slow, steamy stream brought the blood coursing back to his fingertips. Shaking his steaming fingers, there was nothing to wipe them on, he made his way back through the grill door and out onto the slimy footpath at the side of the building.

Two raucous gulls wheeled overhead as he pushed the door open with his shoulder. He stamped his feet as he entered the café, more in an attempt to get the blood flowing to his feet than cleaning anything from his soaked boots. The choking, nauseous smell of cooking fat and damp clothing drifted on a cloud of steam and stale nicotine. Small rills of condensation ran down the inside of the windows and there was a musty, unloved air to the place. The small interior had a number of wooden tables covered with plastic chequered tablecloths that had seen better days. Huddled around the tables were worn, tired looking chairs arrayed in a defensive pattern, almost defying anyone to sit down. An array of beach balls, buckets and spades that looked out of place and longed for the summer visitors festooned a rusted and lopsided rack that leaned drunkenly against a small meccano like bookcase come display cabinet. Dog-eared picture postcards and unread holiday novels vied for prominence amongst the 'Kiss me Quick' hats. In the corner a single counter containing a glass fronted display case stood with a steaming boiler casting clouds of steam over it from behind.

Francis Martin, nineteen and Frank to his mates, surveyed the scene in front of him. In the corner of the dimly lit café a couple sat hunched over their half drained coffee cups, staring into the gloom beyond the watery halo cast by the dim lights of the interior. They were the only other customers and looked somewhat embarrassed that they had been brave enough to venture out in such dreary conditions. Both looked quickly down at their coffee cups as Frank surveyed the interior. Behind the tired looking counter stood a very bored looking girl of about his own age, absently peeling the backing from a discoloured beer mat, not even bothering to look up as he approached the counter. A small mound of discarded mat shredding was slowly turning to mush on the wet counter. She was not bad looking with streaky blonde hair falling over her shoulders onto the sides of her ample chest that a tight red sweater was fighting to contain. "Menu up there Duck." She drawled in a bored Lincolnshire twang, pointing loosely behind her head and loosing interest quickly she went back to the beer mat.

He ordered a bacon sandwich and a mug of coffee, watching as she slopped milk from a carton into the brown liquid. "Sugar's on the table. I'll bring your food over." She pointed in the vague direction of a stained table in the corner containing plastic tubs of various sachets and packets. He walked to the table and emptied two sugar sachets into his coffee, NATO standard, and took a sip of the hot bitter liquid, burning his tongue in the process. With the offer of food he suddenly remembered he hadn't had breakfast after his shift and hunger now gripped him as he walked away from the server. He took a seat at one of the Formica topped tables near the window, after disentangling the chairs, and watched as the persistent drizzle turned to a squally shower and wind rattled the door against its rusting hinges.

The ride over had taken longer than expected due to the howling Fenland wind that made him lean the bike against the buffeting at every bend in the road, and the rain had very quickly soaked through his gloves and ran in rivers up his arms. Fortunately, his waxed cotton jacket had kept most of his upper body dry, if not warm, but his jeans were now matted to his legs, soaked through. A puddle had formed in each of his boots and his toes were almost as frozen as his fingers. The long, white fisherman's socks had held it back as long as possible but even they had succumbed in the end. He slumped back in the chair and rubbed his sore eyes with the edge of his hand. The accumulated tiredness and the battle with the wind had made him feel exhausted and the hot coffee at least had started to revive him, even it it did taste like bilge water.

His reason for making the effort to come to a rundown, out of season and very cold seaside was something of a mystery. The note he discovered shoved under the door of his room on return from the night shift that morning had started the saga. "Sorry mate. I hate to do this but I have to go. There is a boat tonight and I must be on it. I want to explain, so meet me at the café by the beach. You're the only friend I have." It was scribbled on the back of a scrap of log pad and signed 'Yorkie'. Frank had been totally baffled by the note, but then Yorkie did have a tendency for the dramatic, and very often baffled him with his mildly off the wall behaviour. He usually put it down to his sheltered upbringing in a small industrial town in Yorkshire.

The café by the beach in the note could only mean one thing. They had both spent a couple of days off in the town a few weeks ago, catching the end of a brief Indian Summer. Mainly to kill the time of three days off between shifts and break the boredom of the usual endless beer nights in the club on camp. They were both on the same 'watch' and it tended to split into three bits at the end of the shift pattern. The married men, there were no women on their watch, would go home to their families on the married patch and the singlies, as they were known, would either go back to their home towns or spend the three days camped in the NAAFI bar.

Frank could only stand a very small amount of this very insular existence and tried to get away from camp when time off allowed, he had suggested to Yorkie they spend the 'stand down' on the coast and they had managed to get a reasonably priced B & B near the beach. Both had come armed with their newly purchased Zenit SLR cameras and brim full of enthusiasm that they were going to be the next Lord Litchfield or David Bailey. They had spent most of the first day taking snaps of everything that moved, and most of what did not, until they had both realised that without talent, enthusiasm was an underrated thing. Finally, having exhausted every angle of the Victorian pier with its middle collapsed into the North Sea, they had come to the run down café a number of times to sample the brown liquid that passed for coffee and the bacon rolls.

Kev Biddle, or Yorkie to everyone, was his closest mate. They had gone through training together at the sprawling camp in the Midlands to become Military Signals Operators and later when they specialised in Military Signals Intelligence at another out of the way and nondescript outpost of the military machine. Now they both worked deep 'underground' at the Top Secret facility on the Lincolnshire Wolds. The 'underground' bit was a running joke with the operators that served there. In reality the unit consisted of a hurriedly erected 'H' block built sometime in the 1950s perched on the edge of an old wartime airfield that had not seen an aircraft for at least thirty-five years. It stuck out like a sore thumb against the flat Fenland landscape and, due to its Top Secret work, would be very high on any list of Soviet targets should they chose to unleash nuclear death and destruction on the good people of Lincolnshire.

Yorkie, was older by two years and came from Barnsley in South Yorkshire, hence the nickname, Yorkie. He had previously been a Police cadet until he was asked to leave due to his 'lack of authority'. He was quiet and unassuming, probably the reason he was asked to leave the cadets, although he had a wicked sense of humour that erred on the dark side. Unlike Frank, he was totally unsporting and considered walking upstairs as enough exercise for one day, thank you. During basic training he had always been the one singled out by the Physical Training Instructor, or PTI in military speak, for extra reps when found to be slacking, much to the amusement of the rest of the squad. They had hit it off straight away and had become close friends over the previous eighteen months and were now junior tradesmen working rotating shift patterns analysing Soviet communications activities, or they had been until the Monday of the previous week.

Frank had been home on a couple of days leave and spent the day with some of his civilian mates in Cardiff. Finding that he now had very little in common with his old school buddies he had returned to his parents house early to a message from the local Police to return to camp immediately. They had received a message from the military, as was normal practice, to deliver the instruction in person rather than it be communicated by phone. Rumours had been circulating on the camp jungle telegraph for a few weeks about an upcoming surprise inspection exercise so he had guessed this was the callback that would kick it off. Far from being concerned at the message he was more than a little excited at the chance to play in his first real operational exercise. They had participated in many contrived exercises during training but this would be the first one at an operational unit, and the rumour mill had it that they were to deploy in full battle mode for this one. He made his way back to camp on the bike making up imaginary scenarios in his head during the three hour ride and trying to guess what form the exercise might take.

It was only on arrival at the Guardroom, he was told to report to the Officer Commanding the Administration Section, that he realised things might not be OK. The Guardroom Corporal had almost a look of glee on his face as he had imparted the directive. He had quickly stashed his stuff in his room in the barrack block and made his way across camp, skirting the sacred ground of the parade square that was always under the watchful eye of the Station Warrant Officer from his eyrie on high in the headquarters building. The imposing Station Headquarters, a relic of the stations flying days, was somewhere you only went to when ordered, and never entered through the front door.

Reporting to the Chief Clerk, an old school Warrant Officer with a fearful reputation, he was marched down the long back corridor and into the Admin OC's office. The Officer Commanding the Admin flight had barely looked up from his desk as he was shown into his office, had grunted something about Military Police and told Frank to take a seat in the corridor outside. The Warrant Officer had then marched him out again! He spent the next two hours kicking his heels sat in the austere corridor outside his office. Pictures of wartime flying aces and previous Station Commanders adorned the walls and there was an all pervading smell of floor polish. Eventually he was summoned, again marched in by the Warrant Officer, to a room upstairs.

The room was a vast space on the top floor of the building and was used by Senior Officers for briefings and meetings. Old style, wartime, lamp shades painted in the military's favourite colour scheme of drab green sheltered single bulbs at intervals down the centre of the room. A large, highly polished, conference table almost filled the space, with just enough room to get chairs around it. Black roller type blinds covered the metal framed windows that allowed the single bulbed lights to cast pools of eerie yellow illumination over the scene. Seated behind the table, both at the far end, were two 'gorillas' from the Special Investigation Branch of the Military Police. Frank only knew this was who they were because one of them had screamed at him "We are from the fucking SIB. Sit down!" It would appear that adding the unnecessary expletive to their organisation somehow made them feel even more important.

There was a fug of cigarette smoke drifting up to the high ceiling, swirling to meet the heat of the bulbs, and used butts were spilling from an ashtray onto the highly polished table. Whatever endeavour the two thugs had been embarked upon it would seem they had been at it for a long time. He was ordered to sit in a leather backed chair with polished ornate arms facing the two goons. One was about six feet tall, bald with a heavy set jaw that made him look like a bulldog. His shoulders stretched the material of the ill-fitting suit he wore so that it bulged at the chest. His fingers were nicotine stained and his face had the pallor of someone who didn't see fresh air or the light of day very much. It was his voice that had barked the order to sit down. The other was much shorter and scrawny looking with a dark moustache covering his top lip that made him look like one of the 'Village People' pop group. His sandy coloured hair had receded so much that the little that was left at the sides gave the impression of two rugs skirting a highly polished floor. It was 'Bulldog' who spoke first. "Right then." His voice was loud and echoed off the empty room. "We are not here to piss about. Just tell us what you have been up to with this mate of yours, and we can get this done and go home." As Frank had absolutely no idea what they were on about the 'interrogation' took a little longer than 'Bulldog' had anticipated.

During the two hours they made him stay in the room he was accused of everything from incest to murder, and had him guilty of it all until proven as innocent, the usual military way of doing things. Through the constant babble of 'Mr Bulldog Nasty' and 'Mr Village People Nice' he managed to make out, that they were talking about something that Yorkie had allegedly been up to. It allegedly involved one of the Corporals and an act of a very unsavoury nature involving homosexual acts, which were illegal in the military, but beyond that he had no real idea what they were trying to get at. He had no idea about any of the things they were putting to him, but this just seemed to piss them off. He got the distinct impression they wanted a confession from him, any confession would do, so they could call it a day and go for a pint.

Eventually, after what seemed like hours, they let him go with the threat of further harassment, and physical violence, if he spoke to anyone about anything. There was a fat chance of that as he didn't know anything, unlike, it seemed, the rest of the camp. He had suspected from the moment the Guardroom Corporal had given him a sly wink on delivering the message, that maybe whatever the issue was, it was already common knowledge amongst the troops. On returning to his room in the barrack block his suspicions were confirmed and the place was alight with the story. It seemed they all seemed to know everything, or if they didn't they made it up anyway. The truth was never popular in the military when invention could produce a much better yarn. The story, which grew bigger with each telling, was that Yorkie had been the centrepiece of some sordid homosexual gang bang involving increasing numbers of otherwise unidentified Corporals, and higher ranks, the details of which became more and more depraved and sordid as time progressed. By the time Frank had showered and made his way to the club for a well earned, and desperately needed drink, Yorkie was the only topic of discussion on camp.

The unelected council of barrack room lawyers that exists in every military unit had decided unanimously, that whatever the charge was, then Yorkie was absolutely guilty of it. The fact that he was not around to defend himself and offer some kind of explanation to the increasingly wild allegations mattered not one bit. His guilt was definite and if by some chance he made an appearance the gallows would have been quickly erected for the prosecution of the ultimate sentence. But as no one knew where exactly he was, that eventuality never came to pass.

13

No one really knew what was going on beyond the mere presence of SIB on a base makes whatever the incident is, a very serious one. Most day to day 'crime' on any camp is normally dealt with by Squadron or Station Commanders rather than the military police, whose job is mainly harassment, which they excel at, and standing guard on the main gate, which they do not. After a couple of days the hysteria had abated to such an extent that the cook-house chatter had returned to its usual fare of football and who was organising the next troop piss-up.

Frank was none the wiser, really, until he was called into the Watch Commanders office during the first night shift following the hysteria and Yorkie's disappearance. "Sit down Martin." It was an order, not a request. Frank dragged the chair from the corner of the office and sat down facing the officer. "I understand you and Biddle spend a lot of time together?" He said without looking up from the desk where there were a number of forms loosely arranged. Flight Lieutenant Mills had been with the watch less than Frank and Yorkie, about six weeks. He was slightly older than the usual troop commanders who were usually in their first post after officer training. Rumour had it that Mills had already done two tours, one as liaison to the Special Forces Flight. This was the first opportunity he'd had to pull any of the operators in for anything other than a friendly chat. The unit was a Joint Services Signals Unit, or JSSU, and much to the Army's disgust had officers and operators from all three services, although the Navy tried to avoid the posting if they could, preferring to serve with their own kind if at all possible. Frank had replied in the affirmative which to his surprise was met with a smile and a gentle nod from the other side of the desk. "Well I'm not too bothered about all that. I am sure SIB will get to the bottom of it all. Young Biddle won't be coming back to us, unfortunately, and I understand something unsavoury has been occurring within the camp of which he has been a part."

Frank nodded and smiled weakly. "I thought it was about that Sir, that you wanted to see me." If it wasn't about Yorkie then he had no idea, unless SIB were still trying to implicate him in something he really had no clue about. On the night in question, as the legal people liked to say, he had been on nights and had not seen Yorkie until four days later as he had gone straight on his rest days in Wales. Yorkie had been given a 'stand down' from the final night shift and had supposedly gone to Nottingham that night with some of the guys from 'D' shift, which was unusual for him, and this had turned into a 'long weekender', even though it was midweek. It had struck Frank as slightly odd at the time as Yorkie was not really one for the nightlife but he had guessed that, being at a loose end with his own watch on nights, he had been persuaded to tag along. Although no real pattern had emerged, thinking about it now, Yorkie had been spending more time away from the camp than he normally did. Frank had just shrugged that off as meaning he had found some interest more suited to his reclusive nature and had not given it much thought.

Shuffling the forms on his desk Flight Lieutenant Mills cleared his throat. "I understand you've put in a request to try for CSS. Is that correct?" Frank was taken aback by the quick change of direction and was momentarily taken off guard. He had indeed applied to try for selection to the Combined Signals Service, a highly trained specialist unit, drawn from all three services, that provided Communications and Intelligence to Special Forces, but with so little experience in the job he doubted if his application would even leave the camp, never mind actually making it to the department in MOD that dealt with such things. In addition no one could in reality remember the last time anyone from the RAF had actually been successful in getting beyond the application phase. Most of the posts were given to the Royal Signals Special Operators, or Spec Ops as they were known. Was this going to be the gentle let down from the OC with a 'try again another time' added on the end?

Mills continued without waiting for an answer. "Well, I am very pleased to tell you that you have been accepted on to the next selection course. It would seem that our Army colleagues are trying to be inclusive. I wish you all the best, I may see you at Selection as I have been offered the chance to try for the Troop Commanders Cadre." Another first if he was to be successful as there had never been an RAF, or Navy for that matter, Troop Commander at CSS. He handed the paperwork across the desk "And let's put this Biddle nonsense behind us shall we?" Frank had been doubly gob smacked, that not only had his application been accepted but that the OC was going as well. Although on different elements of the selection process, the Troop Commanders Cadre was a temporary pool post, he hoped he would see the CO during the course.

Footstepsand the shuffling of feet brought him out of his reverie. The blonde stood over him with his bacon sandwich extended in her outstretched hand. "You Martin?" She chirped, somehow more awake than she had first appeared. "Some bloke left this for you, said he couldn't wait." She offered him a brown A4 envelope, complete with greasy smears from being sat on the counter amongst the cooking debris.

She smiled at him and pushed her chest out. The tight, thin top she wore made her breasts look bigger and her nipples were trying to explode from the front. Frank, making sure his observance did not go unnoticed, took the envelope from her, carefully avoiding contact with the offered mounds. "Yes, I'm Frank Martin. Thank you."

She made her way back to her beer mat and managed to wiggle her tight jeans enough to catch the eye of the only other people in the place, who quickly turned away when she stopped to collect their mugs. With a scrape of chairs they stood and made their way out of the café. The performance had been purely for his benefit and he was

16

now the only one left in the building. On returning to her place behind the counter she leaned forward towards where Frank was sitting, making sure he had an ample view of her assets as they sat on the counter. He turned away from the smile and the proffered delights to concentrate on the envelope in his hand.

He had been in two minds anyway, when finding the note, as to why he should make the trip at all. Yorkie had obviously either done a bunk or been removed to somewhere known only to the powers that be. Since the meeting with the Watch Commander and the resurgence of the rumour mill adding more and more to the story, he felt he wanted nothing more to do with Yorkie Biddle. The gossipmongers had now added passing secrets to the Russians to the increasingly sordid homosexual antics, and he just wanted to get himself right for the forthcoming selection process. But, Yorkie was his best mate and he felt he owed him the chance to at least explain himself, so he had struggled against the elements to get here even though he was knackered from the night shift, and now the fucker hadn't even turned up!

He ripped the top from the envelope with an aggressive yank and removed the hand written A4 sheet it contained, at least he hadn't written it on a log sheet this time! The unmistakable scrawl of Yorkie's hand covered both sides of the paper.

'Hi mate, sorry I'm not there to talk to you. I had to get away from the base pretty sharpish and I expect the balloon has gone up and they will be after me bloody quick.

Not sure what you have heard about me or what you believe. I expect there are lots of rumours about me and what I've been doing. The truth is mate I didn't mean to do any of it but it just sort of took me over and now I can't undo it. I'm scared shitless mate but I can't hang about. They have told me I will go to prison and not a military jail, probably the Scrubs or something. I can't do that mate.

You've probably heard about me having sex with one of the Corporals. Well mate that bit is true. I got drunk one night, after that night out in Nottingham, and ended up naked in his bed in the block and we did stuff to each other, and I went back the next night and did it again. I didn't want to mate, but once I was doing it I couldn't stop, trouble is there were others and I liked it with them as well. I'm not gay or anything pal but I just can't stop when we start doing it.'

Frank couldn't quite believe what he was reading from the note. He had slept in the bed next to Yorkie in a sixteen man room all through training and had never suspected him of being gay or having any tendencies in that direction. Yes, he was a bit quiet and reserved when it came to the opposite sex but he was a bit quiet and reserved anyway. Frank put it down to his Yorkshire way. As far as he was aware he was straight and fancied girls as much as they all did. He always joined in the sexually explicit banter that seemed to dominate barracks conversation, especially in the NAAFI after copious amounts of beer, and he would have said he was as 'normal' as the rest of them. Shit, he'd even seen him pick women up at the 'grab a granny' nights in the club. Now he was reading that his best mate was a fucking queer!

'It's been going on for a bit mate and it's sort of got worse. I was going to Corporal Webb's bed most nights mate, he was the first. Do you remember that trip to London I went on?'

18

Frank had been in the Midlands at the Air Force Athletics championship and had thought it a bit strange that Yorkie had gone to London, but never really asked him why.

'Well I went down there with Corporal Webb. We met this guy in a nightclub and they both had me in a big four poster in some posh hotel. He was a Russian. After that Webb asked me to start bringing out some stuff from work. At first I wouldn't do it. But he promised to do all the things I liked if I did, so I was bringing stuff out to him.'

All the material they worked on was highly classified and most of it was above TOP SECRET. No written work was allowed out through the security check points and even scrap paper had to be destroyed at the end of the shift. He just couldn't get his head around where this was leading, how fucking deep had Yorkie got himself? A bit of illegal rodgering from a queer Corporal was one thing but this was way, way beyond his comprehension.

'I've been taking stuff out of the bins mate and carrying it out after nearly every shift. I met the Russian guy down town a few times and I've been taking the stuff to him. When SIB interviewed me about the sex stuff they didn't seem to know any of the other stuff mate. I just sort of blurted it all out. Trouble is Webb told them it was all down to me and I'd made all the sex stuff with him up. They believed him for a bit, as he is a Corporal, but they have since pulled him and the others in. Anatoly, that's the guy I met said he can get me away. SIB took me to Wyton, RAF Wyton but I wasn't locked up or anything. They put me in a block with other guys waiting for investigations to finish. They kept dragging me in for questioning and kept telling me I was going to prison, so I just walked out. Anatoly was waiting for me mate and he and another guy, don't know his name, took me to a hotel up here. They told me we can't hang around though. They have arranged for me to go tonight mate. Sorry Franny, you are my best

19

mate and I don't want to go. They say we are getting away out of Hull mate on a boat to somewhere. I don't want to go, Frank, I just want everything back the way it was. We could come back here and take photos again mate. I think we sail about 2100 mate, not sure what the boat is called. You need to come and get me Frank, I can't go where they are taking me. Maybe I will see you later?'

Frank dropped the note into the coffee dregs that had formed a lake on the Formica. The light had now gone from the day and the pale yellow street lamps were casting insipid shadows that seemed to dance in the wind. The girl was turning off switches behind the counter and half-heartedly sweeping a cloth back and forth over the stained surfaces. Outside the windows the gulls screeched and wheeled in the wind. "Is everything all right?" She asked as she wiggled towards him flicking the cloth at the tables on her way, making sure her breasts swayed as she walked. "You seem a bit shocked?"

He looked up from the table at the once more proffered breasts as she came closer to him. They seemed to have grown in the last half an hour or was she just thrusting them further towards him? Her tight jeans followed the curve of her hips and he was drawn to the tight cleft between her legs that seemed to be accentuated by the stretched material. "I'm OK. My best mate has just done a bunk. Nothing serious really. He was supposed to meet me here but never turned up. Bit of a wasted journey." He didn't really know what Yorkie expected him to do. He had obviously got himself into something he could never get out of. If SIB tracked him down he would go to prison for a long, long time. Maybe the option to get away is the best for you mate?

The girl smiled at him. "That's a shame." The sympathy was forced but she continued to lean towards him. "Maybe you could give me a hand, I'm locking up now, cheer you up like?" She walked to the door and locked it and jiggled her way to the small stockroom behind the counter. Frank stuffed the envelope into the pocket of his jeans and followed her out to the back room, maybe it wasn't going to be a wasted journey after all. As he reached the small back room the girl was reaching up to close the window high up the wall with her back to him, her jeans had slid downwards revealing the swell of her buttocks as she arched up towards the window. Frank reached up to support her as she closed the sash on the ancient window. As she turned to face him his hands slipped around her body and lightly rested on her chest. Taking his right hand she pushed it beneath her top and leaned against him. Frank eased the material of the top further up with his other hand and unfasted the front clasp on her bra. Her large, unfettered breasts, now released from their confinement, spilled towards him.

Yorkie must have known what he was doing Frank thought as he made his way out to the bike. He just couldn't believe that he would have allowed himself to be taken in by these people. He checked his pocket to make sure the folded beer mat with the girl's phone number on it was securely lodged. Don't know about you Yorkie but I definitely prefer my dates with big tits and a nice arse, he thought as he swung his leg over the bike's seat and secured his still soaking gloves on to his, now warm hands.

The long ride back had given him time to think about why Yorkie had done what he had, and more importantly why. But even in the days following he could not come up with a reason. The camp had returned to something like normality in the last few days before Frank left for his CSS Selection Course. No one was really giving Yorkie a second thought and it was if he had never existed. Frank for his part had to concentrate on his preparation and was probably as guilty as the rest in letting the whole incident fade away. He did manage to make two further trips back to the coast though!

2017

ONE

Through the mist and smoke figures could be seen desperately trying to find cover amongst the scrub and bracken. Tracer laced the sky in sheets as a maelstrom of red hot horror ploughed into the advancing, smoke shrouded figures. High on the slopes to the front, machine guns rained down from their concealed and protected positions. Starting in the last remnants of the dark night, the advance over the open moorland had slowed as the opposition now trained their heavy machine guns on to the troops below, aided by the lifting dawn light.

From their concealed vantage point on the hillside the SAS intelligence unit could only observe the unfolding carnage below. "For fuck sake Fifer. Have we got permission to engage yet?" The question came from a scrape at the edge of the hollow the patrol was concealed in. Operating as forward close reconnaissance the eight man composite team had observed the battle unfold below them as the Paras crossed the open ground towards the settlement. Composed of four troopers from 22 SAS and three specialist Intelligence operators the team led by a CSS Officer were concealed at the side of the slope, relaying identifying intelligence back to the Brigade Headquarters at the beachhead. They had been active for almost two weeks after landing covertly and had covered a large amount of ground providing in-depth intelligence on the movement and positioning of the enemy. As the beachhead had been established and the Paras and Royal Marines had been given their orders to engage the patrol had started to withdraw, its job completed. As they made their way back to the beachhead they had received amended orders to confirm enemy positions at the settlement before continuing their withdrawal.

From their concealed positions on the hillside they could see troops caught out in the open as the torrent rained down from the hidden guns. Their role was one purely of Intelligence collection, their job had been completed and they were about to depart when the attack had commenced. No one from Brigade had thought it necessary to tell them that an imminent attack was about to take place on the settlement they had been observing for the past twelve hours. The Intelligence they had gathered and relayed had obviously formed part of the planning but the position of the guns on the ridge had either been ignored or deemed to be a necessary obstacle to overcome. Although the approach had commenced a few hours earlier in the protection of darkness, early morning daylight had now revealed the approaching troops to the defending guns and they were sitting targets out in the open with little or no cover. Someone, somewhere up the chain of command had decided a full on frontal assault was the best option, somewhat negating the need for Intelligence gathering. Although only lightly armed for team protection, permission to engage from their concealed position had been requested from the Head Shed through Special Forces channels, by the Troop Commander, bypassing Brigade. Although having only personal weapons the SAS troopers felt they could make a difference to the carnage that was unfolding before them. Fifer had transmitted the signal using the new battlefield satellite system, one of only two in operation, via the encrypted fast burst radio he carried.

23

"Permission denied Sir. Proceed with withdrawal out of area." The answer was not what any of them wanted, but it was an order. Standing by and watching your fellow troops hammered was not in their nature. They were elite operators and this, in their opinion, was what they were there to do. Much of the equipment they carried was highly sensitive and it was to be protected at all costs. It was the role of other troops to fight the war whilst theirs was to provide the Intelligence to enable them to do so. The three specialist operators as well as being highly trained in their fields were also competent special forces soldiers and not just along for the ride.

The Troop Commander, Flight Lieutenant Mills, rose to his feet in a half crouch. "I'm going forward. I can't watch this." Although an RAF officer, he was highly regarded by the SAS men, he was one of the better CSS cadre officers. Mills' talent was recognised by both the men in his troop and the senior officers in the regiment for his military ability and the leadership and compassion he showed. He had only taken five crouching steps out into the open before the heavy rounds started to stitch a pattern towards him over Fifer's left shoulder. As he ran, the rounds danced over the ground and sought out their target, slamming mercilessly into his back and legs. Out of the corner of his eye Fifer saw the Troop Sergeant, a burly Scottish SAS man, lung forward after the CO. "Get down Sarge!" His call was lost in the cacophony of sound from behind and the stammering gunfire as the rest of the troop opened up. The Sergeant dived for cover amongst the peat and provided some protection to the prone form of the CO as he lay thirty metres in front of Frank's position.

Frank, Fifer to the troop and his call sign, crawled forward, his hands trembling and shaking, until he was alongside the CO. Frank had a deep respect and affinity for the Officer, having served with him in his previous role. He had also gone through his CSS training at the same time as Mills had joined the Officer Cadre. This was the *first action he had encountered since joining the troop six months ago. They had trained and trained for moments like this, but now it was here his body was reacting. Pulling the boss over, he strained to cover him as he brought his weapon up to his shoulder, struggling to control the spasms in his arms, rolling on to his back he directed his fire, firing one handed, in the general direction of the incoming fire storm, adding to the rounds being laid down by the Troop Sergeant. Using his legs, and his free arm hooked through the officer's webbing, he drove into the wet peat and dragged him back, inch by inch, to the shallow scrape. The ground was shaking from the impacting shells that were now seeking out his position. Wet peat clods, earth and bracken flew into the air and covered his face and arms. He rolled the inert body of Mills into a slight downward slope behind their position, facing away from the direction of the onslaught.*

As the patrol formed an all round defence on the shallow cover Frank pulled a field dressing from his webbing and applied pressure to the wounds in the officer's legs and lower back. He broke open the OC's morphine ampoule and thrust it into his arm.

Wakingwith a start and rolling on to his side, wiping the sweat that was pouring into his eyes from his face, now fully awake, Frank Martin eased himself out of the side of the bed, trying not to wake his sleeping wife. The sheet he had been lying on was soaked with sweat. The dream was always the same one and this time of year, approaching Remembrance Day, came more frequently. He still had a great fondness, and feeling of guilt over the loss of Mills. Over the years the images and memories had become more vivid, he could almost feel the wet peat and smell the cordite laced smoke. It was a long time ago but always fresh in his mind. He had been very young then, but also an experienced operator. That first raw exposure to combat had left scars deep within. For years he had hidden the memories away, locked them in a box deep inside his head, along with many others gathered along the way. He had managed to get on with his career, get on with his life. There had been other horrors over the years, but that first time on that desolate hillside was the one that kept returning. Time and again in his head Frank battled to save his Commanding Officer, battled to cover his wounds, battled with his own embedded guilt, battled to no avail.

The CO hadn't made it despite his, and other's, efforts. Within minutes of the action that morning the troop had again been ordered to leave the hillside. Leaving the unfolding carnage around the settlement had been the hardest part. They had recovered Mills' body and taken him with them as they withdrew. At the subsequent board of enquiry the blame had been squarely placed upon their CO for endangering the whole patrol, disobeying a direct order to withdraw and recklessly sacrificing his own life. Frank and the other CSS members had been kept quiet with promotions, something he had accepted as part of being in an elite military unit but now regretted, and the SAS guys had just got on with their jobs. No awards or commendations were ever made and their role in the attack, or even the conflict, was never acknowledged and hidden in heavily redacted documents even to this day.

In his mid-fifties now Frank was still very fit for his age and very light on his feet. Many years of maintaining the highest level of fitness and nearly as many years on covert ops, both in and out of uniform, had made a habit of stealthy movement. These days however, as a deskbound warrior, his only opportunity to practice field craft was creeping up on the cat in the kitchen! That he no longer filled the role that he had loved for so long sometimes fell heavily on his shoulders. He had loved the job, both in and out of uniform, but age was catching up with him and others, younger and more able, had taken over the front line job. Not that there was much of a front line job left, the focus these days was on cybercrime and combating extremist recruitment on the Internet.

The fitness though was another thing. Right from the early days of his military career, and before, he had been a dedicated and successful distance runner. At school it had been the one sport he had excelled at, beating boys much older than himself and winning area and county championships at an early age. It was the running fitness and endurance that had given him the edge all those years ago during the CSS Selection. Competing alongside potential SAS recruits he had surprised the Army by coming top in all the physical endurance tests, his slight frame belying his strength, even when carrying increasingly heavy loads. The years of endurance training had also given him the depth of mental fortitude to withstand the deprivation and fatigue that built up over the course of the selection process. He was one of only three CSS applicants to pass out, the other two from the Royal Signals, and one of only fifteen in total from a starting number of eighty-five.

The distance and, eventually, marathon running combined with the physical stress of his two careers had eventually taken it's toll. A serious illness, cancer, twelve years before had almost derailed him but the deep determination and will to survive, developed over many tough times, had allowed him to beat it off and he was probably as fit now as he had ever been, allowing a few degrees for age! Five days a week he still drove his body to its limits, admittedly more in the gym these days than the hours pounding the roads he had done at his peak. Back to very close to the fighting weight of his younger days, he still had the competitive streak that kept him striving to be as fit as he could. His hair was thinning and turning increasingly grey but his relatively slight frame still had a hardened, toned edge.

Sunday mornings were the one luxury he allowed himself. No gym, late start and a couple of hours with the papers. When the dreams allowed, a lie in with his beautiful wife, Samantha and never Sam, a day just re-charging the batteries. He had married Samantha following his illness and a following dark period in his life. Samantha was so different to anyone he had known before. She was highly educated, intelligent and most of all she loved him for what he was, not for what she thought he should be. They loved to lie in bed on a Sunday, reading the papers, with nothing to really get up for. Unfortunately, this time of year, the dreams seemed to intrude on most of his mornings.

Filling the kettle, he flicked on his phone, he hated the intrusion that work issues might bring and to be fair to the duty officers they very rarely called him unless something really needed his attention. Most of the stuff that arrived overnight was mainly follow up details from the Americans on operations they were running. Very little of it these days was a priority, plus the other agencies had already cherry picked the good stuff! He punched open the voicemail and listened to the message alerts as he spooned coffee into the mugs, there was nothing of any real urgency, just updates from ongoing operations. He quickly scanned the drivel on Facebook, used mainly these days to keep track of his grown up children who were spread far and wide with careers and families of their own, stopping at the "friends request" that flashed in the corner of the screen. These were usually from people he had never known and were usually deleted without reading. Although lately he had received some contacts from long forgotten military colleagues that had rekindled memories, not always good ones.

Takinghis cup through to the lounge he idly flicked open the request. The screen flashed open 'Friends request from Kevin Biddle.' Just seeing the name made him recoil after all this time. "What the fuck?" He half dropped and half placed his cup on the coffee table, startling the cat who had taken up residence in the chair opposite. Someone must be taking the piss. Kevin Biddle? Yorkie? It must be nearly forty years since all that had blown up and he had disappeared. He thumbed the name to take him to the Facebook page, no photo. Scrolling down to the 'About' details he didn't really know what he was hoping to find, but was a little surprised to find 'Royal Air Force Retired' written under the occupation banner. The only Air Force you ever retired from was the Russian one, you fucking ran away from ours!

The memories of the aftermath of the 'incident' were all too vivid. Almost as vivid as the recurring dreams but not as painful. He remembered the day he returned to camp after his ride to the coast all those years ago. The place was crawling with Military Police officers, Royal Military plods and Special Investigations Branch. A lockdown had been called, all leave cancelled and everyone confined to barracks for the foreseeable future. On returning to his room in the block the doors on his personal locker had been forced open and all his belongings were strewn around the room, along with those of the other occupants. Red capped RMPs were rampaging through the block, seemingly under no ones control or authority, forcing open doors of locked rooms amid a cacophony of shouted abuse from the blocks inhabitants and the running of studded boots on the polished floors.

The invasion of their living quarters continued for a number of days with no explanation as to what exactly they were looking for until the Commanding Officer, determined to restore some order, ordered them off the camp until such time as a logical plan could be presented. Unfortunately, as he did not deserve it, he was fairly soon after relieved of his duties, but the camp did return to some kind of normality. The investigation into what exactly had occurred continued for many months and it was eventually decided there had been a small ring of conspirators, led by a Corporal called Don Webb from the same shift as Yorkie and Frank, who had been luring young operators, of which Yorkie was one, into compromising acts and then blackmailing them. Webb, it emerged during the lengthy investigation that followed, had been passing information to his Russian contact for many years, himself having been compromised during a posting in West Berlin, and was now acting as a recruiter.

A number of the ring ended up in court at the Old Bailey. The enormous pile of documentary evidence produced by the prosecution had them guilty as charged. Due to the intervention of a team of very expensive defence barristers and evidence of confessions gained under duress, the duty Police Sergeant and his team had basically kicked the shit out of them to obtain a guilty plea, no one was ever punished. Yorkie and one other had taken the offer from the Russians and left on a boat from Hull the night it all kicked off. The other guy, a young lad called Davies with only six months service, was eventually handed back in Berlin in a prisoner swap and joined the others at the Old Bailey. Yorkie, for a reason no one could work out at the time, seemed to be treated in a very different way to the others and seemed to have something else that kept him useful to the Russians. There was never any suggestion of him being handed back, nor any evidence to suggest he wanted to come back. Frank had learned much later as part of the Intelligence community that many attempts had been made by MI6 to negotiate an exchange but had been rebutted by Yorkie himself and not the Russian authorities.

The only person to suffer in the whole sorry saga was the Commanding Officer, Wing Commander Welsh, who was Court Marshalled and stripped of his commission for allowing the ring to operate on his camp. Exactly how he was supposed to have stopped it was never explained. If SIB, Special Branch and its army of goons had no inkling it was going on then how was he, as Commanding Officer of a secret signals unit supposed to find out. His role was the efficient day to day running of an operational echelon not spying on every member of it. Frank had been alarmed to learn many years later that he had committed suicide. It transpired that he had been the son of a decorated Battle of Britain Ace and he could not live with the shame it had brought on the family.

He clicked the 'accept' button on the friends request, his professional brain had been alerted, but still thought this was just someone taking the piss. After all, anyone could create an account in any name, but why the fuck would you want to create an account in the name of a traitor that had been missing presumed gobbled by the Russians, literally, for thirty-eight years. He placed his mobile on the coffee table and re-boiled the kettle to take Samantha her coffee in bed, another of their Sunday morning rituals.

While he waited for the water to boil his mind drifted back to those times many years before. Little more than a month after Yorkie had disappeared Frank had gone on his three weeks selection course for the CSS. Two weeks of the most physically gruelling activity he had ever done followed by a week of intense technical testing and examination. The physical part of the selection process had been taken in his stride as he had pushed his body to the limit and beyond in preparation. The week of intense technical and academic testing on the other hand had nearly been his downfall. Although he considered himself averagely intelligent, the depth of technical understanding required had explained why not many Air Force operators made the grade. The Royal Signals training provided to the Spec Ops at that time was far superior to that offered to the RAF, hence the number of Signalmen that made it through.

He had been successful, despite struggling to make the required grades in the technical tests, and almost immediately had been posted for nine months intense training, both infantry based with the Parachute Regiment and at the Royal Signals School at Blanford. He had immensely enjoyed the regime of getting stuck into learning new disciplines. One of the most intense phases had been Pegasus Company, or P Company as it was known by the Paras, a five day testing period designed to weed out those not suitable. The aggressive physicality of the testing period had played to his strengths and he had emerged as one of the top ever candidates.

On successful completion of the training he joined number 12 Combined Signals Troop attached to the Second Battalion of the Parachute Regiment. The attachment of CSS to the Paras had been extremely unpopular since its inception due to the overwhelming elitist feeling within the regiment. Within a few months of Frank joining the unit the MOD, under intense pressure from the Parachute Regiment hierarchy decided that the CSS would be better deployed with the Royal Signals SAS support unit 264 Signal Squadron, so they were subsumed into the Squadron, but kept their very unique identity by wearing a CSS flash on their battledress. The CSS were not just signallers, 264 had enough of them, but were experts in Intelligence in the spheres of Advanced Communications, Radar and Electronic Warfare. When the conflict with Argentina blew up CSS operators were very quickly deployed with the SAS Intelligence gathering teams as the Task Force gathered to sail South.

Over the following nine years Frank Martin had supported various elements of the Special Forces in many of the hotspots around the World, but it was that first operation that had left the vivid memories, recurring dreams and scars, both physical and mental. Until recently he felt he had it all safely locked away in the mental strong boxes, nailed down, that still existed in his head. But the dreams were becoming more and more real and sometimes he awoke with the smells and sounds of the intense battlefield all around him.

He did not know why after all this time such images and memories should return. He had carved out a successful career in the Intelligence world, both Military and Civil, and had raised a family to have successful careers of their own. Over the many years since that conflict he had never given any of it a second thought. Yes, he respectfully paid his respects to fallen colleagues at Remembrance time each year, but otherwise the memories were well hidden. It was only in the last few years that those vivid retentions had made a return. He could not explain why, and his usual response of throwing himself into hard gym work no longer seemed to work.

With his military career behind him, his technical and operational experience had led him, after a number of abortive attempts at self employment, to the Intelligence Services. His twenty-five years service milestone had been reached a number of months ago and he was now nearing retirement from his second rewarding career. He had married Samantha eight years ago, she was an Intelligence Research Analyst and they both worked for the same organisation. They had met when Frank had spent six months attached to MI5, where she ran a team of analysts. Following his illness, he had been seconded to the service while he had been convalescing, and not fit for operational work. In the Aftermath of the 7/7 London bombings he had been attached to a small team looking at long term Terrorist planning, reconstructing previous attacks in the hope of gleaning possible pattern data and pointers to future attacks.

Although it had been a worthwhile exercise it was not what he was about and seeing all the operational activity going on without him in the weeks following the attacks had depressed him. He had worked alongside some excellent analysts, one being Samantha, who had supported and encouraged him to prove the medical people wrong and to get his fitness back to the required standard. He and Samantha had grown closer together in the few short months he was with the team and they had married a year later. They were both happily looking forward to the day they could head for the sun. Samantha herself had left MI5 not long after marrying Frank and was now the leading Research Analyst in the office.

Spooning sugar into the cup, he returned to see the screen of his mobile flashing. A 'personal message' box filled the screen from 'Kevin Biddle.' He clicked the dialogue box open. "Hello mate. It's been a long time. Yes, it is me. Your old mate Yorkie." He just stared at the screen for a few minutes. After forty years it really was Yorkie, what the fuck was going on?

"I'm back, back in the country mate. Been away a long time I know but I really needed to come back. Lots of things have happened, lots of things I need to deal with pal. I got things to do mate. Can't explain on this thing Franny. Not very good at this technology lark. I thought I would look my old pal up though. Come and meet me mate. You know the place. See you tomorrow about 12." The dialogue box disappeared from the screen. He quickly pulled up his 'friends' list, no sign of Kevin Biddle. This really was bollocks! A guy he had heard nothing about or from for nearly four decades, suddenly appears on Social Media asking him to meet like long lost buddies in a shitty seaside town one hundred and fifty miles away. For what? A chit chat? Catch up on old times? Someone really was fucking him about.

Frank had enjoyed two brilliant careers, served his country well and was now, so he said, winding down towards retirement. But what about you Mr Biddle? Where have you been all these years? What have you been up to? What does your appearance now, if indeed it is you, mean? One thing he had learned in all his years in the intelligence community was never take anything at face value. Most things were not what they first appeared and he was not about to start now.

Following his disappearance all those years ago nothing more had been heard about his close friend but it had been assumed that he had been taken in by the Russians just as the net was about to close around him. It was discovered during the investigation, and after, that he had been snared in a wide ranging operation by the KGB that had been infiltrating military communications and intelligence units for many years. Their targets, and successes, had ranged far and wide to most areas where the British military had bases including the UK, Germany and Cyprus. They had dug deep within the established units dedicated to watching and listening to them, keen to learn the methods used and block the access. They had probed and recruited the most vulnerable and weakest, and those that were stronger they

34

had trapped, usually, as in Yorkie's case, with drink and free sex, the squaddie's favourite vices.

With the help of one of the Corporals, himself previously compromised, on the Squadron, Yorkie had been identified, lured and trapped. Frank himself had been told during his own questioning after his disappearance, that Yorkie had been a willing participant in some of the more extreme forms of gay sexual practice which in those days of the late 1970s was seen as both illegal in the military and very definitely immoral.

The operation had been running for a number of years until it was finally stopped with a very public trial of a number of service personal who had been passing material to their handlers while stationed in Cyprus. As in Yorkie's case it was more about those involved getting cold feet and admitting their guilt than the authorities actually uncovering any wrongdoing. The British system of security vetting had been found wanting on many occasions over the years and there were many cases of traitors giving themselves up rather than being caught. To this day the system seemed to chew up a large amount of resource, piss people off, and never actually prevent would-be traitors from working in the field of Intelligence. In fact modern vetting practice had now discarded the probing of political leaning and sexual practice to concentrate solely on how much money people had in their bank accounts. The powers that be, frightened to death by political correctness, had decided that anyone considering betraying their country would only be doing it for money.

At the time it was a complete mystery as to how Yorkie had been lured into the seedy world of homosexual sex in the first place. Originally from North Yorkshire, hence the nickname Yorkie, the guy had been as straight as a die and down to earth, or so it seemed to everyone, including Frank. His straight forward Northern approach to everything was the reason he and Frank had got on so well. His brother had been a professional footballer and the family were grounded and down to earth. A 'spade was a spade' in Yorkie's book and there was never any time for pissing about. Just how Frank liked it. But following his exit the rumours gathered momentum and stories emerged that not only was he a willing homosexual, some of his more extreme interests included sex with animals amongst other pleasures. This was probably more imagination from the barrack room gossip-mill than actual fact.

Franktook his coffee and sat in his leather recliner and mulled over the message again trying to make some sense of it, if there was any sense to be made. If it was genuine what did it mean? Was Yorkie back after all these years? If he was genuine, why was he trying to contact him? Did he just want a friendly chat after all these years or was there more to this approach? As far as he was aware Yorkie had no knowledge at all of Frank's life after he had done a bunk that night. It was a bit of a mystery as to how he had managed to identify him on social media as Frank did not use his own name, but it would appear that maybe Mr Biddle was more computer savvy than he was admitting to.

Before taking any action he was going to find out if this was a genuine approach, and not some kind of wind-up by one of his colleagues from the office. But then none of them knew about Yorkie. Most of them were too young to even know about the scandal that caused mayhem throughout the military intelligence community all that time ago, and those that did had only read it as source material during their training. At one time the whole sorry saga had been used as one of the scenarios on the Counter Intelligence course run at Fort Monkton by MI6. Nowadays, though, the new recruits were prepped on the perils of an approach on social media rather than through old fashioned sexual blackmail. Today's Intelligence Officers and Analysts were more likely to be recruited from the local comprehensive School after responding to an advert in the press than the time honoured method of the tap on the shoulder at Oxford or Cambridge University. As a result they were more likely to be spending hours hunched over their computer games in their bedrooms than frequenting seedy bars and clubs that might leave them open to sexual approach.

One person would be able to help though, if only to establish if the post had been genuine. Frank picked up his mobile and called Si Radford, his number was always top of Frank's dialling list, but as usual got only his voicemail telling him to leave a message. Si was, officially, the office technical intelligence leader and this was normal practice for him and he was probably listening to the device anyway, along with watching various computer screens and webcams that he constantly monitored. As well as being the office technical manager Si was, in reality, its number one geek and spent most of his time reviewing, playing with or inventing new technical gizmos. Even at home, or his HQ as Si liked to call his small London flat, and even on a Sunday Si was constantly monitoring, analysing and mapping various feeds from around the world. Frank left a short message asking him to run the name Kevin Biddle, alias Yorkie, through his systems and check also on the message that had just been received on his Facebook account.

He refreshed his own coffee and took the second cup back up to the bedroom. Samantha was lying on her back with her blonde hair draped over the pillow and the sheet only half covering her naked form. Six years younger than Frank she was beautiful and perfectly formed. The sight of his wife's partly exposed breast, nipple and the gentle curve of her pubic mound made him stiffen as he approached the bed. Every time he saw her naked the effect was the same, their was still plenty of life in the old dog. Placing both cups on the bedside table he leaned over and gently stroked her breast, slowly circling the deep red nipple, that stiffened to his touch, while lowering his shorts and exposing his now full erection.

Samantha meant the world to him and was the reason he was still working, all be it a little less. She had supported him fully in getting his life back on track and the time was fast approaching when they could put their many retirement plans into place. As well as the deep love and affection they had for each other, both had a healthy sexual lust for the other.

She moaned gently as he bent forward to take the erect bud into his mouth, reaching forward, pretending to be half asleep, she started to slowly rub his lower abdomen. Yorkie could wait, for now. Another Sunday ritual had to be enjoyed first.

=

Thegym was quiet on a Sunday afternoon, most people used it before or after work in the week in their busy London lives, as Frank cranked the pace indicator up on the treadmill. There were only three other people in the fitness area and a couple down in the 'Monkey House' as Frank liked to call the free weight training room. This was where the over-eager youngsters strained to lift over heavy weights in the pursuit of the body beautiful, most of them failing miserably. The sweat ran down his face and he wiped a hand across his forehead to stop it from streaming into his eyes as he cranked it up a further two notches. He very rarely came to train on a Sunday but the message on his phone that morning had frustrated him and he had felt the need to come and blow away some cobwebs. Old habits died hard and he had always used the endorphin rush of an 'eyeballs out' session to clear his mind. The thought processes seemed to work much better once the body had been stretched to its limit.

He pulled his headphones from his ears as he increased the pace, a sure indicator that he was running close to his maximum. Not for him the current fad of High Intensity, or HIT, training but sustained aerobic effort at close to maximum heart rate, the traditional runners method of attaining peak fitness. Holding the pace for another fifteen minutes he focused straight ahead, in the old days this would have seen him pounding some road somewhere, but these days the treadmill was his weapon of choice. His toned arms provided the drive for the knees to follow as his stride and cadence increased in time with the moving belt.

Easing the machine down to a steady recovery jog and wiping the sweat from his eyes with his gym towel he mulled over the events of the morning. He had spent a couple of hours talking over the implications of the message with both Samantha and Si after the latter had confirmed that the message was genuine. They both knew enough about Frank's military background to understand the stirring of those old memories would bring other issues that maybe he did not want to confront. Despite his attempt at shielding Samantha from the dreams that were increasing in intensity, she knew only too well how they were affecting him. She had seen the evidence of the soaked sheets and the tossing and turning as he fought the recurring demons. Maybe coming face to face with someone from that long ago in his past would allow Frank to at least confront the nightmares if not fully deal with them.

Following the message to Si and his confirmation that all seemed genuine in the messages, Frank and Samantha had walked from their apartment just off Victoria Street to St James' Park. They had strolled around the footpaths alongside the lake, Sunday afternoon was normally quiet and their favourite time to visit the park. Si had joined them at the café on the lake and they had discussed the approach that had been made to Frank by his old colleague. Frank had told them both the story of the disappearance and the resulting furore, leaving out some of the more sordid details of the military rumour mill, and re-telling the tale of his cold and wet dash to the coast that had ultimately been fruitless.

Despite his reluctance to proceed on what could be another wild goose chase to the Lincolnshire coast he had accepted their reasoning that maybe Yorkie really did have something he needed to get off his chest after all this time. While Si and Samantha had finished their coffees he had called the Director and ran the events passed him. The STAG director was very much an old school Intelligence Operator and going on ones gut instinct, he agreed with Frank, nearly always brought results. They had both been in the business long enough to know that even the remotest connection to something could open up a new avenue of investigation. It was agreed that he would make the trip the next day as the two experienced Intelligence Professionals agreed looking into what was a long forgotten case of internal spying might prove intriguing, and if nothing else would give Frank a much needed day out of the office!

TWO

Franksteered the big Honda through the late Monday morning traffic. The weather had been dry lately and unseasonably mild for the time of year which had brought the hardy day trippers back to blow the cobwebs away. It had been a typical British Summer, a bright fairly warm Spring followed by the usual rain sodden middle and a short lived 'Indian Summer' in early September. Following some sharp, frosty days late October had now brought a few days of weak sunshine. The trip had been uneventful and quite boring until he had joined the twisty Lincolnshire roads. Leaving the Motorway just south of Nottingham he had stopped for a coffee and to top-up the bikes huge fuel tank. On leaving the petrol station he had seen the black Range Rover with the blacked out windows pull out behind him about three vehicles back, but had not paid it much heed. Although the favoured mode of transport of most Special Branch teams, and used by the Intelligence services when they wanted to portray their power, Frank also knew that it was the tool of choice now for aspiring middle class professionals. The same Range Rover had sat a few vehicles behind all the way to the coast and was still there as he had exited the big roundabout as he approached the outskirts of the town, probably not a local businessman then. Confident that the driver was expecting him to continue on the main road he had made a late decision to take the left hand fork towards the back roads for Ingoldmells rather than the direct route into town. He noticed in the large fairing mounted mirrors that the driver had been caught off guard by his late manoeuvre and the Range Rover had circled the roundabout twice before following him. Opening the throttle on the big machine Frank had launched the bike into the sharp, twisting bends. Dropping the electrically operated screen two snicks to elicit a more nimble response from the bike, he quickly opened up a large gap. Frank had never lost his love for large, powerful motorbikes and now savoured the refined delivery of power that the bike gave.

As he entered the main road towards the town from the North, Frank took the opportunity to make sure the pursuer had definitely lost him. Passing the large number of caravan and camp sites along the coast road he turned quickly into one of the entrances. He aimed the machine down the short driveway and turned the bike in behind a caravan that was 'For Sale' behind the brick reception building. Making sure he had a good view of the coast road he flipped his visor up and sat observing the passing traffic. After two or three minutes he was rewarded with the sight of the Range Rover passing, at speed, heading into the town. Happy that there was not a second pursuing vehicle he gave it a few more minutes then resumed his ride down towards the centre of town and the seafront, at a more sedate pace.

Cars lined the beach road as a few families wandered up and down the main drag alongside the seafront. This week was half-term in many areas, the last school holidays of the year, and little gaggles of people were trying to make the most of the Autumn sun before the Winter arrived. Skegness was much as he had remembered it, although it had benefited slightly from recent attempts to revive the British seaside holiday, it gave off an air of bygone pleasures. The major part of the pier was long gone, although the part anchored to the seafront remained, but the side shows and cafés still clung on in the forlorn hope of a major upturn in fortunes. The anaemic sunshine gave the place a brighter feel although some of the shops still had a run down aura about them. The car park looked exactly the same with the familiar café and toilet block still looking desolate despite an attempt to brighten it with a fresh coat of paint.

He manoeuvred the big beast into a space, dismounted and eased the bike onto its stand. The bike gear had definitely changed since the last time he had arrived here. In those days his only protection from the elements had been an old and extremely smelly waxed cotton jacket and a pair of plastic road workers over-trousers that made you wetter from the inside than out. Synthetic materials and high grade leather riding suits had made riding a motorcycle much more enjoyable these days. Next to keeping fit, and of course Samantha, bikes were still Frank's great love. He had owned many different models over the years, including the cutting edge sports machines, but these days his middle-aged body was very definitely more suited to a big tourer. His hands were still toasty warm despite the three hour journey, courtesy of the heated grips on the handlebars. The big barn door of a screen on the front of the bike had kept the wind away and apart from the usual old age aching and creaking he was fairly fresh. The on board music system had kept him alert and amused whilst the big 1300cc V4 engine had made the mostly motorway trip smooth and fast, just as he liked it. Things had definitely changed in the bike world over the last forty years.

The decision to make the trip had not been made in haste or on a whim, as it appeared, but had been helped by the information that Si had sent to him after his message and the discussion they had had over coffee in the park. The post, in Si's opinion, was very definitely genuine and he had also tracked and mapped the location of the phone to the Lincolnshire area. This had still not been enough for Frank, but encouragement from Samantha had convinced him that his old mate probably deserved a fair hearing at the very least, even though he could not fathom why after all this time Yorkie had reappeared, nor why he wanted to speak to him. Yorkie had left his life that day and nothing more was ever heard from him. He would have no idea in what direction Frank's life had gone since, nor what he was doing now.

Leaving the military after fifteen years service Frank had applied, like many other ex-service personnel, to join one of the Government Intelligence Services. His application had been accepted and he had attended the selection panel, only to be rejected by letter a few weeks later. He felt he was ideally suited to the work they performed, with his experience in the Military Intelligence world, and was completely deflated when the letter arrived. No explanation was ever given, as is normal from such organisations, and he went to work in the private security industry. Not as prolific as it is today, however he managed to get a number of very lucrative short-term contracts, mainly on the recommendation of ex-military colleagues.

Why he had been rejected had baffled Frank. He felt he had acquitted himself extremely well in the battery of technical tests and written papers that formed the bulk of the application process. He knew he did not possess the same degree from a 'Red Brick' University as most of the other applicants did. He fully accepted that he was not as young, or blonde and beautiful, as most candidates were, but he did feel he had vastly more experience. Apparently this was not deemed to be enough as only he and one other ex-military applicant did not get an offer of employment. All the other young graduates were snapped up by the Security Service, MI5.

A number of months later he had been approached whilst on a night shift, as it happened on a Government site, by a visit to the gatehouse by someone purporting to be from another Government Department. Frank had been suspicious by the form of approach. He had been asked a few short questions by a very smartly dressed women in her late forties, while a much younger but equally smartly dressed guy stood behind her. They had both produced what looked, to Frank, like genuine Government ID cards and produced a letter on Home Office headed paper inviting him to an interview. The whole meeting that evening had only lasted around five minutes but had pricked Frank's curiosity. The almost as short formal interview, in a London hotel a few weeks later, had delivered the beginning of the career he now loved. It had all proved to be very genuine and had been the entry to a small and very specialised organisation, very secret and very detached from the mainstream British Intelligence Community. It appeared that far from being rejected Frank's name had immediately flagged up for having the right experience, skills and knowledge that the fledgling new service was looking for.

The Specialist Tasking and Action Group, or STAG, had been set up in the late 1980s to provide direct action against the rise of extreme crime and, later, terrorism that could not be dealt with by legitimate Police or Court actions. Following the terrorist attacks of 9/11 in the US and 7/7 in the UK they had taken on more and more of the deep and diverse threats to the United Kingdom as the mainstream Intelligence Services concentrated, almost in its entirety, on the threat from Islamic extremists. The remit and scope of operations for both MI5 and MI6 was very heavily controlled by the Political hierarchy and policed by public opinion. Every move they made was scrutinised in the popular press, that in Frank's opinion, had far too much freedom when it came to matters of National Security. STAG, on the other hand, had deliberately been kept as a relatively small and publicly deniable outfit and its existence was a very closely guarded secret, even within Government circles. You could not apply to join STAG, you were only ever covertly recruited, almost like the way the traditional agencies had operated but were now not allowed to do.

Frankhad started at the bottom, been given more and more responsibility, and risen through the grades over the years and was now leading a team of Analysts, IT Experts and Covert Operators looking at threats from areas around the World, and was in effect its Operations Director. The work was diverse and covered serious crime as well as Counter Terrorism, many of their recent operations had involved taking down organised crime gangs flooding the UK with hard drugs. Although primarily an intelligence unit STAG also possessed a very lethal cutting edge when required. Although never acknowledged, and always accredited to the Police or Military, they had been authorised to deploy lethal force on a number of occasions. All its personnel, including Si Radford, were qualified and licensed to carry weapons in the UK, but it also retained its own, highly trained, strike team.

For the last five years he had been mainly office based, much to his disdain. The only time he got to travel these days was to represent the office, usually under the cover of one of the other agencies or a Government department, at high-level meetings and conferences in the US and Europe. The plan was to retire in a year or so and enjoy other pursuits. Despite this, he kept himself operationally fit and attended the Special Operators course run by the UK Special Forces every year along with others from the organisation, including the Director who was an ex-Special Forces Brigadier.

He left the bike in the car park and walked slowly towards the café. Nothing much had changed on the outside. A new block paving walkway led towards the front door from the old rutted surface of the car park, that had unfortunately not been replaced. The paint was still flaking and weather-beaten on the outside but bright lights now illuminated the entrance. The wind still blew eddies of sand from the beach to the seafront walkway, a few hardy gulls wheeled and screeched above, even on this near Winters afternoon. Inside was now a modern and brightly lit coffee shop with leather armchairs, drop lights and stainless steel counters. No sign of the 'kiss me quick' hats or buckets and spades.

Frank ordered a latte from the young barista who smiled politely as she turned, times had changed. "Is that a large sir?" She asked in a heavy Polish accent. "would you like cakes or pastries with that?" He ordered a tuna melt pannini, handed over a ten pound note, the prices had changed accordingly, and made his way to one of the comfortable looking chairs near the window. In the town beyond, just visible through the watery haze families could be seen making their way to and from the seaside attractions still desperately vying for their trade. Although getting colder now as the afternoon approached there were still many people around. As he gazed through the slightly steamed up window he caught sight, but only just, of a black Range Rover parked at the roadside next to the grass play area alongside the seafront. It was difficult to see from that distance if it was the same one that had followed him but Frank guessed it was. You didn't get many brand new top of the range, high-end vehicles in this part of the world.

He eased down into the pleasantly worn seat, placing his helmet and gloves on the table, and stretched his legs to loosen his taught calf muscles. Old injuries from many years of running marathons had left both of them brittle and tight, and the pounding he had given the treadmill the day before hadn't helped. The long journey even on his armchair of a bike had caused them to stiffen up. His leathers creaked as he lowered himself down. Bike gear had moved on in recent years and most old bikers like Frank went for the softer textile clothing, but he still liked the assurance and confidence that a good set of leathers gave you. His daughter's called the bike his 'midlife crisis', but as he had been riding bikes since he was sixteen years old, he didn't see it that way. Over the years, along with the physical venting running allowed, he had used the bikes as a stress buster. He loved nothing better than spending a day on the tight mid Wales mountain roads pushing the bike to its limits, and always came back refreshed and relaxed. A number of advanced riding courses over the years had taught him how to enjoy the limits of himself and the machine without extending either too far.

The sunshine had started to fade outside the window and an early Winter afternoon was getting into its stride. The coffee shop was quite busy with half-term trippers. The barista brought his food to the table with a smile. "Is your name Frank?" She asked politely, smiling again.

"Yes, I'm Frank." He replied, returning her smile. She offered him a brown envelope with her outstretched hand.

"A gentleman left this for you earlier. He said you would be coming in to collect it. He was very nice."

Frank took the envelope from her. "Thank you very much. How long ago was he here?" She looked back at the clock on the wall behind the counter. The time was now 1.30.

"He was here about half an hour ago." She turned and made her way back to the counter where a small queue had formed and the one remaining staff member was trying to juggle orders. Steam rose from behind him as he strained to keep up with demand.

Again? Frank opened the envelope with an angry flourish that almost dislodged his coffee from the table. Was Yorkie, if it was him, fucking about again? Inside was a piece of A4 paper, just like last time, only this time the paper was blank. What the fuck was going on? He looked through the window again. The Range Rover had moved on. What was going on here? Was someone playing games? Had he been too quick to believe all this was genuine? He bit into the hot, and surprisingly tasty, sandwich. The hot cheese burnt his tongue and dribbled down onto his lip. He continued to stare into the distance through the window as his anger swirled in his head. He did not like the piss being taken.

"Hello Frank mate. It's been a long time." The broad Yorkshire accent was still very evident. "'ows you doing pal?" He turned his head back from the window scene. The voice was very definitely familiar but the figure stood before him was not. Stooped and round shouldered, the remaining hair grey and wispy encircled the bald and bony head and sunken red-rimmed, watery eyes peered out from a thin cadaverous and very lined face. The skin on his head, face and hands was taught and stretched with an anaemic sickly pallor. Yorkie had been slightly taller than Frank's own five feet eight inches, but the person now stood before him was hunched and shrunken. The old grey greatcoat he wore loosely hung about his shoulders made the figure look small and frail.

Frank climbed to his feet and held out his hand. "Kev? Yorkie?" The outstretched hand was taken, the grip weak and soft. "It's been a very long time mate. I had given you up for dead a long time ago. Forty years is a long time mate. We all thought you were fucked for sure when you didn't come back that night." Frank's mind was now racing. Was this wrinkled, sallow wreck really his best friend from all those years ago? Could he really have come back from the dead all this time later? He sat back down and the figure painfully lowered itself into the empty seat alongside the table. He seemed to be hurting, and the act of sitting took his breath away and it took a few seconds before he could talk.

"Yes mate, it is me. I meant to get in touch with you and the others but it was never the right time, or the right place." he coughed heavily and wiped spittle from his lips with a bony finger.

"But why now Yorkie?" Frank offered him his drink but it was waved away by the unsteady hand.

"Sorry Frank, I'm not doing too well at the moment. It's sort of the reason I have come back now. I owe everyone some kind of answer mate I wanted to see you all again, one last time. I'm dying Frank. I don't have long and there is some stuff I must do."

Outside the coffee shop, obscured from them both by the gathering gloom, the Range Rover turned into the car park. On the far side of the grass play area another identical vehicle mounted the kerb and traced tracks along the damp turf as it was steered on to the beachside walkway.

THREE

Alexissteered the big van into the parking space. The motorway rest area was bustling even at this early hour of the morning. Trucks were arriving and leaving every few minutes for destinations all over Europe. This was a major changeover point for goods being brought into Europe from the French ports. Drivers from the United Kingdom handed over their loads, and sometimes the whole vehicle, before heading back over the channel with goods from Europe and beyond. Alexis' nondescript grey van was one of the smallest vehicles in the parking area. He stretched his legs and rubbed both his shoulders. He had been on the road for a day and half. The stubble on his face scratched as he rubbed the tiredness away from his eyes with both hands. Outside the van a light watery sun was trying to break through the lifting darkness. The torrential rain from the day before had faded and stopped as he had driven West through

France towards the channel port. He had battled the elements and had wanted to stop and sleep but knew he had to keep to the schedule he had been given. He had to make it to the meeting point at the truck stop and hand over his cargo for onward delivery.

The remains of his last stop lay on the seat next to him, a plastic wrapper with a half eaten sandwich and the cold remains of his coffee in a plastic cup. The job was nearly over though. All he had to do now was wait until he was approached and hand over the load and the van. He had been promised a First Class rail ticket back home to Donetsk the next day and a night in a top hotel tonight to sleep off the journey.

The van had been loaded when it had been delivered to him, the satnav set for his destination and an envelope containing a large amount of Euros for his expenses was waiting in the glove box. There was no explanation of what the load was, who it was for and there was no key to give him access to the load in the back. His instructions were just to drive and hand over.

The situation at home was grim, Western sanctions were biting deep and there was no work for Alexis. The war between the Ukranian Government Nationalists and the President Putin backed and loyal so called 'rebels' had been raging for a number of years. Ceasefires had come and gone and although the conflict was receding in the eyes of European leaders and the Western media things were getting worse and neither side wanted to give in. The ordinary people, as always, were suffering in a conflict they didn't want. Much of the rubble had been cleared from the streets but there was still an air of conflict, mistrust and danger as Alexis made his way to the agency office each morning.

Alexis, like most Eastern Ukranians, thought of himself as Russian and believed the Crimea should once again be under Russian influence but this was not his war. He just wanted to be left alone with his wife and two small children to get on with his life. Before the conflict he had made a reasonable living as a delivery driver. His small rented truck allowed him to take work all over Ukraine and beyond at times, sometimes driving for days to make a small delivery. But due to the war, work had now dried up and he was finding it increasingly difficult to provide for his family on the meagre wage he was able to earn. Many of the medium sized international companies that he relied upon for most of his income had relocated back to the safer parts of Europe.

Despite the lack of regular work Alexis had made his way to the small agency office each morning in the hope of securing at least some of the dwindling work that was being offered. Many of the agency drivers had given up hoping for work to return and moved away to other towns and cities. It was while he was making his way to work one morning, having parked the van a street away, that he was approached by the two men. They had known who he was, knew about his wife and the children. They had talked to him about his loyalty to Russia and the struggle that he now found himself in. They encouraged him to think how he could, with very little effort, make a difference, a big difference. They had offered him a week of work driving long distance across Europe to a French port, nothing dodgy, nothing dangerous, just straight forward and honest delivery work. He would use a truck they supplied and the load would be loaded and ready to go. All he had to do was deliver it to another party waiting not far from the port.

Alexis did not want to leave his family but the offer of good money, very good money, was too good to turn down. He really was struggling to feed them, struggling to buy shoes for the children. He had told himself many times he was not a fighter, this was not his fight, but many times he had felt ashamed and guilty that others were fighting for him. Now he was being given the opportunity to do something for the cause, no longer would he be ashamed.

The truck was delivered to his small apartment at the arranged time with instructions for the drop and the route he was to take already programmed into the Satnav. The route he was to use was long, avoiding busy border crossings and major towns and cities. The truck was registered in Germany, but Alexis had an international driving permit so he encountered no major issues crossing borders and no one had paid much attention to the sealed load. All the border and customs paperwork had been waved through and at some crossings he did not even have to leave the driving seat.

The truck he had been given was brand new and easy to drive and the journey, although long and tiring, had been easy enough with no major issues. He checked his watch for the fourth time since he had stopped and slipped from the drivers seat out into the cold morning air and reached back in to retrieve his coffee cup so he could go for a refill. As he turned away from the cab door the silenced automatic round hit him in the centre of the forehead. He was dead before he hit the ground.

FOUR

Frank swallowed a mouthful of his coffee, it had gone cold in the cup. "There ain't many of us left any more Yorkie and no one is doing the same job." The coughing erupted from across the table again.

"I know Frank mate. I have kept up to date as best I could. Sorry to hear about your rough time but I always knew you would come back up."

Frank couldn't quite take in what he was hearing. What was he babbling about? The guy had disappeared nearly half a century ago and he now rocks back up out of nowhere and says he knows all about his life and his problems. Bollocks! Someone was taking the piss. Anyway, he couldn't know all about his life, no one could. Not even Samantha knew all about his life, but probably knew more than most and could probably discover the rest if she wanted to. He wasn't even sure this dick across the table was even Yorkie. Okay, the voice was somewhere near to the broad Yorkshire he remembered but the rest of the hideous husk opposite afforded no memory of the Yorkie he knew. He would have to do better than this to convince Frank that somehow he had risen from the dead and come back for a reminiscing chit-chat.

The voice from across the table was weak and almost inaudible."I know it seems strange mate after all this time." The coughing and spittle started again."I know you all thought the worst of me and it was justified in so many ways. I did some really bad things and I betrayed you all, betrayed my country, my family but most of all my friends." The eyes filled with water as the coughing wracked again.

Frank stood and walked over to the serving counter. "Could I have a glass of water for my friend, please?"

The young girl stooped and pulled a bottle of mineral water from a shelf under the counter. "You can have this. Is he OK? He doesn't look very well?" She looked over to where Yorkie was now bent almost double over the table coughing and hacking with the greatcoat flapping about like a grounded walrus.

"Thanks. He will be OK I think once he has had some of this." He returned her smile and walked back to the hunched figure who was

53

wiping his mouth again with his hand. Frank reached into the pocket of his leathers, making them creak, and offered him a handkerchief. "You don't look too good mate. Do you need a Doctor or something? I'm not sure if there is a hospital in the town any more?"

Yorkie took a large mouthful of water from the bottle and handed it back. He took a deep breath and the coughing subsided. Outside the light was now fading fast and misty shadows were being cast by the lights through the window. "I'm OK mate. It gets like this if I have been walking. Aye, it's not good but there's nowt they can do for me. The lungs have gone mate and the rest is going fast." He chuckled deep in his throat, through the phlegm and spittle and for a moment the eyes creased into the old Yorkie smile. Yes, it was him alright!

"I got right wankered that first night you know Frank. Completely off my face. I didn't know what he was doing to me or why."

The shock of the statement took Frank off guard.

"Once it was done though it was done. He took pictures of me and his mate, the Russian guy, took pictures of both of us. I think the Russian did me as well, but I was out of it by then. They both fucked me all night mate."

Frank raised his hand to halt the torrent of confession. "But they attacked you Yorkie. Why didn't you report it?"

He sipped some more of the water. "They didn't attack me mate, I loved every minute of it, I couldn't get enough. Why do you think I went back the night after and the night after that. I bet the bright eyed boys from SIB didn't tell you that bit. I had known for a long time I was different to the rest of you mate. I wasn't turned on or excited by the normal things, but I knew this was what I wanted. I enjoyed it Frank. I still do."

The words were coming out of his mouth but Frank could not take them in. Was this guy, was Yorkie, his best mate from so long ago telling him that the belief he had kept with him all this time that he had been forced, coerced, attacked and blackmailed was wrong? Was he telling him it was all a lie, that he himself had instigated it? Was he telling him that he was the leader not the led? His head was reeling. A little over twenty-four hours ago this was all a long, long way in the disant past and now he was being told by this 'thing' in front of him that far from being pulled into some sordid, immoral entrapment he had gone willingly, and even enjoyed himself.

"I don't know what the fuck this is all about mate but I don't want any of it." Frank stood with his fists clenched, the remains of the coffee spilled from the mug and the dregs washed down his leathers on to the floor as it tipped over. His building frustration joined the coffee and spilled over. The heads of the other customers in the coffee shop turned to identify the source of the raised voices. "I've got my life, got what I want, you threw yours away when you pissed-off pal. Why the fuck have you come back now just to tell me you enjoy being fucked by men? I really don't give a shit mate." He grabbed his helmet and headed through the door into the now almost dark and rapidly cooling afternoon gloom. The seafront walkway was almost empty now as the few remaining visitors headed to their cars. The anger and frustration banged in his temple as he jogged to the bike through a fug of exhaust fumes from the cold engines as the fleeing day trippers queued to leave the car park. His tight calf muscles complained as they reminded him of the long, cold and dark, journey he would have to get home. Slinging his leg over the wide seat he thumbed the starter button and the big V-4 engine willingly throbbed into life. He turned the bike out of the parking bay to see the hunched figure of Yorkie shuffling towards him, hunkered down in the depths of the greatcoat.

Frank had not seen the black Range Rover parked in the gathering murk at the end of the car park until it pulled across in front of him as he eased the bike round in a tight, feet up turn. It was heading into the space between him and the slowly advancing figure shuffling after him, its two occupants could be plainly seen in the front two seats. They were dressed identically to the two figures that were pacing quickly no more than ten feet behind Yorkie. All four wore the unofficial uniform of Government Intelligence and Security goons the World over, long dark overcoats, over business suit, white shirt and dark tie, two of them even had their sunglasses on even though it was now almost dark!

They brought the car to an abrupt screeching halt in front of Yorkie, almost taking him off at the knees with the swinging open door. Frank, seeing what was unfolding before him, gunned the motor and aimed the bike directly at the door, bringing his boot up to connect with it just above the door handle as he swerved the big machine away at the last moment. The door slammed into the outstretched leg of the driver as he tried to leave his seat causing him to scream in agony as the full weight of the door and Frank's power assisted boot thudded into his kneecap.

The two foot men attempted to grab Yorkie by the shoulders as Frank veered towards them but only managed to get hold of the empty greatcoat as he shrugged his already wasted body further into the coat. "Yorkie, get on!" Frank cracked his kevlar covered fist into the face of the nearest goon as he felt the slightness of the body clamber aboard behind him.

The traffic was much lighter as he aimed the big Honda away from the seaside car park, leaving chaos in his wake as the now coatless Yorkie clung to the seat behind him. He headed right along the seafront, weaving between the departing day trippers and ignoring the oncoming flashing headlights and blasting horns. He knew that he had only slowed the goon party down and he had to put distance between him and them. They may not have been the only team in the area. He could be riding them both into a waiting trap. He didn't even know who he was riding from. Were they ours or theirs? Were they MI5, Special Branch, Russian Security? What the fuck had he got himself into? Why had he not just turned away and left him to whoever they were? Yorkie was obviously in deep shit and it would appear he was too. But he knew he couldn't leave him, despite what he had been telling him, Yorkie was his mate and he had obviously come back for a reason, whatever that was, not just to spill his guilty guts. That reason would now appear to be in hot pursuit in a black Range Rover.

The road ran parallel to the seafront and out towards Mablethorpe to the North. A glance in the huge side mirrors showed the Range Rover, and what appeared to be another black pursuing vehicle, about half a mile behind as he urged the bike along the straight seaside highway. They re-passed the caravan and camp sites. Soon the holiday camp on the right hand side of the road appeared, and Frank knew this area from many years of visiting the bikers weekends held there. Just before the camp the road curved in a series of sweeping bends hiding the entrances to the myriad of caravan parks scattered on the outskirts of town.

Just beyond the holiday camp there was a left turn that took you on to narrow Fenland lanes and away from the town, the same lanes Frank had used to outrun the Range Rover on his inward journey. He made the turn without slowing and felt Yorkie's body almost catapulted from the bike over his shoulder as the momentum of the turn took hold. He screwed the throttle open and the massive engine whined as the speed built over the rough, potholed surface. Despite its size the bike seemed to dance over the grooves as Frank aimed it forward with the lightest touch on the bars, the big headlight picking out the bends as they raced towards him. This was Frank in his element, throwing the surprisingly agile machine into the bends and sweeping the bike from verge to verge, clipping the overgrown hedges with his elbow. There were no pursuing headlights in the mirrors.

After what seemed like hours, but in reality was only about twenty minutes, and a screaming trip of breakneck riding through the flat Lincolnshire countryside, Frank steered the bike off the road on the outskirts of the City of Lincoln. He pulled into one of the many Fenland gateways that usually had a concrete hardstanding for loading trailers with the sugar beet and other staples of the Lincolnshire farmer, many of them old wartime Bomber Command airfields now turned to more peaceful use. The only thing wrong with Lincolnshire was it was as flat as a pancake with no hills or valleys to hide in, but this hardstanding still had banks of stored hay bales that offered some concealment as he killed the engine. By contrast parts of Lincoln were built on a dirty great hill topped off by the impressive Cathedral that was now brightly lit away in the distance in the Winter darkness.

Frank had almost forgotten about Yorkie clinging to the back of the bike but the coughing and shaking from the thin hunched figure soon reminded him. He would now be freezing, without his greatcoat. Frank knew he had to warm him up and somehow ditch the bike as their description was likely to be spread to every copper in the County and beyond. He propped the bike on to its side stand and after pulling his jacket off, fed the padded fleece liner from the inside and handed it to Yorkie. "Put this on mate. I'm going to get us into the town to somewhere warm. Then you've got some talking to do I think." The shrivelled and emaciated figure was shivering uncontrollably and the coughing was now a deep bark coming from his lungs. Despite the cold, a sheen of sweat still coated the bony, skeletal face. With help he managed to struggle into the fleece jacket and spare gloves. Frank pulled his spare helmet from one of the bikes side cases and jammed it on to his head. At least they might just get away with looking like they were returning from a Sunday ride out, until they could get into Lincoln which was now about ten miles away. He didn't bother plugging Yorkie into the intercom, he could do without the constant coughing.

As they approached the city's outer limits the traffic became busier and Frank had to steer the big machine around the waiting queues at junctions and traffic lights. His knowledge of the street layout was now well out of date and new conurbations had grown up where there had been fields. He followed the signs towards the University and the canal basin and managed to locate an express hotel on the inner ring road. Steering the bike into a parking space he helped Yorkie dismount and shepherded his shivering form towards the hotel lobby.

Frank paid for the room, the last one available as there was some kind of convention in town, and ushered Yorkie into the lift before too much attention was paid to the strange figure now clad in an over big quilted jacket. The corridor was bright and airy but smelt of paint and plastic as he half pushed and half carried Yorkie down its length to the room at the far end. The room was pleasant enough and comfortably warm. It was directly opposite the University campus and anonymous enough not to arouse too much suspicion when they had booked in. Once he had settled Yorkie into the large leather armchair that sat in the corner and wrapped him in the quilt from one of the two beds Frank returned to the ground floor by the stairs. Checking that the goons in the Range Rover had not yet managed to locate them, he strode across the car park to the bike.

Gunning the big machine into life he made one more all round check of the car park before aiming the bike back towards the City centre. Much had changed in the intervening years but the main pedestrian shopping precinct remained, and was much as he remembered and the multi-story car park was still halfway up the hill. He negotiated the entrance barrier and took a ticket from the machine and rode up to the top level and parked up in the designated motorcycle parking area. The car park had twenty-four hour access should he need to retrieve the bike in a hurry. He stopped on the way back to the hotel to get some cash from a hole in the wall and buy some sandwiches and hot coffee, neither of them had eaten since leaving the coast.

There was a text waiting for him when he checked his phone on the way back from Samantha. He had quickly replied but did not tell her anything, he didn't have much to tell, he still didn't know what the hell was going on. She hadn't questioned him too deeply but he got the impression that she maybe knew more about Yorkie than he had actually told her. He had known as soon as he left to ride up to the coast Samantha's analytical research skills would have rolled into action. He had no doubt that she had been in touch with Si and would have started putting together a current profile of his long lost buddy. He liked to keep in touch wherever he was and gave her rough details about the meeting in Skegness, but left out the details of the chase into Lincoln. Once he knew what was going on he would call her, if she didn't contact him first with some newly discovered details.

Yorkie was still sitting in the chair when he returned to the room. The colour, such as it was, had started to come back to his face and the coughing for now had subsided. "Sorry to dump myself on you like this pal, but I do have my reasons. I had my reasons all those years ago too but they don't matter now." He wiped the side of his face where his eyes had been constantly running. "I didn't go willingly but I had to go all the same. The net was closing on me from all directions and I just ran mate. They offered me a way out of the mess and I took it and in some ways it was for the best. I discovered things about myself that I would not have know if I had stayed here Frank. Things people tried to keep from me." The

60

coughing started up again but not as bad as it had been and he quickly regained an element of composure.

Frank sat on the opposite bed and waited for the hacking to stop. "But why have you come back now? What the hell have you got yourself into and who is chasing you?" He threw a plastic wrapped sandwich onto the bed and watched as the bony fingers struggled to open the package, eventually swapping it for the one he had already opened. He tore the second one open and bit hungrily into it.

"They are Met Special Branch mate and they want me for playing both sides at the same time, amongst other things, but I need to warn you Frank before its too late, this time you had better listen to me." His voiced tailed off to a feeble croak and the tears rolled again down his now flushed cheeks. He continued in a subdued, hushed tone.

"After I left that night I was met by the KGB and Military Intelligence. They had been running me back here and my contact case officer travelled with me. We ended up in some Baltic seaport and they gave me a place to stay and eventually a job. As far as I know nothing was done from this end to get me back. They just let me go, mate, washed their hands of me."

Frank amazed at what he was hearing raised his voice. "For fucks sake Yorkie." Maybe that was too loud, he lowered his voice to a more measured tenor. "You had turned them over Yorkie. You were passing information to the Russians. Did you honestly think they were going to come running after you and say it was OK? Do you know the mayhem and devastation you left behind?"

Yorkie coughed and hacked again. "I thought they might have tried to stop me going. They knew the reasons, the real reasons." He paused and wiped the spittle again from his mouth. "Anyway, pal, I was passed through various Military and Police camps, and they bled me dry of everything I knew, before ending up at Meritopol, amongst other places, where they got me working on telecoms research projects. A lot of their technology was more advanced than ours, in theory. We always thought they were backward in their application of modern equipment, but they were light years ahead of us but their materials were crap and nothing lasted long enough to be deployed." He stopped to finish the food. Frank made them both another cup of coffee and handed one over.

"After a few years of analysing and comparing their radio gear they realised I had more to offer and they moved me to work under a General Roganov who was working on prototype small yield battlefield nuclear devices. One of the areas he was struggling with was the interface between the device and the remote trigger. Roganov was old school Soviet and was very well respected inside the military and polit bureau. I worked on the technology with a team of really clever people to work out where they were going wrong. The device became a reality within a couple of years but was only ever theoretical. Computers were beginning to become more widespread and they encouraged us to look in that direction. Internet technology was just emerging and the US military were starting to make use of it. The Russians managed to get hold of it fairly early on and I became fascinated with coding and protocols and they encouraged me to continue with it. I found I had a natural talent for writing code and producing cyphers.

MI6, who had been watching and keeping tabs on me through an agent that they had on the team, made contact about this time. They had unearthed the project through their contacts but had no real detail and thought we were still pursuing a mechanical outcome. He had passed them the outline of the project but did not have the expertise, and was not close enough to the technology, to give anything of real value. I wasn't happy, homesick and not doing too good mentally, so I agreed to pass them a few details every now and again. Old habits die hard mate." Frank, for the second or third time that day, could not quite believe what he was hearing. Was this really his quietly spoken, insecure and introverted friend? A double agent for MI6 and the KGB?

"I passed them the Radio Frequency technology I had been working on and also some of the basic nuclear details I could get hold of, but it was difficult as Roganov kept most of the technical detail within a very small group which I did not have access to. The work was very compartmentalised and only a few really trusted men had all the knowledge, a bit like here Frank." The hacking cough come laugh returned. "Things started to change politically in Russia around the late 80s, as you know, the new military elite lost interest and the work was mostly shelved. Roganov was removed for backing the wrong side, MI6 felt they weren't really getting anything of interest to them now as the Cold War was over, so their contact tailed off.

My interest in computer technology increased and I continued to work on the theory of a remote computer controlled trigger in secret. We had a very small team funded by a group of generals that were syphoning money away from other projects. They eventually brought in a new project director, a very bright new style military leader called Gregorio Alexayev. He was a Major and had worked closely with their special forces and came from the Crimea. The work was hidden in projects for more conventional weapons and was never on any of the disarmament agendas. It was all very political and the different factions within the Government of the time were busy building their retirement plans and they didn't really care who they did business with."

Frank re-filled the kettle and took the cups, there was the usual two sachets of coffee and four milk portions. "What happened mate? Why the change? I thought you were homesick and wanting out. Why didn't you get MI6 to work on a deal to get you home? Times were changing and things did relax a bit for a while in Russia." The kettle boiled and he sloshed water into the two cups and poured the last of the milk in an effort to make the brown liquid look at least a little inviting. He couldn't imagine MI6 would have walked away from a golden opportunity so close to the break up of the Soviet Empire.

Yorkietook the cup in both hands. The wetness around his eyes appeared to get worse. "Do you remember me talking about my Dad Frank?"

Frank took his own drink. "Yes, mate. He had some kind of accident didn't he? I remember you saying he was in a special hospital for a while."

Yorkie seemed to shrink even smaller and his voice weakened to a croak. He seemed to be looking into the far distance, his face was somewhat unnerving. "He was hit by a runaway freight wagon on the railway, so they said, and badly injured mate, he didn't last long. There was an investigation of sorts and some kind of conclusion like there always is. The truth was never made public though, something I want to put right Frank." The tears seemed to increase again and the coughing returned.

He wiped his face with the tissue that Frank held out for him. "I love my family Frank, my real family. My Dad deserves the truth to come out. My Mother has been in some kind of home for the last ten years Frank, she doesn't even know I am still alive, not sure she even cares. Same deal there mate, I would like to do something for her."

Although feeling some sympathy for him Frank felt the dialogue was just one of self-pity and even an attempt to make himself out to be a victim. After all, no one had forced him to flee, he could have held his hands up and taken the rap. OK, he would have done some considerable time in prison but not almost forty years. Also, something just wasn't ringing true in all this and what was meant by 'my real family'? As far as Frank was aware Yorkie's parents were his real parents, he had never indicated that he was adopted."Yorkie, I'm not sure what you are trying to tell me here mate. Some of you is saying you wanted out and some other bits are saying you wanted to stay. Is there more to this than you are telling me? What was really going on?"

Yorkie looked straight ahead with his head slightly down. "I fell in love mate. Gregorio was young and beautiful." Frank rolled his eyes. Each to his own, Frank preferred his lovers with tits and a shapely arse, but if that's what floated your boat then he didn't really care as long as they stayed away from him.

"For twenty years we lived together and worked on perfecting the trigger to use the devices in a targeted and precise way. I had a talent for computers and he encouraged me to explore the technology more and more. Gregorio was being guided by the senior Generals to provide a means to quell the former states that were causing Moscow major problems. Gregorio was well respected both by the generals and the men who worked for him, or he was until Putin sacked him." He finished his cup of coffee and stared wistfully out of the window into the darkness towards the Cathedral that could be seen haloed in a watery light on the top of Steep Hill. The Cathedral was the major landmark of Lincoln and stood on the top of the only real hill in the city, and was actually called Steep Hill. "Do you remember racing me up there that day Frank? I was bloody knackered by halfway and hanging on to the railing but you just kept on running. You look like you've kept it going mate, that was impressive back in the car park."

Frank stood and walked the three paces to the opposite side of the room and sat awkwardly on the end of the bed Yorkie was on. It must have been the intervening years playing with his memory but he couldn't remember the race up the hill. If it had happened Yorkie definitely hadn't run very far, he hated exercise with a vengeance. "Are you telling me, that you have got this device to work somehow? That this is what it is all about?" The body sat next to him started coughing and hacking again and looked somewhat strange and Frank had real difficulty equating it to his friend from so long ago. When he turned towards him he could see tears running down the lined and pallor faded face. These were not the wet rheumy eyes of earlier, these were real tears.

"We perfected it about ten years ago mate but the political scene in Russia was so changeable no one wanted to approve it or sign it off. We were both pushed off on to lesser projects and Gregorio was passed over for further promotion and then sacked from the military. We had four workable devices and Gregorio started using his contacts outside of Government circles to sell to the highest bidder, and there was a lot of interest. As well as these devices we have been dealing in conventional arms for a long time. Gregorio has a lot of contacts and we are now well respected in many circles Frank. It is just business to us and we have to make a living. Recently though Gregorio had been dealing a lot with the more extremist end of the arms trade, I don't really know who, and he was also helping his Crimean contacts." The words were uttered without much conviction and once again Frank felt the truth was a long way from the yarn he was being spun. "I decided to come back to do something for my Father but Gregorio didn't think it was a good idea, he tried to stop me, but I came anyway."

"I managed to get out through Germany, I still have some contacts from the old GDR days and they arranged for me to travel up to

Bremerhaven. I came across to Harwich on a freighter a few nights ago mate, but it would appear that someone, has alerted the authorities here and fed Special Branch something they want. I know Gregorio has been dealing with a lot of very nasty people lately mixed up with the Ukranian stuff mate, he has a lot of contacts in the Russian backed militia and he would love to prove that his, yes he calls them his, devices work. I have been trying to contact him all the way across but with no luck. My contacts in the militia have told me he has left the country to meet a possible buyer for one of the devices. He is planning some kind of demonstration, or so they say."

"I came back to see my Mother pal. I want to see her one last time, even though she doesn't know who I am. I am full of radiation mate, it's destroying me from the inside out, but the Branch don't care about that they just want me to pay for my sins." Frank thought the self-pity had returned. He still didn't quite get what this was all about, there was something he was missing. He could understand Yorkie feeling sorry about his Mother and Father, but he had been away for so long and as he had said she didn't know who he was.

Yorkie coughed and wiped spittle from his face again. "I want to see my Mother and do something for my Dad mate. I still love Gregorio but those devices work pal and they will be used. It will be quite a party."

FIVE

The grey van inched its way towards the ferry loading ramp. The queue in front of them seemed to stop every few seconds as the drivers of the myriad of 4 X 4 vehicles and small trucks negotiated the wet slope up on to the ships lorry deck. The smaller vehicles below them seemed to be loading much more quickly onto the lower car deck. The spray and heavy sleety rain meant the wipers had to be constantly on to allow them to see the signals from the deck hands waving them forward as the process of loading meandered on. The driver jumped on the brakes at the last minute as she only just saw the raised hand that stopped her ploughing into the back of the van in front.

They had been in the queue for what seemed like hours but in reality had only been about fifteen minutes. Finally, the front wheels of the van made contact with the ramp and spun briefly as they struggled for grip on the oil swamped surface. They made it the short, steep distance up the ramp and they were steered at the top into a line behind two coaches carrying out of season pensioners back from a getaway trip to Paris. The line of vehicles came to a halt amongst a hissing of air brakes and the coach doors were instantly flung open and bodies spilled onto the deck. The overexcited throng filled the gangway as they spilled from the open door, none of them knowing exactly what to do next and too pre-occupied with their bags and coats to care. The fussing multitude turned into an unwieldy snakelike procession and spilled through the door that opened on the bulkhead opposite. Like some out of control school party the pensioners finally all made their way through the open hatch unscathed.

Magda turned the engine off and removed the key. They had been waiting at the service area when the truck had pulled in. Petrov had killed the driver with one well aimed shot from the silenced pistol and they had quickly pushed the body into a flatbed curtain sided truck that sat on the other side of the van. Magda had already loosened the straps and the process had taken less than a minute.

They had secured the straps and returned to the van without being observed, as it was still early and most of the drivers were still asleep in their cabs. Within minutes they were on the autoroute heading for the ferry terminal. By the time the body had been discovered they were loading onto the ferry leaving for Dover. Petrov had disabled the CCTV camera covering that part of the truck park so no one would be looking for the van. This route had been chosen to avoid the more intense security surveillance that would be in operation if they had come using the channel tunnel trains.

They were both from the Crimea and had been fighting on the Russian rebel side for the cause together for a number of years. Both had been involved in low key attacks on Ukranian Military and business interests before the latest offensive a year or so ago. Petrov was ex-Russian Special Forces, had been in the death squads in Afghanistan in the late 80s and served with distinction in operations against the Chechens. Now in his early fifties he was a trusted operator within the militia ranks, he also had links to the military even though he had left under a cloud for very personal issues that still haunted his tortured mind. Over exposure to combat had dulled his spirit and he now carried the burden of serving his country in silence, elective mutism. He had left the army, officially, because he could no longer follow the orders he was given but his old commander, the Major, had looked after him. It was the Major that had ignored his deviant personal behaviours. It was the Major that had given them this task to perform for the militia. He was still regarded as a top assassin and he had been given the job of protecting Magda, and their cargo, during its delivery to the target.

Magda had become both trusted and respected by Petrov by the way she willingly offered her body to him on demand, and the fearless way she took on every task the militia gave her. She had been orphaned by a Ukranian army attack on her village. Both her parents, her Mother was Ukranian and her Father Syrian, had been killed in a machine gun attack on the market where they earned their meagre living. At seventeen and homeless she had willingly accepted the militia's offer of shelter and had not objected when they had offered her up to Petrov to quench his perverse needs. She had surrendered to him in bed each night allowing herself to be taken again and again. She quickly learned to love Petrov, despite his mental anguish and demanding sexual release.

Magda had enthusiastically participated in many operations and had proved herself time and again. She was intelligent and resourceful and the Major had given her more and more responsibility. Together with Petrov she had taken on an increasing load of the most daring, and most dangerous attacks. As the flow of more sophisticated weaponry from Russia, and other sources, had increased, so had the magnitude of attacks. For this operation she had been told to deliver the equipment they were carrying to England and await further instructions. They were to have no personal contact with the director of the operation and would never know his identity, he was always referred to as the 'Controller', but had been told that their efforts would result in a spectacular that would never be forgotten. The Major had assured them that they would be highly rewarded, highly respected by the militia and definitely remembered by the World.

They both climbed from the cab and made their way behind the fussing pensioners up to the amenities deck for the crossing. Magda glanced behind her as they climbed the stairwell to just catch a glimpse of the large blue camper van park in the lane next to their van. She could feel Petrov's breath on her neck as he closed up behind her and slipped his hand under her top and on to her unsupported breast. He steered her away from the throng on to an intermediate deck. She could feel his hardness against her as he eased her away from the steps and into a cubicle of the toilet on the mid level deck. It had been almost two hours since Petrov had killed the truck driver and she knew he would be desperate for release. She lowered her jeans and underwear hurriedly to accommodate him and he drove into her with his usual passion and arousal. Their coupling was frantic and short lived, as usual, but for the second time that day, already, his primeval lust satisfied her deeply within.

Magda steered Petrov into the busy cafeteria on the top deck of the ferry. She found him a seat in the corner and joined the frothing throng of the coach party at the food counter. She could see the strain and unease in his features even from across the length of the saloon. She quickly filled two mugs from the self-serve coffee machine, leapfrogged a gaggle of overexcited grey travellers, paid at the cashier and made her way back to his side. Despite his undoubted skill and bravery in the face of any enemy, Petrov could not tolerate being in any crowded space. Magda gently took his hand and attempted to soothe his panic. She knew he would very soon need her carnal services once again to bring his anxiety under control.

Following the short crossing the ferry docking proceeded without incident and they made their way back to the vehicle deck in the midst of the coach party rushing to form the usual pensioner priority queue at the door. The melee around the coach's open doorway hid their approach and they skirted around the front of the van as the ruckus reached a crescendo of clinking duty free bottles amid the pushing and shoving. One of the pensioners managed to slip on the greasy deck and lay sprawled half in and half out of the door which sent the multitude into an even greater frazzle.

The sliding door of the camper van was open and they both climbed in, unobserved, and slammed it shut behind them. The two large black metal carrying cases had been transferred from the van into the camper. The large head and broad back of the driver, already seated in the front, blocked the view to the two of them as they settled into the rear seats. As the driver eased down the off loading ramp Magda leaned forward into the front cab and threw the van keys through the

71

opened window into the black water of the dock. As she sat back in the rear a scene of chaos was erupting around the abandoned van on the deck of the ferry. The second coach that had been parked behind the camper van would not start, Petrov had cut the fuel pipes, and the riot of disgruntled, and increasingly loud and pompous pensioners, only added to the roadblock.

The driver of the camper van negotiated the post ferry queue and made his way to the waiting customs shed. The small vehicle shed had very little activity in it and the customs officials seemed to be concentrating on the stream of heavy vehicles leaving the boat. They were waved through the overhead gantry by a bored looking customs officer. Happy that they had not triggered any of the detectors he cleared them to proceed and turned his attention to the car towing an oversized caravan that was following them. The lead lined cases had done their job. The driver negotiated the tight roads around the port and steered the camper out towards the motorway.

Magda stirred from her restless dozing as the driver turned the camper van off the motorway. The soporific drumming of the wheels on the surface had caused her to drift into a fitful sleep. Petrov sat next to her staring out of the tinted rear window as the lane they had turned onto narrowed as it skirted the town of Redhill in Surrey. In the gathering dusk of the late Autumn afternoon the overhanging trees glistened in the headlights. The driver pulled the van off the road into a partly concealed lay-by, surrounded by a small copse of trees. Parked in the far corner, was a large silver estate car and he pulled up a short distance behind and quickly opened the door and climbed out. He jogged to the trees, unzipping his trousers as he went. Petrov, who had stepped from the other side of the van, silently closed up behind him and sliced expertly and quickly through the driver's neck with his knife in one slick movement as he stood and relieved himself against a tree.

Together they dragged the lifeless body into the back of the camper and removed the two carrying cases. Petrov carried them to the estate car and loaded them into the boot before climbing into the passenger seat. Magda could already see Petrov's reaction to the killing beginning as she pulled a large jerry can from the vehicles boot and poured petrol from a can over the van and set it alight with a burning rag. She stood and watched as the flames started slowly then erupted into an inferno as the petrol tank exploded sending large gouts of flame spiralling into the air.

As she joined Petrov in the car she focused on his usual reaction to having killed. His trousers were already agape and pushed to the top of his thighs revealing his throbbing and engorged penis. He stroked and pulled at the bulbous mushroom and his full and heavy balls bounced against his legs. Magda lifted her top to reveal her breasts, leaned forward and took his pulsing penis deep into her mouth, sucking and licking greedily at his manhood. Loosing her grip on his shaft she pulled her jeans and panties down and off her legs. She leaned over Petrov and straddled his pulsating root and slid her wetness down into his groin until he was fully buried in her. Their coupling was once again frenzied and frantic as she worked away the tension and tremors arcing through his body. It took only seconds before he exploded his seed deep inside her.

The journey from the lay-by into the gathering gloom was conducted in silence. Magda drove as Petrov, now in a hazy post release state, dozed in the passenger seat. She followed the directions of the pre-loaded satnav and negotiated the country lanes, not venturing back onto the motorway, towards the town in the distance. The traffic was building up and the home time queues meant she had to inch the car along towards their destination.

Magda steered the estate car into a free parking bay in the Redhill Travel Lodge car park. The hotel had a worn down air about it, as they often did, but its position on a hill into town made it suitably anonymous. There were a number of other cars parked up, but the late afternoon hour meant the surge of overnight commercial travellers that were its stock-in-trade had not yet happened. Another hour and the place would be buzzing with the arrival of the one night stayers. Magda left the car and quickly scanned the car park and adjoining road to make sure they were not being observed. Leaving Petrov in the passenger seat she walked across to the reception area that was separated from the body of the hotel and booked them both in under assumed names.

Satisfied that no suspicions had been raised while booking in Magda returned to the car and tapped the window for Petrov to join her and opened the boot using the remote key. They eased the two cases from the car and Magda leaned briefly into the boot, closed and locked the doors. From the car park they could see the railway sidings, and beyond to the platforms, but there was no direct route from the hotel. Each carrying a case they walked out through the entrance of the car park and down the steep hill to the roundabout now clogged with homeward bound commuters. The walk to the Railway station took them ten minutes, Magda left Petrov standing outside while she went to the ticket office to purchase their tickets. On her return she handed him a cup of coffee and a chocolate bar that she had bought from a vending machine.

Standing together on the platform, drinking their coffee they gave the impression of being just two of the many weary travellers around. It was a busy interchange with a lot of London bound services and they did not have to wait very long for a direct service to flash onto the overhead screen. At this time of the afternoon most of the commuters were coming the other way out of London, so the platform was not overly busy. They were able to make out the approach of the train as it entered the confines of the station. Magda retrieved the keys of the estate car from her pocket where she had put them as they had left the hotel. As the train slowed to a halt alongside them she held the keys in her right hand and pressed the door unlock button. A loud bang was heard from the far side of the sidings, near to the hotel, and a sheet of flame erupted into the darkening sky from the Travel Lodge car park. They both stepped aboard the London bound train, dragging the carrying cases with them as they tried to blend into the rush of passengers at the doorway.

SIX

Frankhad listened for most of the night as Yorkie had explained the details of what the device could do and what devastation it would cause if detonated in a built-up area. It was the only time that he was able to speak coherently and without his hacking cough. It was as though the immense pride in what he had developed and built had somehow erased the illness that was racking his frail and wasted body. He had gone into detail about the design that would bring an abrupt end to any localised battle, the detonation would lay waste to anything within six to ten miles radius, depending on the terrain. He had also talked, very vaguely, about this Gregorio's alignment to a Crimea militia. Frank had listened again to the self-pitying whine that seemed to accompany this whole sorry saga. There were several mentions of his 'real father' and the family that loved him, and wanting to do something to honour his father and tell the truth. But when Frank had probed deeper into what he was talking about he would dissolve into another animated round of spittle flying convulsions. Frank was still completely mystified as to why Yorkie had involved him and why Special Branch were so interested. He was after all a seriously ill man and apart from some spurious involvement in building a computer trigger, which Frank assumed there were many, he really could not see what this was all about. He was definitely missing something and would need to enlist the resources of his STAG colleagues to uncover what exactly was going on.

He stepped out of the hotel and made his way into town to check on the bike. He had left Yorkie fast asleep, himself having woken again to the recurring dream although not as severe today. He turned on his mobile as he walked over the river bridge and out towards the main street. Many years ago when he had been here, stationed close to the City of Lincoln, the old railway lines had still been across the street and there had been a level crossing leading to the second of the two stations. The St Marks station had long been removed and much of the cities development, including the University, had been built on the old layout.

He would call Samantha as soon as he had found some decent coffee. The phone vibrated in his hand and a message flashed up as he glanced at the screen. It was from Si. "Ring me as soon as you get this." He had forgotten, amidst all the excitement of yesterday, to get back to him. He had promised to do some more checking on Yorkie's most recent past. He had no doubt that Si and the team had been busy tracing as much of Mr Biddle's past as they could piece together.

Si answered on the second ring. "At last mate. I've been trying to get hold of you since yesterday afternoon." Frank apologised and explained quickly what had been happening. "Yes mate I'm up to speed with your flee across Lincolnshire." Frank wasn't surprised as he knew Si would have been tracking his mobile until he had turned it off, and probably after, knowing Si's gizmos and toys. He was, though, very surprised with what came next.

Si's voice was very deliberate and his tone was measured. "I started running some traces on your mate yesterday afternoon Frank. I kept coming up against file access issues, which I wasn't surprised about, but even my clearances couldn't get me in. Samantha eventually got in via some old MI5 contacts and I managed to call in some favours on the electronic side of things." Si had been a highly respected network analyst within MI5 before joining STAG and Samantha had always kept her contacts with all the agencies she worked with. It was seen as a two-way street by the research analysts and they were always willing to help each other out, despite the sometimes displeasure of their respective agency bosses. Si continued. "His details are on 5s paranoid list, there are only five targets on there and he is one of them. It would appear, mate, that 5 and 6 have been watching your pal, and a guy called Gregorio, for some considerable time and not just because he did a runner. An hour ago Frank I was in Thames House being read onto one of their extreme security compartments that is dealing with a threat to the UK from a probable Russian terror group. Guess who is leading it mate? MI5 and Special Branch have been trying to locate you since you left the coast. They had been trailing him from the time he arrived in the UK and were about to lift him when you appeared on the scene. They backed off while they checked with us, but it would appear you went on the offensive and they lost you!"

Frank stopped in mid stride as Si spoke. Shit, they were the good guys after all. He could not believe what he was telling him. Yorkie had spent the last night telling him he was only involved because of this Gregorio and now Si was telling him something completely different. He cut across Si as he continued to give him the details. "Is there any mention of where this Gregorio might be Si?" There was a pause before Si continued.

"No Frank, they have only been following your mate. He was known to be a Major in the special forces group, according to the details we have, and was involved in some Top Secret work on missile technology but nothing nuclear, as far as we can tell, but the report I have been given is that he died suddenly about three months ago on some kind of arms selling trip. Incidentally, mate, this was around the same time that your mate started to be watched closely. That report cannot be confirmed and there is speculation that Gregorio may still be around somewhere."

Frank turned back towards the hotel. 'Hi, I'm heading back to the room. I will call you back." The reply was quick and slightly louder.

"OK, mate but just so you know, MI5 are all over this now and are probably not very far from you."

Frank didn't doubt it. They would also be loving the fact that he was involved. Although they worked with all the recognised agencies on a professional level STAG was not well liked by the hierarchy, particularly MI5, due mainly to the slightly looser reign and accounting they enjoyed. STAG were only ever given the muckier jobs to do and operated very close to the edge, unlike the regulated agencies who had to be squeaky clean and legal. In addition all the regulated agencies had to subsume some of the budgeting for STAG into their own, very tight, operating finances.

He took the steps to the first floor room two at a time, deciding not to wait for the lift. He put his key card into the reader and pushed the door open. The room was empty. Frank pushed open the door to the en-suite bathroom, but that was empty too. Where was Yorkie? He quickly turned and made his way back down the stairs to the reception area that also doubled as a dining room. No sign of him in there either. Through the large plate glass window Frank saw the two black Range Rovers draw up at the kerb, closely followed by a large black saloon car. He jogged out through the automatic doors to the roadside as the cars stopped and the doors of the leading Range Rover swung open and two black suited figures stepped on to the pavement. At least they weren't wearing their overcoats today, but one did have his sunglasses on.

The saloon car did an elaborate U-turn in the middle of the road, causing a hooting of horns from other cars, and came to a sharp stop with two wheels on the pavement. Another dark suited figure left the passenger seat and opened the rear door to allow the long legs of a woman to stretch out onto the pavement. "Good morning Frank. Fancy seeing you here." The prim, Oxford educated voice was unmistakable. Avril Wentworth-Smyth, one of MI5s upwardly mobile operators appeared on the pavement next to him. Her elegant, sleek form was dressed in a figure hugging dark two-piece suit, with her trademark black leather three-quarter length coat loosely draped over her shoulders, her blonde hair swept back from her face. She walked slowly towards him, followed by the driver who had now joined her on the pavement. "I didn't know STAG had started protecting traitors?"

Frankknew Avril well from a number of operations that they had both been involved in over the years and to be fair to her, she was one of the more amenable and undoubtedly talented middle managers the Security Service had. In fact Frank had tried to recruit her to STAG a number of years ago but the lack of public image and instant upward mobility had not been to her liking. He also knew her background and the way she operated. Much of his information had come from Samantha who had worked with Avril for a number of years prior to leaving MI5. Avril had a reputation for being ruthless in her pursuit of reaching the top and was not beyond using her feminine charms to achieve her goals. Indeed there was a rumour spreading that she was currently romantically linked to one of the senior division heads. She had been touted as a possible future division head for MI5 and Frank had always found her to be professional, even though he thought her a little lacking sometimes when it came to security. The word around the bazaars, confirmed by Samantha, was that she was not averse to leaking the odd snippet of operational information if it achieved results. Not something Frank, or the other members of STAG, would countenance. The very nature of their operation, working on the edge of legality, meant they kept everything as tight as a drum. The old way of doing intelligence work.

Before Frank could reply Avril smiled and held out her hand for him to shake. "Don't worry Frank. There has been no real harm done by you joining in our little spot of 'chase me' with Mr Biddle apart from a few bruises to the SB Boys you had fun with last night."She pointed towards the two Range Rover "But, we do need to talk to him rather urgently, and bring you up speed on what he has been up to. I trust Si Radford has given you in outline? Is our Mr Biddle still in bed?"

Frank smiled back at her and gently took the offered hand. "That would appear to be the problem, Avril Yorkie has scarpered."

=

From his viewpoint high up on the castle ramparts Yorkie focused the telephoto lens of his camera back down Steep Hill to the area around the University and the City Centre. He had been observing the frantic activity by the local Police for the last fifteen minutes as they had scoured the lower reaches for him. Unfortunately, for them he had left the hotel in a waiting taxi the minute Frank had gone to check on his bike, and had been dropped off at the corner of Bailgate, between the castle and the cathedral, and had made his way painfully over the cobbles to the entrance gate. The taxi, driven by one of the network set up to support him, was now waiting for him to finish his business. The camera around his neck and the rucksack over his shoulder had marked him out as one of the many tourists milling around the top of town, the padded jacket he still had belonging to Frank just added to the image. As well as providing him with the means of leaving the hotel the taxi had also contained the equipment he now carried. MI5 had not been the only ones that had tracked him last night, the taxi driver had discretely followed them into Lincoln and been ready to move him as planned. He had observed the Special Branch cavalcade leave the city and now made his way down the crumbling stone steps to the Castle keep.

He sat awkwardly down on a stone bench and weighed the camera in his hand. Funny how much lighter cameras were these days he thought, remembering the afternoon all those years ago he and Frank had spent taking pictures of a decaying seaside. He also remembered the heavy photographic equipment they had given him in the lab when he started working on 'The Project' as they called it. The Soviet era lenses were solid but unwieldy and the development acids were crude and burnt his hands. He placed the camera inside the rucksack and pulled out his laptop. Two icons flashed up on to the screen as he opened the lid, he opened one to reveal a real time tracking app that showed the current location of a particular mobile phone. The phone was in the hand of his operator and showed it was where it should currently be in the South East of England. Gregorio, or the Major to the two operatives, had again chosen well. His influence in the separatist movements still ran deep, his reputation earned on the battlefield had allowed him to recruit the best veterans to his cause. Everything was on track and going to plan. He closed the app and opened the screen for the Internet search engine and typed in the name of a retirement home in Leeds. The address and telephone number flashed back to him under a picture of an elegant looking country house. Noting the address he closed the laptop and returned it to his rucksack.

After fleeing that night all those years ago he had missed this country and all that it stood for. He initially regretted doing what he had done and felt ashamed that he had become a traitor. But as time had progressed and his adopted country had provided him with meaning and reason he had come to despise the place he had grown up in. Most of all he had come to despise people like Frank Martin.

Thebriefing room on the sixth floor of Thames House, the London
Headquarters of MI5 or the Security Service as it was officially
known, was a clutter of paper and discarded coffee cups as the
meeting broke up. Frank and Si Radford had listened intently as the
MI5 lead, Paul Whittle the head of European Operations, had
outlined what detail they had so far. Whittle had taken over the
operation from Avril Wentworth-Smythe as MI5 had now decided it
had become a European issue and were very reluctant to see any
wider potential terrorist angle, to the disgust of Sir Anthony Baxter
the head of the Met Counter Terrorism Branch who was sat next to
Frank and Si. Sir Anthony had argued that all potential threats
against the Capital had to be taken seriously, but Whittle seemed
quite disinterested and let the discussion meander and finally die out
as it did not rank highly enough on his priority scale. Whittle was an
old school Intelligence officer who served his time mostly in Berlin
during the cold war, but had also run informers in Northern Ireland,
that had secured his reputation. He had risen to division head level
but was unlikely to rise any further and resented all the younger
elements that were gradually changing the service to something he
did not recognise any more.

The others called to the meeting had been representatives from other
areas of MI5, MI6 or The Secret Intelligence Service, GCHQ and the
Joint Terrorism Analysis Centre or JTAC and the Met Special
Branch, although Whittle was happy to have MI5 as the lead agency,
or so he thought. The involvement of Frank would now ensure that
STAG played a major part in the operation if it progressed.

Frank had politely declined the offer of a lift back to London by
Avril the previous morning and made his way to the STAG offices
after retrieving his bike from the Lincoln car park. Despite a

thorough search of the City by Special Branch and the local Police no trace could be found of Yorkie. Avril had filled him in, over a much needed coffee, about her operation so far and the assumption up until then that Yorkie was involved in some kind of elaborate computer hacking and espionage game against British interests. MI5 had kept his file alive and periodically, over the years, added anything they managed to glean from contacts with agents and MI6 officers. They had dismissed any notion of a possible terror issue due to Yorkie's contacts with Crimean separatists under the assumption that he was just selling knowledge to the highest bidder. The compartmented working group that Si had been allowed to join, and that Frank was now also privy too, were concentrated on counter arms dealing and not particularly about any specific threat. As with most of the rest of the Western Intelligence community MI5 were concentrating any efforts on fighting Islamic terror and the increasingly unstable situation in Syria and the Middle East. Since British jihadists had started returning to the country more and more of their resources were targeted at keeping them under observation.

Frank had found great difficulty in accepting their dismissal out of hand of any connection to the Ukranian issue having heard Yorkie's explanation the night before, much of which he had edited for Avril's consumption. Throughout the journey back he had been in constant touch with Si via his mobile and the bike's on board intercom system, relaying the information Yorkie had offered. Si had gone straight to work, keeping Frank up to date on progress, and by the start of the meeting had uncovered what was, in their opinion, very quickly turning into possible attack planning against the UK.

Frank and Si had briefed into the meeting as much detail as they thought would keep them busy for a while, hinting at a possible plot against UK interests that it might be worth following up. Despite the information, albeit slightly truncated, being presented to the meeting Whittle had directed the other agencies to pursue the leads at a low priority, much as Frank had thought he would. The only people at

the meeting that had shown any great terest in their slant on things
were Sir Anthony and Dylan Jasper fr n the long-term analysis
team in JTAC. The Joint Terrorism A lysis Centre had been set up
in the wake of the 9/11 attacks in the l 5 and had been the first joint
centre of its kind anywhere in the Wo l. It maintained contacts with
the various offices around the globe th t had quickly copied the
model and set up their own joint ventu es. As a joint organisation,
with a rotating head officer from the r in agencies, it kept its remit
wide reaching and for that reason it tr ted all potential threats with
equal gravitas. Dylan Jasper was one (its more senior operators,
originally from the Defence Intelligen Service, very experienced
and highly regarded.

Two hours before the meeting Frank a d Si had been with the
Director of STAG at the Cabinet Offi briefing the Home Secretary
with full details and their thoughts. Th Home Secretary had
immediately taken an interest and had iven them the go ahead to
run the operation to counter any threa He had placed the other
agencies under the direction of STAG nd those other agencies
would be briefed in due course later in he day as to their support
roles, another rise in STAG's popular no doubt!

As they both left the meeting and head d for the lift to the ground
floor they were joined by Baxter and J sper who had both been
appraised by Frank prior to the meetir on where he felt the
information he had might be leading t m. Sir Anthony was
particularly keen to be abreast of any rther intelligence gathered by
STAG, hence his opposition to Whittl s apathy, as it was his
officers that would be at the front of a counter to the threat. The
JTAC man had agreed to put his team t the disposal of Samantha as
a conduit for information from the An ricans, especially anything
coming from the CIA, although lodge in the MI5 building JTAC
were a separate agency staffed jointly om all the counter terrorists
groups and delighted in scoring points against their hosts whenever
possible.

84

Si and Samantha had been hard at work since Frank had returned from Lincolnshire and had unravelled most of the intricate web that Yorkie had spun, and it was a web. He had indeed been welcomed by the Russian system after he had fled all those years ago, he had also been set to work, almost immediately, on the control systems associated with battlefield weapons. Where the truth was beginning to differ from the story he had offered to Frank was in the post Cold War era where he had, according to his story, been employed on projects secretly funded to continue the research into those same weapons.

They had spent the last twenty-four hours, when not in briefings with the other agencies, mapping and piecing together Yorkie's movements and contacts over the last forty years. Using the most up to date technology and computer tracking systems, most of which he had either developed or had a hand in developing, Si had put together an in depth picture of Yorkie's life history. Samantha, using her numerous contacts within the Government establishment and a few in the more unstable commercial sector had produced an extensive dossier on his life in his adopted country. He had indeed lived with Gregorio for more than fifteen years but they had both divorced themselves from the Russian Government machine very soon after Glasnost and been freelancing. They had effectively been selling themselves to the highest bidder within the dodgy side of the arms industry, the story line that MI5 were happy to follow. Along the way, they had started to associate with extremist groups and individuals intent on causing mayhem, with or without a cause, around the World. It was also becoming clear that Gregorio, at least, had furthered his connections with the unrest movements in the Crimea, and possibly beyond.

Gregorio had, apparently, disappeared off the scene just over three months ago, which seemed to fit in with the official line that he had died. Yorkie, it would appear, had taken on the business on his own and continued to deal with some increasingly dodgy characters, including some of the leaders of the anti-Ukranian terror groups. It was around the time of Gregorio's, apparent, demise that Yorkie's interest in his work on the remote computer trigger seems to have taken on a greater urgency. But there was still something that wasn't fitting right in the story Yorkie had been telling. It wasn't unusual for the Russians to put defectors to work on the projects they had expertise and knowledge on, brought from the West, but they usually kept them on a very tight leash and did not afford them the freedom Yorkie had seemed to enjoy. In fact the life of most military defectors once in the hands of the Russian machine was one of misery. There were numerous stories of ex-allied personnel being squeezed dry of current information before being denied support, many finding themselves begging on the streets for a living. For Yorkie to have lived the life he had described there had to be something else.

The piece of the puzzle that was causing them all some considerable issue was why he had now reappeared in the UK. He had told Frank that he had come back to see his Mother, who was now a resident in a Leeds retirement home, and to 'do something' for his Father. In Yorkie's own words he had 'come home', although he must have known that he was still on the radar as far as MI5 and the British authorities were concerned. There were many things the British were bad at, but forgetting about someone who had committed treason, as that is what it was, was not one of them. Even after this amount of time the authorities would like nothing more than to put him before a court, convict and imprison him for a long time. There were probably a few ex-service colleagues of Yorkie's that would like to do far worse things to him. Most of them also had long memories when it came to reliving the clampdown that the military authorities had placed on them following his bun

Now, as the meeting broke up, both Si and Frank knew that was the key to finding out what this was all about. What did he intend doing for his Father? Was he intending to arrange a commemoration of some description for him? He could not imagine that you would come all this way, under the glare of the British authorities, and go to the extent he had just to erect a plaque or install a bench somewhere. They both thought there had to be more to it and maybe Gegorio's influence on him stretched much deeper than facilitating his geeky interest in computer triggers.

They arrived back at the office after a ten minute walk along The Embankment and up Horseferry Road past the Home Office. It took almost as long to negotiate the traffic on Victoria Street and even longer for Si to negotiate the queue in the coffee shop before they finally made it into the building. Frank turned on his desktop computer and logged on to his emails. Amongst the list of messages waiting his attention was an update from the Special Branch team that had continued the search for Yorkie after he had left the Lincoln hotel. It had been agreed at the earlier meeting, reluctantly by Paul Whittle but at Frank's insistence, that Avril would continue to be the liaison between the operation and Special Branch and Frank noticed that the email had been addressed to her, with Frank copied in.

He opened the attachment that had come from the leader of the team conducting the search, it was in the form of the usual Special Branch Ops report from all constabularies around the country. Traditionally known as the 'Morning Report' in these days of instant communications the reports tended to be re-issued throughout the day to update ongoing operations. The report contained numerous items from various Special Branch teams, some for ongoing operations and some with adhoc report items. They had searched the City and beyond but found no sign of him or where he may have gone. They had checked all the local taxi companies, the coach operators and at the Railway station. No one fitting Yorkie's description had been seen by any of them. It would appear he had just vanished. Frank was about to clos the document when he noticed an item in the adhoc reports a he bottom. Surrey Police Special Branch had reported an unexp ined death in a wood. They were treating it as Murder as it was in ie vicinity of a burnt out Camper van. There was also an item a out an explosion in a Travel Lodge Car Park. They were treating it s possibly connected as the car involved in the explosion had beer een in the vicinity of the wood by a taxi driver having a nap. A led to the bottom of the item, in italics, was a report from the Frencl Police via Interpol of a murdered driver discovered with a gu hot to the front of the head at a motorway rest area not far from Cal s. It had been included due to it's close proximity to the Channel po Avril had attached a highlighted note in bold type under th report suggesting this might be connected to Yorkie. I bet she hasr told Paul Whittle Frank thought, but noted she had copied and ighlighted it to Sir Anthony Baxter. Never one to turn down poten l brownie points Avril always made sure she was kept in the ague table for praise, both during and after an operation.

He turned to Si, who was stood in the rner of the office spooning more sugar into his plastic coffee cup. rank often wondered how he still had any teeth the amount of suga ie consumed! "Yorkie told me he had come in via the port of Har ich. Have we had this confirmed by Special Branch?"

Si brought his coffee over and Frank i inaged to move his away before he knocked it from the desk wi his elbow.

"Yes, they are fairly certain that was l route into the Country. It was their Ports Officer that flagged up possible Alien entry when he checked the scanned passport. Why "

Frank turned the screen so Si could re it over his shoulder.

"It's just this item that has come in fro the Branch, there is a report from Surrey of some unexplained acti ty including two apparent Murders that have the hallmarks of an ssassin at work. I'm not sure

Yorkie is capable of cold blooded murder, but I just thought if he had been assisted somehow coming in, whoever assisted him might have wanted to cover their tracks. He definitely didn't have any bags big enough to carry an explosive device with him so maybe he is having them delivered. It looks like Avril might be having the same thoughts. Could you have a chat with the guys in Surrey and get some details from them?" Si nodded and headed for his desk.

The phone on Frank's desk rang and he picked it up. "Hello, Frank Martin." The voice on the other end was instantly familiar. Avril could not have lingered at the meeting after he left. She spoke without preamble, as was her way. "I've just had a call from the Special Branch guys still in Lincolnshire. They put out an 'All Ports' for our friend and have just had a contact from West Yorkshire. The local Police in Welbeck in Leeds, it would appear, had a call from a Residential Home in the area reporting a man attempting to visit one of their residents. It appears this place is very high-end and they don't get many casual enquiries for people to visit. They were very concerned that no appointment had been made, as is usual, and that he looked ill so they called the station. By the time the local bobby got to the home the man had disappeared. You did say Yorkie was talking about looking his Mother up in her retirement place. Could this be our friend?"

As Avril paused for breath, he agreed with her that it could be Yorkie, told her he would call her back and ended the call. Si, who was busily writing notes while on his call to Surrey Police mouthed 'Yorkshire?' and nodded as Frank made his way to the door using his mobile to call the movement clerk for a train ticket followed by the car pool controller to arrange a ride to the station.

SEVEN

Magda and Petrov had endured the almost ninety minute journey on the cold and crowded train into Victoria in silence. The train had picked up passengers at every station along the route and they had been packed together, almost touching. Magda knew he did not like being in confined spaces and despite the low temperature in the crowded carriage she had seen him sweating and fidgeting from the tension. He had stood next to her as she squatted on the edge of a three place seat that was almost filled by an obese women clad in a dirty fur coat, the folds of her stomach rolled on to her knees as the train shook and jolted. His broad six foot plus frame was taught as he had braced himself against the movement of the train. His face was fixed in a hard grimace but despite the cold there was a fine sheen of sweat covering his bald head. He had kept flexing and unflexing both his fists, and Magda had gently stroked his arm in a soothing gesture. As the train clanked and jerked to halt at the platform she had pulled Petrov close to her and they had waited for the throng to heave its way off before they made their way through the door. Inching behind the crowd they had made their way through the ticket gates and out on to the brightly lit concourse.

Magda steered him to a small coffee shop at the side of the main thoroughfare and bought two small, strong coffees. In her hand she clutched the mobile phone that she had used to send a text to the contact number they had been given. The instructions for the next stage would be passed to them when they arrived at their London destination. The Controller had arranged everything and all they had to do was pass through each stage and deliver their cargo. The Major had told them that the Controller had made sure their contacts would be where they needed to be. All Magda had to do was carry out the instructions given to her and keep Petrov in one piece, he in his turn would keep her from any danger.

As they sat finishing their drinks Magda brought the phone up to her face so that she could look at the contents of the message with some limited privacy. Someone would meet them when they arrived at Paddington station, a ride on the Underground away that Magda was not looking forward to. The journey on the overground train had been bad enough for Petrov but she knew it would take all his resistance to endure the trip deep underground. They had to follow the plan to allow further directions to be given. Their orders were always relayed in this way. They were never given the plan or instructions for the whole operation. Should they be intercepted or arrested they had no information other than the next immediate command. Neither she nor Petrov had been told the ultimate outcome of this operation, of any operation, they had not been told what the cargo was, their directions were merely to deliver it.

The twenty minute journey across London on the underground passed without incident. She had held Petrov close as he had sat, still heavily perspiring, next to her on the filthy bench seat of the worn and dirty carriage. On arrival at Paddington they quickly immersed themselves in the tide of scurrying travellers heading for the exit gates and the main concourse. They walked close together and tried to look like they were deep in conversation with each other, heads slightly bowed to avoid the CCTV cameras that they knew must exist. Her grip on Petrov's sleeve tightened as she felt the tremors increase as the phalanx of commuters closed around them.

Climbing a short flight of stairs and exiting the gate from the underground platform they crossed the mainline station concourse heading towards the overhead destination boards and away from the platforms. As they neared the boards they were approached by a stout, auburn haired women in her early forties dressed in the green uniform of one of the train companies operating out of the station. She was pulling behind her two wheeled crew bags, which she quickly passed over, and carrying a brown envelope in her hand. As she closed within a couple of feet of Magda she whispered in a strange accent. "All the details are in here." She handed the envelope to Magda and without any further interaction walked away towards the platforms. Without acknowledging or making eye contact with the woman they both headed out of the station.

In a small coffee shop in Praed Street, behind the station, Magda opened the envelope as Petrov sipped the Latte that she had given him, the amount of caffeine in his system was only adding to his wired state, but they had to try and look as normal as possible. The place was crowded with tourists from a myriad of nationalities speaking in an overexcited babble of languages and affording them no interest or attention as they scrutinised itineraries and folded maps. On a piece of A4 the instructions for the next day were typed in Russian Cyrillic along with the address of a cheap hotel not far from the station where they had been booked for the night. Attached to the sheet of paper were two Rail Staff ID cards to be fitted into the holders that were in the bottom of the envelope. In the crew bag they would find two Railway uniforms and outdoor coats. Along with instructions for delivering the package they carried to agreed locations, the final lines of type contained the times, destinations and departing platform numbers for three high speed trains leaving for the West Country the next morning.

Finishing the drinks they made their way along the street to a shabby double fronted hotel, set back from the road. The reception area was brightly lit and furnished with large fat leather armchairs and solid looking wooden coffee tables. Magda stepped over to the polished reception desk to be greeted by a young bubbly, and over familiar Polish girl. She presented both their passports, more assumed identity, and filled in the formalities of the form the girl presented to her. She politely declined the offered breakfast upgrade at a reduced price and took the key card from the proffered hand.

There was no lift and after climbing three flights of stairs and banging the cases and trolley bags against the walls of the narrow and uneven hallway they found the room was at the back of the hotel, above the hotel kitchens. The hallway had a pervasive smell of mustiness mixed with floor polish that was replaced by cooking smells as they entered the room. The hotel, much like the one they had booked into, but never used in Redhill, was sufficiently anonymous for their uses and offered the cover they needed. The extended militia network had done its job and Someone, they did not know who, had done the legwork and found them a hideaway for the coming hours. Neither Magda nor Petrov had been to London before but they had no time for sightseeing. Precise instructions on how to navigate the area of London they were in had also been inside the envelope. The mission they had been given was likely to be their last, they knew, because of their experience and the trust placed in them, that this was a one-way trip. That they would become infamous for the devastation they were about to have a hand in causing was reward enough for both of them. Although they did not know the true capabilities or operation of the packages they carried, they both knew it would have a major importance to the group to have attracted this amount of planning. That the Major was the driving force they had no doubt and they knew the preparation would have been meticulous. Their own involvement, they were regarded as the best, guaranteed what was about to happen was of the highest magnitude.

They lifted the cases on to the bed and propped the trolley bags against the wall. Magda let herself into the small en-suite bathroom. It was pleasantly appointed and there was a surprisingly large shower and bath for the size of the small, but comfortable room. She ran the cold tap and splashed water onto her face, before pulling a large and fluffy towel from the wall mounted rack and rubbing her face and hair.

She knew Petrov would need de-stressing after the journey into London and the aftermath of the killings he had already performed. She returned to the cramped room from the bathroom to find him naked on the bed waiting for her in an agitated state of arousal. She quickly shed her clothing and joined him on the bed and grasped his engorged manhood with her tiny hand.

EIGHT

Frank thanked the taxi diver and made his way around the neatly laid flower beds on the brightly coloured and very crunchy gravelled path. He spent the journey from Leeds station studying the glossy website the home had on the Internet. The pictures portrayed a very select and high-end establishment in a quiet suburb of the city that catered for the well-off retired of Yorkshire. The double automatic glass doors swished open as he approached them and he entered a high ceilinged and luxurious lobby that would not have been out of place in a very expensive hotel. On reflection, he thought, this is a very expensive hotel, for wealthy retired people. He was greeted by an elegant, manicured and smiling young receptionist. "Can I help you Sir?" The accent was very much Yorkshire but with an effected and polished delivery.

"Yes." He replied, returning the smile. "My name is Frank Martin. I have an appointment to see Mrs Biddle."

"Welcome Mr Martin to the Later Years Retreat. Please take a seat." She turned back to her computer. "I will tell them you are here."

Frank thanked the receptionist and made his way through the deep carpet to the seating area that looked like it belonged in some grand stately home.

He settled himself into a large, well upholstered, chair with plump cushions that almost enveloped him. He had spent the journey from Kings Cross to Leeds reading the latest information on the search for Yorkie and the developing operation in Surrey that Si had emailed to him. Forensic information had connected the killing of the driver in France to the body in the wood outside Redhill. It appeared that whoever had carried out both murders was also responsible for the explosive destruction of the car at the Travel Lodge car park. CCTV footage from the station, that fortunately had also covered the car park, had clearly shown two figures, one male and one female, leaving the vehicle in the car park. The images from the platform cameras had also shown the clear detonation of a device inside the vehicle, by remote control, by the female. Some in depth investigation, and intervention by Interpol, had identified the two figures as known operatives of the Russian Crimean separatists. SO15, the Met Police Counter Terrorism Command, had now taken over the operation in Surrey and were liaising with Avril, who was also sending him updates. Sir Anthony had made it a priority and his detectives were making progress and currently tracing their journey towards London.

He now waited to be taken to talk to Yorkie's Mother who he had last seen forty years ago when he had been invited for the weekend. He remembered the visit fondly and the way the whole family had made him feel so welcome. How had it all gone so badly wrong for Yorkie? They were such a lovely, stable, warm family. She now resided in this very comfortable home in a Leeds suburb paid for by Yorkie's younger brother who had been a professional footballer and was now a successful art dealer and TV pundit. Frank had spoken to him by phone on the journey up to explain what was happening and to ask if he had had any contact with his brother recently. He had been told that they had not spoken since he fled all those years ago, and as far as he was concerned he did not have a brother. He had been quite concerned that Frank had felt the need to contact his Mother and had started babbling about a Solicitor being present until Frank had assured him that it was nothing more than a quiet chat and he would not unduly stress his mother. He knew the family had not taken Yorkie's disappearance very well and as far as he could remember they had not been treated very well by the Military authorities. He did recall a story in one of the tabloid newspapers a few months later that accused MI5 of hounding the family, but he had suspected at the time that it had been instigated by the football club his Brother was playing for.

The elegant receptionist caught his eye and beckoned for Frank to follow her down the corridor. The home was tastefully decorated in pastel colours with high end furnishings and Frank noticed the number of large paintings that adorned the walls and suspected he knew who had provided them, probably at a price. Yorkie's brother was now a very well known art dealer and from time to time was seen on some art programme on the BBC, as well as his usual contribution to a Satellite Sports Channel as a football pundit.

At the end of the passageway he was shown into a very comfortably decorated lounge with subdued lighting and a number of large sofas covered in luxury throws and more plump cushions. There was a feint smell of lavender and a number of small flower arrangements sat on highly polished low tables. Seated in an armchair under the window was a very small framed woman dressed in a knitted cardigan and plaid skirt, her white hair was swept back off her face but flowed over her shoulders. Frank recognised her immediately, even after all these years, and smiled as he entered the room. On a small table in front of her stood a coffee pot, two cups and a large ornate plate of chocolate biscuits.

The women smiled and held out her small, delicate hand. "Frank, how lovely for you to come and see me. I know Kevin would be so pleased. It must be at least forty years since he brought you up for the weekend." She made it sound like he was visiting his favourite aunt. It had been a very long time since Frank had seen her but she appeared just as he had remembered her, and she looked very well."Would you like some coffee?" Frank nodded and took a seat in a sofa alongside her. "Sugar?" She asked.

Frank shook his head. "No thank you."

They spent the next ten minutes chatting over generalities and she very much remembered the weekend Kev had taken him to meet his family. Pausing to sip her coffee gave Frank the opportunity he needed. He knew the reason for his visit had been explained to her by the local Leeds Special Branch so he wasted no time, in fact he had no time to waste.

"Mrs Biddle. It is lovely to see you looking so well and it has been nice talking about Kev and the old times but I have some very important questions to ask you. I know the local Police have been to see you so I must ask you do you know where Kev might be?"

She poured two more cups of coffee and offered him the sugar bowl, which he declined, for the second time. "Yes, I know you are looking for him and the Police have told me he is in some kind of trouble. I didn't even know he was still alive." Her eyes appeared watery and it looked like there might be tears, but she held it together and stared straight at Frank. "Kevin left us in 1979. He broke my heart when he went and I could never work out why he had done the things they said he had done. He never got in touch, not even when my husband passed away. His brother tried to pass messages to him via the Foreign Office and they assured him the messages had been delivered, but we heard nothing." She had a far away look in her eyes and seemed to be re-living those far off times.

Frank gently interrupted her. "Don't you mean his Father?" The frail old Woman smiled.

"No Frank. My husband wasn't Kevin's Father. Although Tommy, my husband, brought Kevin up as his own he was not his Father."

"Yorkie, I mean Kev, had never mentioned he was adopted."

"We never told him." She sipped the coffee and blew her nose in a delicate handkerchief as the tears threatened again. "I worked in London before I had Kevin, and in those days it was frowned upon to have a child out of wedlock." She smiled again weakly across the table at Frank. "I was very young and London was full of charming young men. I worked in the typing pool at the Foreign Office and we girls were always being invited to parties by the Civil Servants and Diplomats. I am ashamed to say it now, but I had a brief relationship with one of them and fell pregnant. Once it was found out I was carrying a foreign Diplomats child I was sent back to Yorkshire and it was all hushed up. Kevin's Father was Russian, Frank."

Frank almost fell off the sofa as her softly spoken words started to sink in. "Are you telling me that after everything he went through he was actually Russian?" He must have looked even more surprised than he had sounded as the reply was accompanied by a subtle chuckle.

"Yes Frank. I'm afraid I was a very naughty girl all those years ago."

She went on to describe how she had married Thomas, Tommy, Biddle a few months later, just before Yorkie had been born. Tommy had been her childhood sweetheart and when she had returned to Barnsley, even with someone else's child, he had been more than keen to rekindle the romance. Tommy had brought Yorkie up as his own child and two years later she had given birth to another son, Roger, who had gone on to become a fairly decent Professional footballer before turning to the art world. She also told him that far from being employed on the Railway, as Yorkie had always told him, Tommy Biddle had worked in the local industry of glass making and had died not in a railway accident, but from Silicosis associated with his work.

"I was never allowed any contact with his Father once I returned to Yorkshire." The far away look had re-appeared. "I received an official letter on Foreign Office headed paper sometime later to tell me he had been involved in an accident and had died, and that was that. My Tommy loved Kevin and we were very happy together, but our Kev never really fitted in with the other kids around us. Tommy was overjoyed when the RAF accepted him." She again wiped her eyes with the lace edged handkerchief. "It broke my Tommy's heart when he did what he did."

Frank had thanked Mrs Biddle and promised to come and visit her again when all this was over. He had contacted the local Police, not wanting to waste any more time with train journeys, and was now sat in the back of a Special Branch BMW as it made its way at speed, escorted by the blue light traffic car ahead, down the M1 towards London. He was trying to put some sense into what he had learned over the last day or so but so far was struggling to work out exactly what was going on. He had no doubt in his mind that whatever it was had to be connected with the incidents the Counter Terrorism Branch were now pursuing. Using the encrypted in-car radio he had discussed his thoughts with Sir Anthony Baxter and had his commitment of full support to STAG as the operation progressed. He had also spoken to the STAG Director and given him a full appraisal for onward communication with the Home Secretary. Yorkie had obviously come back for a reason or maybe several reasons, but at the moment none of them were obvious.

Si Radford, back in London, was now urgently trying to track down the Russian angle. Avril, who had previously worked in the Foreign Office and had many contacts, was working the possible embassy connection. SO15, on the direction of Baxter, had now added Yorkie's disappearance to the operation they were now running and were making progress identifying the images from the CCTV at Redhill. The trail had led them so far back to Paddington Station and footage from there was now being analysed. Although progress, of a sort, was being made it still did not make the why, where or when any clearer.

=

Yorkie placed the paper cup on the small pull-down table in front of his seat. The hot liquid burned his throat as he swallowed the first sip of his coffee. The rocking of the train carriage as it rattled over a dip in the track slopped the coffee almost over the rim of the cup. He fumbled the plastic lid back onto the cup and eased his aching shoulder against the seat back. The coffee you could get on the train definitely had not changed in forty years and the carriage was cramped and overcrowded, much as he had remembered. Many Friday evenings he had made the long and tedious journey from the Midlands back to his home in Yorkshire. Most Fridays the trains had been packed with students returning North so the ancient carriages had been crammed, cold and if it was Winter damp with condensation running down the inside of the windows. Nothing much had changed, although the coaches were slightly more modern but still packed from end to end. During his time in Russia he used to remember those Friday night journeys with a rosy fondness. He had been proud to travel home in his uniform, and even prouder stepping off the train to be met by his father and then the short walk to the local and a pint before one of his Mother's famous Yorkshire fry-ups. But it had all been a lie and a charade and his real home had been with his real family and now he despised them and the grotty county.

He had just made the last train out of Leeds after his aborted attempt to see his Mother, not that he really knew why he had even tried. Growing up in Yorkshire oblivious to the fact that his family was not his family was something he could not ever forgive her for. What he was going to do if he had been able to see her was irrelevant now, but the sense of betrayal, anger and hatred he felt for her was still an aching poison in him. Never telling him, in all those years, that the man he called dad was not his father was in Yorkie's eyes a nasty and vindictive move on her part. It was only after fleeing to Russia, a place he now loved and called home, and meeting Gregorio did the truth of who he really was reveal itself to him. Far from being the son of a working class Yorkshire industrial worker he was in fact the product of a Russian military dynasty.

His life had changed that day amid the storms of the North sea as he had huddled in his tiny cabin. He had been terrified, very sea sick, confused and not sure of where or what he was going to. The reality of what he had done was dawning on him. He loved his life in the Royal Air Force but knew that he did not fit in from day one of basic training. There was something about him that he did not understand. Something that made him different. He joined in the barrack room horseplay and piss-taking but never felt a part of the group. His slight, slim stature had marked him out for some of the piss-taking but he just shrugged it off. Frank Martin had been his only real friend and had often stood up for him when the taunting got too much. So why had Frank not followed him that night?

He had felt alone and betrayed for weeks, no months, after his escape from the UK. Betrayed by the person he thought would come and get him, take him back, explain it all. Frank Martin had looked after him when the mocking started, protected him from the insults. He had been there for him when he couldn't hold his drink and the pushing had started, had taken him to his room, had put him to bed. But he had not come that night, had not come when he needed him most. Frank could have explained it all to them, explained how weak he was, how it was not his fault, explained how he was different. But he had not come.

He stared out of the window at the lights of the outskirts of Leeds as the train negotiated the twists and turns of the tracks. After a fearful and nauseating journey he had finally arrived in a holding camp in Russia, as he had told Frank earlier, and his evaluation had began. During many months of questioning and appraisal things started to make sense. The Russians had been extremely appreciative of the information he had passed them over the previous months and were keen to exploit the skills that he had brought with him. Within a couple of weeks they had moved him from the camp to a small and comfortable apartment. Although escorted everywhere he went he was given a fair amount of freedom and began to settle into his new way of life. It was made very obvious that there was no going back to the life he had left.

After six months of intense questioning he was moved to a small town in the North where he was offered an education programme and a chance to learn the language, which he took to and found very easy. The Russian words and pronunciations held no difficulty for him, reading and writing in Cyrillic came to him almost naturally. It was during the programme that he was given a personal mentor and the Russians had started to explain to him what his real background was. They had spoken to him about his real father and the family that he had come from with all its honour in the Russian military. They had showed him photos of his father, his grandfather resplendent in his Generals uniform, showed him the lineage, accepted him, welcomed him home. At first, he had been disbelieving but when the documentary evidence, both from Russian and British sources, had been presented to him the reality of who he really was, far from alarming him, made him feel finally at home.

He engaged fully with the education he was offered and sought out opportunities to become more integrated, to become a Russian. His hosts encouraged him to immerse himself in the family pedigree and he took on the Antonov name. He became engaged in the Radio technology projects they were working on, as he had told Frank, and the Russian authorities had encouraged him to allow the MI6 contact. The information that he then fed back the other way was worthless and stage managed by his superior officers on the project. He had felt alive for the first time in this new and exciting World. But deep inside him, even in those early days, he felt a sense of betrayal. He had been betrayed by his Mother by not revealing to him his real identity and bringing him up as someone else's bastard. He had also been betrayed by Frank when he had needed him most.

He pulled the laptop from the canvas bag at his feet and opened the app to find the strongest Internet signal, not relying on the feeble on board offering. The hacking cough returned and he doubled over until it abated. The Russian system had taught him well and now he was deploying those skills in the role he was now committed to, returning the Crimea to its rightful place in the Motherland. He and Gregorio had planned this day for many years. Gregorio had taught him how important the cause was, how he would be revered by the Crimean people when his task succeeded. Gregorio had encouraged, pushed at times as he had dedicated his hours and days to perfecting the technology. There were moments when it felt like Gregorio had the zeal and force of a company director demanding a product be perfect for release, but he knew it was his way of serving the people they both loved. Their lives in Sebastopol had been comfortable, thanks to the now open arms trade, but both had been committed to the cause of returning her to Russia.

His intellect, intelligence and ability to learn quickly in those early months had been identified and remorselessly exploited by the Russian machine. He had been quickly moved from the pursuit of conventional technology when they had identified the natural ability and ease with which he assimilated the emerging computer technology. He was moved to the newly constructed nuclear city of Pripyat and embedded into the process of nuclear trigger evolution, met Gregorio and fell in love.

He opened the tracker to full size on the tablet screen. The location of the couriers, personally selected by Gregorio and used successfully many times, were highlighted and showed they were static in London, as they should be, as everything was going to plan. The tracker, another of his technological creations, also showed the location, close to them, of the four devices they now had in their possession. Soon they would deploy them to the arranged locations, nothing could now stop him celebrating his Father, and leave Gregorio's legacy. Gregorio had been insistent that they use all four devices in this one hit. He had presented four perfect triggers and their associated software and Gregorio had closely supervised the team they had employed to match them to the battlefield weapons. He switched tracker mode and the system brought up the location of a mobile phone that he knew was currently sitting in Frank Martin's pocket heading down the M1. Frank Martin, like all the rest, had let him down all those years ago.

Frank Martin, someone he trusted, had betrayed him that evening. Instead of following him to Hull, his plea for help had been obvious in the note, he had left him to his fate. He could have made the short journey, he could have raised the alarm, he could have saved him. Self-pity was a way of life for Yorkie. None of it had been his fault. He had been trapped, coerced, betrayed but then finally loved, wanted and respected. Frank Martin had forgotten him. He knew Frank Martin would be involved in his pursuit, he knew Frank Martin would want the glory. He would now show all those that had let him down, all those he despised and hated. His would be the final play.

NINE

*Sweat poured into Frank's eyes from the effort of pulling the CO up
the bank into the relative safety of the scrape. The smell of cordite
and smoke filled the air all around him as he dressed the wounds in
front of him. The CO was still breathing a heavy, ragged and
wheezing breath that whistled as he exhaled. As he applied the
dressing the blood seeped through onto his hands and he wiped them
roughly on his combat smock. In his ears, through the Bakelite
headset still clamped to his head, an incoming message clamoured
for his intention. The beeping grew louder and louder as if impatient
for an answer.*

With sweat still stinging his eyes and running down his cheeks Frank
woke with a start and to the streaming of the lights of oncoming
traffic in the back of the Special Branch vehicle. They were now
racing through the outskirts of North London, heading for The
Embankment. The blue light from the escorting car now washing
into the rear seats through the darkness. The mobile in his hand was
vibrating and the increasing volume of the ringtone demanded
attention. He flicked open the phone cover, it was Si Radford.
"Evening Frank. Get the driver to bring you straight to Thames
House. Operation meeting being stepped up and COBRA is being
convened. I have emailed you everything we now have." Frank
acknowledged and shut the phone down. COBRA was the high-level
meeting convened to brief the Government, in this case, on what was
now being treated as a potential terrorist plot.

Flicking open his emails he saw Si's message at the top of the list.
He had called Si after leaving Mrs Biddle at the retirement home and
given him the new lead on where they should be looking. Si had got
to work with the help of Samantha who carried out most of the deep
research and historical analysis for the team. Extremely intelligent

and highly educated she brought a wealth of research technique and experience to the team, much to the disgust of MI5 who she had left to join STAG after meeting Frank.

While Si had concentrated on re-tracing Yorkie's recent movements by retro mapping all his electronic contact points, Frank didn't even try to understand it, Samantha had started digging deep into the complex character that was Yorkie Biddle. The attached report that Samantha had compiled was several pages long. Frank opened the file and started reading.

As his Mother had told Frank, she had trained as a clerical typist at a college in Leeds before being lucky enough to secure a junior typist position with the Foreign Office in London. It was the late 1950s and there were lots of opportunities in Government circles in the late post-war years as Britain grappled with its foreign entities amid the emerging new World order. Large numbers of young girls were offered the chance to work in the Capital as it built on the wave of post austerity. London was propelling itself towards the swinging sixties and Yorkie's Mother took a full and active part in all the social opportunities that came her way. The invitations to Civil Service social functions were many and they were encouraged to attend, particularly when it involved fraternising with members of the foreign diplomatic corps. They were also encouraged to report any contacts they made.

It was at one of these such parties, within days of her arrival in London, held in one of the ornate function rooms at the King Charles Street headquarters of the Foreign Office that she had met Sergei Antanov, a young Russian diplomat attached to the Soviet Embassy. He was a young, handsome and very charming Major of the Russian Army working with the Military Attaché. He was descended from a revered Russian Military dynasty, his father was a senior General as had been his Grandfather, and was destined for a glittering career. They had immediately started a torrid, brief and passionate affair, although it was discouraged by her senior grades. Within a few weeks she found herself carrying the Major's baby. Both authorities moved quickly to avoid the obvious scandal that would have inevitably followed if the news had made it into the press.

She was sent home to her family in Yorkshire and he was moved out of London by the Embassy hierarchy. She, just before Yorkie was born, married her childhood sweetheart Tommy and, with quiet financial help from the Foreign Office, set up home in Barnsley. A second son followed within eighteen months and they all settled down to family life and a very proud Tommy Biddle, with more quiet help, rose to the grade of foreman in the local glass works. She continued to covertly correspond with her Russian ex-lover for a number of months until, tragically, the Major was killed trying to cross a Railway siding while observing the movement of British Nuclear armaments in the West Country. It was reported as a tragic accident and his body was sent back to Moscow with full military honours.

Digging into the Security Service archives and pulling rank to read the non-redacted versions of filed reports, Samantha had unearthed what had really happened to the Major. She had been given full access, begrudgingly, to one of the Service's 'Wendy's' as MI5's paper file storage facilities were known. In a couple of hours with the help of a very junior MI5 officer, again begrudgingly supplied, the full picture emerged.

Major Sergei Antanov was a very flamboyant character with an air of elevated confidence, no doubt boosted by the family dynasty, who liked to work hard and party harder. Although officially attached to the trade division of the Russian Embassy his real role was to spy on emerging British nuclear weaponry. He would spend days observing the delivery of the weapons and component parts to the new V Bomber Force and its subsequent training sorties from various airfields around the UK. In addition he was also reported to have been adept at gaining access to the secure nuclear sidings around the country. It was believed that during one of these clandestine visits he had met his tragic end.

The non-redacted versions of reports Samantha had managed to elicit from the MI5 'Wendy' put a very different slant on the official document that was in the public domain. MI5, tipped off by their MI6 colleagues prior to Antanov's arrival in the UK, had been closely monitoring the Major from day one. His party loving ego had made it easy for them to get close to him. There was some suggestion in the reports that he was possibly getting too close to the new technology, and maybe his end was more engineered than a tragic accident.

Samantha had highlighted the Railway accident and Frank took a moment to think through the possibility that this could be the link they had been looking for. It was not beyond possibility that the 'real' reason for his father's demise was known by the Russians all along and had eventually been fed back to Yorkie. Could Yorkie have come back 'to do something' for his natural father and not for the father that had brought him up? Had they been looking in the wrong direction? If all the information Samantha had unearthed been on record, how the hell did Yorkie manage to join the Military and obtain the highest security clearance there was? The answer to that one was annotated to Samantha's report in italics, she was thinking ahead of him again:

Application for Top Secret Security clearance following Positive Vetting, in use at the time, approved following scrutiny by MI5 and

MI6. Reasons given that Kevin Biddle was brought up by his Mother and Tommy Biddle who had married before he was born and he never knew his natural father, or even that he existed. It was felt that the risk was non-existent.

Frank read the paragraph again. Well there damn well was a risk. The British system may have deemed it was not a risk and glibly forgotten about it, but the Russian system definitely had not. Did they target Yorkie because they knew his real background? They had obviously filled in the blanks for him.

The car negotiated the mini-roundabout at the end of Lambeth Bridge and glided to a stop outside the front steps to Thames House. Frank ran up the steps two at a time and in through the heavy, ornate, glass doors. Flashing his ID he bypassed the entry pods and went through the disabled entry door being held open by a uniformed security guard. Si was waiting to the left of the entry pods, holding back the sliding door of the lift. As they entered Si pressed the button for the sixth floor. "The meeting is waiting for you Frank. They all have the up to date info, including the work by Surrey Special Branch, and COBRA is meeting in an hour." The lift doors opened and they made their way down the corridor to the conference room.

The room was crowded and MI5 had rolled out the big guns. The head of MI5 Counter Terrorism, Toby Gadsby, was in control although Paul Whittle and Avril were also in attendance. Frank and Si took their seats and it was Avril who opened the meeting, bringing everyone up to date with the operation to track the two suspects from the Surrey incidents. She went over the reports in fine detail that had been coming in regularly from the Special Branch teams that were now on the ground. The trail of the two suspects identified by the reports from Interpol was now becoming obvious.

Avril came to the main point of pulling the meeting together. "It would appear from the CCTV picture we have managed to piece together they are now somewhere in London." Still images of the two walking down the platform at Paddington station appeared on the screen behind her. "As you can see from the images they are carrying quite heavy bags or cases and we believe this could be some kind of device." You don't say, thought Frank. Another image appeared showing the two figures talking to someone in a railway uniform just beyond the ticket gates. Frank spoke quickly as she paused for breath. "Excuse me Avril." Heads turned his way. "Are you connecting these two with Yorkie Biddle?"

The head of Counter Terrorism interjected before Avril could reply. "At this time, Frank, we have no reason to connect these two suspects with your Mr Biddle. They have already carried out at least two murders, are suspected of carrying potential explosive devices, and may be planning an imminent attack on London. Why would a sorry returning traitor have anything to do with this?" He waved his hand dismissively towards Frank. "We are still checking with Interpol and our European colleagues but there is a very good chance that we have an ISIS connection as well. We are now running this as a separate operation Frank, and Avril will be briefing COBRA after this meeting. The Home Secretary has now pushed it to the highest priority and all our resources will now be dedicated to this operation."

A hushed silence fell over the meeting room and Frank could feel the eyes of everyone present staring at him. It wasn't the first time MI5 had used their Political connections to try and pull an operation away from STAG, and the fact that it was Avril going to brief COBRA and not the Head of Section meant their reasons for trying were absolutely political and not operational. If they were proved wrong it would be Avril who was roasted and not any senior managers. Since the London Underground attacks of 7/7 where MI5 had been found sadly lacking in their reading of all the pertinent intelligence, it appeared that lessons had not really been learned and they were still an organisation that thrived, for funding and image reasons, on grabbing the obvious and missing the detail. That was the reason STAG had been created, to focus on the in-depth detail of real and potentially deadly threats, using any available method, not worried by the Political and media fallout.

When he spoke Frank's voice was steady and measured. He spoke directly to Avril, ignoring the eyes upon him. "Thank you Avril for your update. I can see why this part of the threat is a priority to MI5 but obviously we must not rule anything out and we have potentially a very dangerous man somewhere in the country." He caught the flinch in the Head of Counter Terrorism's eye as he continued. "Your two suspects are well known operators within a Crimean separatist group that we know have carried out several attacks in the past, usually confined to Ukranian interests. Why is it in their interest to carry out an attack here in the UK if they are not working with or for a higher authority?"

Before he could continue Toby Gadsby cut across him. "They are Frank. That higher authority is ISIS who have purchased their obvious operational skills and access to weapons. COBRA is about to meet so I must now wrap this meeting up. Thank you all for attending and Avril will forward you the tasks and priorities." He rose from his seat and headed for the door. Frank was about to follow him when Si pulled at his sleeve. He handed Frank his mobile. A message flashed on to the screen. 'Hi Frank. Good meeting? Cheers Yorkie.'

Frank turned and beckoned across the room to Avril who was fielding questions from a gaggle of overexcited analysts. He showed her the screen. "Your boss is wrong. Those two are very much connected to Yorkie. He is very clever and he is very able. They may be the foot soldiers but this man is driving this."

111

Avril sighed. "I know Frank but we have been told to concentrate on the potential attack on London. I can't go against COBRA or the Service. I will keep the reports coming to you." She turned and walked away down the corridor. A text flashed on to his phone. It was from Samantha.'On my way to COBRA.'

Frank stared out of the window to the meandering Thames way below. London was always the obvious target to the mainstream Intelligence agencies despite the not so distant history of attacks in other major Cities by the IRA. He was not so sure. Yorkie was not a Londoner, he detested the place, but did he have a reason to attack it. Frank remembered the long weekend they had spent in the Capital during training. Yorkie had moaned about 'bloody rich Southerners' for the whole trip, but was that a reason to attack them? He didn't think so. He thought back to Samantha's report on his natural father. Yes, he was stationed in London and his mother had met him here but would that alone be a reason for carrying out an attack here. If the two MI5 suspects were the executive end of the attack how was he going to direct it?

Sihad joined him at the window. "I've traced his last message to you. He is at Kings Cross station, or he was fifteen minutes ago."

Frank looked at the location report."Shit, that means he is here in London and he could be about to meet those two. Maybe MI5 are right and we are looking at a London attack?"

Si opened his laptop and leaned it against the window sill. He pulled up a document and turned the screen towards Frank."This is the digging I've been doing into Yorkie's technical skills. This report has just come in from GCHQ. I had a mate of mine down there run a scenario for me through their crypto analysis and real time tacking systems. It would appear that he has advanced his knowledge into the remote control of devices somewhat. Using the Internet, they believe, he is able to control and trigger a device anywhere. He doesn't need to be close by, all he needs is a reliable and strong Internet signal."

Frank quickly skimmed the report. Was this possible or was this Si and his techie mates getting carried away again? "Wouldn't you just be able to jam the signal?" Frank had an ancient knowledge of old radio technology from his past but nothing like the cutting edge brain that Si possessed.

"The only real way to stop it would be to turn off the whole Internet, and that's not going to happen. If you could find the devices then you could, in theory, shield the receiver from any internet signal while you tried to disable them. All he needs is a laptop just like this one with the right software, his software, and he can feed instructions into the devices all day long if we don't know where they are."

Frank looked back out to The Thames. "The two suspects in Avril's briefing were carrying large cases. Could these be big enough to carry any devices or have they delivered them some other way?" A commotion in the corridor behind him attracted Frank's attention and a group of analysts moved aside to allow Avril back into the room.

"One of our suspects is on the move towards Paddington station. We have Special Branch and a tactical unit on the way." She paused to draw in a lungful of air. "The boss is going to the COBRA meeting. My car is outside Frank."

TEN

Magda watched Petrov from the window of their room high up in the roof of the hotel as he crossed the road outside, avoiding a number of black cabs as they made their way to the station. The collar of his black leather jacket was pulled up around his neck and his hands were pushed into the pockets. He walked easily on the balls of his feet with an air of authority and despite his attempt to blend into the busy street scene he appeared to her very much the assassin he was. Fortunately for him London was full of wannabe gangster types so no one paid him any attention. Petrov had the blood of many enemies on his hands and his talent for killing, both entranced and frightened her in equal measure. She had seen his skills deployed many times and also the convulsive, sexual aftermath. He loved Magda in his own way but his only real loyalty and love was for the Major and he would willingly lay down his own life for him and their joint cause.

Hidden behind the grubby net curtains that hung down across the grimy, stained windows she observed him make his way down the side street towards the main road. He walked with a purpose and was almost automaton in his slavish abiding of the plan that they both followed. Just before he disappeared from her view he abruptly stopped and immediately hailed a cab heading alongside the station. As Petrov climbed quickly into the back Magda saw the large, black saloon car move away from the kerb and ease into the heavy traffic two cars back, the two male occupants in the front seat were clearly visible.

She remained at the window observing the street below looking for the surveillance that she knew would be left waiting for her to follow Petrov from the hotel. Across the busy street she could just make out the outline of a female figure in the window of a small coffee shop, and further back parked on the same side as the hotel sat a small blue car with two male occupants. All three had been there for some time and had made no attempt to move when Petrov had walked down the street. The watching team were obviously well trained and had been split into at least two units. It was now up to her to outwit the remaining watchers as Petrov towed his tail away across London.

The first thing Magda had done on arriving at the hotel, after another frantic coupling with Petrov, was to survey the exit plan that had been outlined for her in the details handed to her at Paddington Station. The militia preparation team, comprising of loyal sympathisers living in the UK, had carried out a thorough reconnaissance during the operation planning stage and no detail had been left unplanned. Many of them had family still living under the Ukranian diktat, others were paid mercenaries selling themselves to the highest bidder. So far each stage had worked directly as it had been arranged. The transport had been in its planned locations and the contacts along the way, all paid and deemed as dispensable, had carried out their roles to the letter. Petrov had performed the task of protector and executioner, when required, while she had been given the task of delivering the packages to their pre-planned positions.

Thefour packages that they had carried in the two large lead lined cases were now arranged on the floor at the side of the bed. Magda took two of the packages, one at a time, and placed them both into one of the trolley cases. The third package she put into the second trolley case, making sure to fill the space to stop it from banging about within the case. Happy that all the preparation was complete for the next day she took the fourth, and slightly larger, package and placed it into a small rucksack that lay at her feet.

Taking a last check from the window. All three watchers were still in place, Magda made her way out of the room with the rucksack over her shoulder. She picked up a worn and frayed denim jacket from the bed on the way out and pulled the door closed behind her. She slid the door key card into the hip pocket of her red leather trousers. The blonde wig that now covered her own hair and the heavily applied make up gave her an appearance that would identify her as one of the many foreign students that were around this part of London.

Checking around her as she walked away from the room she made her way quietly to the far end of the hotel landing and quickly pushed open the entrance to the internal fire escape. She stopped and looked about her, listening for any movement, making sure she was not observed she then descended the three flights of stairs down to the basement. The exit plan handed to her by the contact at Paddington Station had outlined the route to be taken from the basement and into the lower level below the main kitchens that housed the preparation area for the hotel dining rooms that were used as entertainment venues. At this time of year there were very few midweek events and this area was unused. Checking that no one was around she made her way out of the back of the kitchens and up a small flight of stone steps into the delivery area of the hotel.

Happy there were no deliveries taking place Magda crossed between two metal wheeled refuse bins and down a small alleyway that took her out to a side street with parked cars along both sides. Continuing to walk away from the hotel she passed a number of small shops, restaurants and wine bars making her way in the opposite direction to the station. Walking briskly down Sussex Place and through Hyde Park Gardens she eventually came to Bayswater Road that ran along the top of Hyde Park. At this time of the evening all four lanes were still busy with traffic. Doubling back a number of times to make sure she was not being followed she crossed the road at a pedestrian crossing into the park. The park was still fairly busy with a lot of people walking through at a brisk pace on their way towards the station. After strolling slowly for ten minutes along one of the many footpaths taking photos on her phone she doubled back on herself to identify any followers, eventually heading for one of the small cafés that were scattered about the top end of the park. She took a seat in the corner of the Italian Gardens café and ordered a latte, sitting for twenty minutes she made a pretext of reading the magazine she pulled from the rucksack whilst observing everyone entering and leaving the café and anyone on the walkway outside. The evening rush hour was in full swing and large crowds of homeward bound commuters were using the park as a short cut to their trains waiting at the station.

Satisfied that she had not been followed Magda paid for her coffee and walked back towards the main road, again observing all around for any sign of any surveillance. A gaggle of Japanese tourists appeared who seemed engrossed in fold up maps waiting for the bus. She joined them and was happy that she was not being followed and the plan was working. The bus, when it arrived was already full and people were standing throughout its length. She managed to join and swiped her pre-paid Oyster travel card that had been included with the plan details, made her way through the crowds to the rear of the bus and stood hanging from an overhead handle with the rucksack wedged between her feet. The bus lurched and jolted its way through the nose to tail traffic and finally stopped outside the station, the doors hissed open and the thronged mass pressed its way on to the pavement. Magda was carried by the rushing onslaught towards the platforms but managed, halfway across the main concourse, to extricate herself and head in the opposite direction.

The station was packed with passengers and a swelling mass was stationed in the middle of the concourse straining up at the departure boards. At periodic intervals, as a departure for a specific destination flashed up, an embryonic floe would break away from the Mother berg and head at a flustered, rushing high speed for the ticket gates. Amid the thronging melee Magda made her way through the sliding doors at the head of the concourse and up the escalator to a small sandwich bar. She plucked a plastic wrapped sandwich and a bottle of still water from the glass display case and handed over the correct money to the cashier. Making her way to an empty table with a view back down towards the concourse she sat for another thirty minutes, again using the magazine as cover, to observe any approaches.

Satisfied she was not being followed she left the sandwich and the water untouched on the table and joined the down escalator to platform level.

In the far corner of the concourse she found the lost property office tucked away out of view but bustling with activity. Waiting in a queue until it was her turn she presented the rucksack to the harassed attendant. The throng of home going commuters trying to retrieve long lost personal belongings, intermingled with hyper American and Japanese tourists, assured the briefest of questioning of where Magda had found the item. A cursory sweep of the x-ray wand, thwarted by the lead wrapping around the package, registered nothing and the bag was tagged and added to the pile awaiting removal to the storage area in a large metal cage. By the time Magda had placed the receipt slip into her jacket pocket and turned away the rucksack had been covered by three other bags thrown into the cage. She side stepped another group of frantic customers and left the office as a shoal of overexcited Japanese tourists entered to berate the attendant about a lost camera.

Walking quickly across the concourse she joined the jostling throng under the electronic destination boards awaiting the identification of platforms for particular departing trains. A shrill announcer's voice, distorted and babbling, triggered a stampede towards the gates, allowing Magda to avoid the gaze of the two patrolling Police Officers and head for the underground. She turned on her heels as the tide swept away towards the far platforms and headed down the steps to the relative sanctuary of the Underground station.

Sliding the Oyster card across the reader and negotiating the automatic entry gate she joined the thinning crowd heading away from the mayhem of the main line station. The Westbound District line platform was sparsely populated, most commuters were now heading in the opposite direction into the crowded rush for home. Identifying the CCTV high on the wall above the platform she sought out the shelter of a chocolate vending machine and slid back against the wall out of its sight line. She managed to sidle behind a pair of suited City types on the platform edge, avoiding the camera as the rattle of the points and the sparking of the electronic contacts on the live rail heralded the arrival of the train. Staying as close as possible she followed the two men into the carriage as the automatic doors slid open.

The carriage was lightly populated and Magda was able to sit alone in a four seat partition at the far end. Her fellow travellers were immersed in their own journey's and did not offer her a second glance. As the train made its rolling gait way through the darkened tunnels she kept her eyes fixed on the network route map above the exit doors and counted off the eight stops to St James' Park. Clanking to a stop the doors jerked open and she stepped down onto the platform and made a play of reading the posters plastered to the wall facing her until the other four or five alighting passengers had walked away to the stairs. Happy that no one was watching her she climbed the steps onto the Broadway end of the station and swiped the Oyster card to open the gate. Walking slowly she made her way onto Queen Anne's Gate, stopping at a newsagent to buy a fizzy drink and pick up a copy of the Evening Standard.

Taking the narrow footpath out onto Bird Cage Walk Magda hailed a black cab and gave the driver the address of the hotel. She sat in the back and stared from the window as they turned in front of Buckingham Palace and up Constitution Hill towards the Wellington Arch. Avoiding the attempted small talk from the driver she pulled her phone from the pocket of her jacket and opened the pre-drafted text, selected the contact and pressed send. She then scrolled down to received messages and opened the waiting message from 'pet', as expected it was blank, that confirmed all was as planned. Petrov had been successful in his part of the decoy operation and it meant the watchers still had no idea what they were delivering or where. Had they known, then Magda was sure that he would have been lifted sometime during his ride around Central London. She also knew that he would not have gone without a fight.

She asked the cab driver to stop in a side street on Bayswater Road, paid him for the full journey, and alighted onto a busy street now thronged with people out for their evenings entertainment in the pubs and wine bars. Taking the usual precautions she took a different route back to the rear of the hotel. Spending five minutes stood in the shadows of the delivery area she retraced her steps back through the hotel, swiped the key card through the reader and entered the room. Petrov was waiting for her, his trousers and boxer shorts at his knees as he lay on the double bed, his engorged penis throbbed at his groin. The strain and tension was etched on his face, even the act of decoying the watchers had built him to a frenzy from which he now required sating. Magda had become accustomed to his post killing arousal and need for discharge, but his every action now appeared to demand her attention. The mission end was at hand and they both acknowledged it could call for the ultimate sacrifice. She dropped to her knees at his side and gave him his release.

=

Avril pulled the earpiece from her ear and turned in her seat to face the rear of the car. They had spent the last two hours following at a discrete distance behind the Special Branch surveillance team as it had toured Central London following one of the suspects. "The cab has just turned back into the hotel Frank. No stops along the way. It would appear our suspect has been taking us on a sightseeing tour."

Frank leaned forward and squinted against the headlights from the oncoming traffic heading along the Bayswater Road in the London darkness. "Has his partner made any move?"

Avril replaced the earpiece and spoke quickly into the handset in her right hand requesting situation report from the watching teams. "No movement at all. She is still in the hotel. Our own MI5 team has been in place all evening."

Frank was about to answer her when his phone rang. He accepted the call and spoke sharply into the handset. "Yes Si. What have you got?" The frustration was building in his voice, no action had yet been taken and they had just been on a pointless tour around London. The reply was calm and measured, as usual.

"I've just had a ping from the same handset we identified on the train from Redhill. In fact two pings. It looks like our suspect has been in touch with two people. Location seems to be somewhere on Constitution Hill, probably from a taxi as I also managed to pick up its locator beacon through the clutter, and on the move."

Frank's question of what time the contact was made was answered quickly from the handset.

"Your suspect number one was already back at the hotel Frank. This was the women and she has definitely not been at the hotel all evening."

Frank ended the call and leaned forward between the two front seats and spoke directly to Avril. "It would appear your MI5 team has been out-foxed."

Throughout the journey back through the late evening traffic Avril kept up an almost constant tirade into her mobile as she extracted a full report from the team that had trailed the suspect through London. Once satisfied that the cab he had been in had not stopped or picked anyone up she immediately ordered the removal of the watching team at the hotel and replaced them with a double compliment of watchers. Frank left her updating her boss who had just left the COBRA meeting as he was dropped off at the STAG offices on the corner of Palmer Street and Broadway.

Ignoring the lift, as he usually did, Frank took the stairs at a run up to the second floor open plan office where STAG did it's business. The whole of the floor was one large office with clusters of desks arranged around the walls. In the middle a large oval table dominated the space with six individual computer monitors rising from its surface. This was the nerve centre for any operation involving STAG personnel and tonight it was where Si Radford and two members of his team were monitoring streams of data from various platforms, some legally and others not so legally. Samantha was sat at her desk in the far corner of the room with a view of St James' Park. She was deep in conversation with a research assistant via a video link to one of the many agencies that provided her, and STAG, with information.

As Frank entered the office Si waved him over to the monitor he was observing. "Your man Yorkie is on the move Frank." He swivelled the monitor to face Frank and pointed to a series of lighted dots traced out on a map of the Eastern side of England. "This shows the tracking of his phone and looks like he is heading North up the East Coast rail line." Frank leaned over his shoulder to see the position just South of Grantham being highlighted. Before Frank could speak Si continued. "I have also managed to analyse the two outgoing messages from the suspect travelling up Constitution Hill. One definitely went to our boy back at the hotel and I suspect it was a pre-arranged signal as there was no content nor any answer. The other one, Frank, was received by Yorkie's phone."

Frank had no idea how Si did these things nor what black magic he used, or illegal entry, but he didn't care. The guy was a genius. He looked straight at Si and the two technical analysts that were now listening to the conversation, Samantha had also walked over to hear what was being said. "So that confirms our two suspects are definitely connected to whatever Yorkie is up to. MI5 are chasing the obvious shadows again and missing the point."

Si interrupted him."Yes, to a point Frank, but I still think these two are the method of delivery but not the method of execution. While I have been tracking the data movements my team have been looking into the potential to detonate a device remotely using commands via the Internet." He gestured to the two analysts sat on the other side of the table.

Si and his team then gave Frank a full technical explanation, about how with the right code and encryption formatting a number of devices could be controlled without the person giving the commands being many miles, or even hundreds of miles, away. All that was needed was a laptop and a steady, strong, Internet signal and the right encrypted commands. The encryption, Si explained, made it impossible to interrupt the commands once they had been made. Even if the Internet signal was lost the command would remain in readiness and activate once re-established. Once they had finished their explanation the two analysts then showed Frank how it would work. They had not only researched it but had reverse engineered it and built their own version.

"So Frank." Si continued over coffee and rolls that had been hurriedly collected from the all night Deli across the road. "The two suspects currently, we hope, being watched by MI5 only have to make sure the device, or devices, is delivered to where it needs to be. After that it is just a case of whoever has the laptop and codes can sit at a comfortable distance and send the commands at a time of their choosing. At this time my money is currently on Yorkie being that person, the reasons why I will leave up to you."

Franktook a swig of his coffee. "I can go along with everything you say, but where did he get the knowledge or ability to build this thing? When I knew him he was bright enough, but this must be way out of his league."Si glanced at Samantha. "I think your wife might be able to convince you otherwise. We haven't been the only team burning the oil tonight while you've been jollying around London." Frank gave him a sideways look as Samantha brought her coffee over and sat next to Si and his analysts. She flipped open the laptop she had placed on the table.

"Yorkie gave you some of the story Frank when you were in the hotel in Lincoln." The smile she gave him was the one she always used when she was about to remind him that she was the experienced research analyst. "My Foreign Office contact wasn't too pleased in being dragged back to the office this late, so some recompense will be required Mr Martin." Frank shrugged his shoulders as Si chuckled to himself. They all knew how good Samantha was and how without her contacts and knowledge STAG would not be as successful as it was. But the banter between them all was good.

She continued after another mouthful of coffee. "Yorkie was employed on Radio Frequency technology as he told you, but he was very soon identified as having a very technical brain. My research tonight has shown that he was sponsored by the military in Moscow to attend several universities in the early and mid-eighties that were carrying out research into fledgling computer systems and their potential military use." She paused and opened a file on the laptop. "There was a reason why he was able to be sponsored Frank." Samantha turned the screen towards him. Displayed was a Russian document, that Samantha had translated underneath, that showed the Birth Certificate of one Yvgene Antanov, Date of Birth 14th February 1959. Yorkie's birthday. "They welcomed their own back Frank."

The research revealed that Yorkie had been bequeathed a large amount of money from his natural father's estate, although it was still unclear if his entrapment was deliberate or a coincidence. The family had welcomed him warmly and he had quickly proved himself to be a true Russian. Family contacts had provided him with the right offices, protected by the right Generals, to allow him to repay their generosity. His obvious deviant sexuality was conveniently overlooked and he was provided with the comfortable trappings of his elevated position and left, socially, to his own devices. Those own devices had eventually led him to meet the vibrant, young Gregorio at a military sponsored technical conference, shortly before Gregorio had taken over command of the research team. They had become friends, and then lovers, and Gregorio had also opened more doors for Yorkie in the world of missile and munitions application.

As the embryonic application of computer and data processing technology merged with the burgeoning nuclear industry the Russians had purpose built a town to accommodate both the civilian and military R & D needs of the Communist State. Yorkie had moved to the town of Pripyat as a major player in the mobile application of remotely triggered devices. When the reactor at close by Chernobyl had exploded Yorkie had been in the vicinity and although evacuated within hours the effects of his exposure were now evident in his deteriorating physical state.

Yorkie's love for the young and ambitious officer, and his own acceptance by the party elite, had provided, unwittingly at first, an opportunity for him to feather his own nest. At the collapse of the Soviet Union and the end of the Cold War, under Gregorio's counsel, Yorkie was able to solicit business from the now freelancing military elite. Their encouragement and funding, skimmed from legitimate sources, provided the continued impetus and eventually potential orders from the many rogue but willing nations.

Samantha's digging into the provenance of the now very much Russian Yorkie had surprised, and even shocked, the normally unflappable STAG team. It was becoming increasingly obvious as the narrative revealed the depth of his engagement that he may not have been a supine collaborator but the principal perpetrator. Si had kept up a running update during Samantha's delivery as to the current location of Yorkie, or at least his phone, which was currently just outside Grantham in a small hotel. The reason for his appearance at Kings Cross was not apparent and provided a perplexing question mark over how or why he had made the trip. That he was connected to, or more likely directing, the two operatives at Paddington was overwhelmingly agreed.

Frank had checked in with Avril to elicit a report from the watchers at Paddington, who had now covertly been joined by a team from STAG at Frank's direction. The two operatives had been confirmed as back at the hotel. He had also touched base with Sir Anthony Baxter who had immediately put two units of SC19 Tactical Firearms Command on standby and asked to be woken at any developments overnight. The night control staff were given instructions to alert them to any changes before they all retired for some well earned rest.

Frank was woken by the thumping of the heavy guns through bleary, sweaty eyes, that was actually the night staff banging on the office door. He and Samantha had pulled the camp beds, kept for such eventualities, out from the cupboard in the corner of his office and grabbed a couple of hours. Si had managed to secure himself one of the six duty berths in the corridor above the operations room, and left one of his colleagues monitoring all electronic movements with instructions to call him for any eventualities. Frank eased himself out of the low slung bed, his knees groaning as he put weight on them, and made his way into the Ops room. The night supervisor handed him a sheet of message pad that had a short handwritten paragraph on it. It was from the MI5 surveillance team, timed five minutes before, informing him that their two suspects had been seen coming out of an alley at the back of the hotel onto Praed Street. As he was about to ask a question Si stumbled, almost sprawling on the floor, through the door. "Just had a message from Taggart." He was referring to Jim Murray, alias Taggart, who was the lead operator for STAG, both surveillance and executive action. "Two on the move towards Paddington. Taggart and his mates are moving ahead of them. SC19 backing up, and an SF team on standby."

Like Si Radford and Samantha, Taggart was a vital part of the STAG set up. He had joined the Scots Guards after being brought up in a variety of Glasgow Children's homes from the age of eleven when his parent's were both killed in a car crash. As an eighteen year old fresh faced Guardsman he had been pitched into the ferocious battle for Mount Tumbledown as part of the Second Battalion, taking a lead role when his section Corporal had been wounded, ensuring the troop advance had not stalled. On returning from the South Atlantic he had applied for the Special Air Service Regiment, passed selection and served with distinction around the world.

In December 2001 as an already experienced and decorated Staff Sergeant he had led a patrol into the caves of Tora Bora in Afghanistan in pursuit of fleeing Al Qaida terrorists. Although badly injured he had continued to lead and take the attack to the enemy against an horrific onslaught. Eventually evacuated back to the UK and discharged from the Army he slipped, as many ex-Servicemen and Women do, into drink fuelled pity. He was diagnosed with PTSD around the same time as STAG came calling. His reputation had gone before him and they had provided the treatment he needed and welcomed him aboard. He was now the Executive Action team leader, in other words he was responsible for any messy outcomes that may be required.

Frank called Avril and brought her up to speed with the developments, although she already knew. The watchers had called her first, as was usual, before informing anyone else. They would now back off and leave any action to Baxter's SC19 officers. STAG had no such formal restrictions and would now lead any action that was required with the Tactical Firearms units ready to deploy on their request. Frank guessed that Taggart may well have already alerted his former colleagues at their London barracks and that was why an SF team was already standing by. Official requests and paperwork could come later.

Frank checked in with the STAG Director by phone, confirming all the actions that had so far been taken, and was given overall executive control of the operation, signed and authorised by the Home Secretary. Permission was also given to authorise executive action, unleashing Taggart's teams, when required. How the Director had elicited such authority at this early hour intrigued him but he guessed that pre-authority had been requested and agreed in the corridor outside the COBRA meeting. It was the usual modus operandi for STAG.

ELEVEN

Magdaand Petrov, dressed in the green train crew uniforms they had been given, left the hotel room and crossed the hallway to the stairs. All was still and quiet at this time of the morning and there was no one around as they walked across the reception area, pausing so Magda could deposit the key in the collection box, and out into a cold and damp London morning. Although still too early for many commuters to be around, the road was surprisingly busy with cabs and delivery trucks servicing the close by businesses. They took their time avoiding a mechanical street sweeper and crossed the street, entering the station close to the deserted taxi rank.

The station had an empty and eerie feel, the platforms were quiet although a number had trains stabled alongside being readied for operation. Magda observed how different it looked to the massed crowded place it had been the evening before. She felt a bead of uneasiness shiver through her as she realised they were now exposed without the cover of the commuter throng she had enjoyed. She felt Petrov's unease and stiffening alertness as he scanned the open concourse ahead of them. Magda feigned an air of confidence and tried to give an appearance of being in a place she should be, and strode towards the open ticket gates. Waiting on the far side of the gates holding the handle of an identical trolley case to those they pulled behind them was the same female staff member from the day before.

As they came out of the shadow of one of the food concessions that sat on the floor of the concourse she walked towards them, stopped and opened the top of the case. Magda pulled a package from her own case and slid it into the offered opening of the bag. Without any acknowledgement the staff member fumbled a piece of folded paper into Magda's outstretched hand, turned and walked away towards the trains. Petrov beside her had started to slightly shake with the tension and Magda gently touched his arm to reassure him. They were now at the final point of their mission, it would soon all be over and she could console and release him once more.

=

High on the overbridge at the far end of the platforms from the concourse, Taggart had observed the not very subtle transfer of something between the uniformed figures. It was obvious that for some reason they had resorted to using an untrained amateur for the final act, probably due to her easy access. His small, highly trained and highly armed team were arrayed below him on the platforms, seemingly part of the hustle and bustle of train preparation on each of the target platforms, in full covert communications with him and the SC19 operators concealed around the station. Sir Anthony Baxter had, as promised, deployed two of his close tactical support teams to the station following a phone conversation with Frank.

Frank Martin had now assumed operational control, the Director would explain the reasons to MI5, but it was Taggart that now had executive ascendence at the station. He now had full control over the under cover surveillance operators from STAG, the SC19 officers and the two SAS Assault Teams that were on their way across London. The Home Secretary had only thirty minutes ago signed the warrant to allow lethal action to end the operation, if required, and it would be Taggart that ordered the action, of any kind, to commence. All concerned were happy that they were about to witness the delivery of, if not the execution, of the devices. No one at STAG, nor any other of the involved agencies, were completely sure what the devices were or contained. For that reason an ordnance unit and a de-contamination team were en-route, under Police escort, through the streets of an awakening Capital. With the main players now on the plot, the local Police had sealed the surrounding roads and all staff were being discretely evacuated to prevent public casualties should action ensue.

The slim tablet he held in his hand, another Si Radford invention to provide real time information to covert operations, vibrated quietly to inform him of incoming data. He glanced down to the display, while also keeping watch on the platforms below, three lines of text emerged, typed by someone in real time at control. *Targets: 3 Trains. Instruction: Take Down. Time: Immediate.*

=

Frank released the send key on the tablet that he held in his hand. It was identical to the one that Taggart was now reading his instructions from. A flash message from Special Branch sources had been received in the operations room only two minutes before indicating the target for the planting of three devices. The information had come from British Transport Police channels indicating that the contact observed by Taggart at Paddington had, it would appear, had last minute cold feet and had informed her train crew supervisor of her involvement in what she had been told were incendiary devices designed to cause panic. Frank hoped the amount of money she had been paid for the amount of trouble she was now in had been worth it. She had been persuaded by Special Branch to continue with the task she had been given and meet the two suspects as planned. His attention was drawn to the large screen suspended from the ceiling above the central ops room table as Si confirmed he now had a feed of live images from the station.

The screen above the central table in the STAG control room was split into four quadrants showing the main concourse at Paddington Station and three of its platforms. Si had electronically highlighted and designated the two suspects, plus the train crew member who was now being treated in the same regard, although she was now a reluctant participant. As the figures moved down the platforms Si could follow and zoom in on each as required. Frank was now in real time communications with Taggart and his team as they compressed around their targets, still holding off until the authority to intercept them was given. Frank's authority was now delegated to Taggart by the instruction 'take down' he had just given. In one of the quadrants the tactical firearms unit could be seen taking up positions on the main concourse, now empty of anyone not involved in the operation.

=

Magda and Petrov had separated as they approached the head of the platforms. Magda headed down platform number Two alongside the train with its doors open awaiting the onslaught of passengers. She had glanced at the instructions on the piece of paper that had been handed to her and read the letters painted on the carriage sides as she counted down the doors she had to walk. She could see Petrov doing the same on the far side of the double width platform, his designated platform Three, but could only assume the staff member contact was doing the same on platform One as the stabled trains were blocking her view. In fact she was now in the hands of Special Branch Officers and on her way to Scotland Yard.

Magda approached the stairs leading down from the overbridge at the far end of her platform, keeping close to the train that sat alongside. The instructions on the piece of crumpled paper in her hand said to enter the train by the passenger door in the coach marked with an 'A'. She glanced across at Petrov who had stopped and started to turn his head back towards the ticket gates. She heard the shouted command before she saw the black clad figure. "Stop and raise your hands." The figure was twenty metres from Petrov as she saw him drop the handle of the trolley case and swing towards the approaching figure. Everything slowed down in Magda's head as she saw Petrov's extended arm, clutching his Makarov pistol, pointing towards the advancing figure. She heard the sound of the two rounds Petrov discharged and saw him dive through the open door of the platformed train. The black clad figure had dived to the platform surface, rolled and returned fire with two shots that had slammed into the train door.

Petrov landed heavily in the vestibule of the doorway, slamming his shoulder and head into the opposite door frame. He clambered to his feet as two more rounds hit the door, covering him in glass as the drop down window exploded. He put his full weight against the door in an attempt to force it open before realising it must be centrally locked. Amid shouts and further shots from the platform he pulled the remaining window frame down on the locked door and using all his strength managed to eject himself through it. The drop onto the ballast below took the wind from him and increased the pain in his already battered shoulder.

Before she could react to what was happening on the opposite platform Magda felt a heavy weight smash into her lower back, her knees buckled and pain seared through her spine as her face was planted into the platform at force. Two figures dressed in black combat clothing who had been concealed on the far side of the overbridge steps stepped out and aimed their automatic weapons from the shoulder, pointed at her head. The person who had dumped her onto the floor followed up with a sharp knee into her kidneys that made her almost pass out with the pain. She tried to turn her head to the far side of the platform to observe the pursuit of Petrov but her arms were pulled sharply behind her to add more pain to that already invading her body and head. She was struggling to breath as her arms were pinned and manacled behind her.

Still gasping for air she was roughly pulled into a sitting position on the platform, the automatic weapons still pointing at her head.

Petrov ran along the ballast towards the front of the train, ducking behind the wheels twice to take cover from shots being fired from figures on the train. Just as he was about to emerge from the front of the train two black clad figures appeared around the front of the driving cab and dropped into a kneeling position with their weapons raised. Four shots slammed into his body as he tried to take cover. His body was raised into the air by the impact and driven backwards, his head smashed into the adjacent rail and the blood from his shattered skull immediately started to coat the stones. One of the black clad figures sprinted forward and rolled his body onto its back then quickly spoke into his shoulder mounted radio.

Taggart, who followed the two SF operators onto the ballast in the pursuit of Petrov acknowledged the report on his radio. He immediately sent a confirmation message of the action to Frank on the tablet. From his position at the front of the train he could see Petrov's body had been rolled back onto its front and the two heavily armed figures were thoroughly searching his remains as the sea of vacating blood spread around it. He climbed back onto the platform to see Magda being taken away by members of his team. In front of him from the steps of the overbridge figures wearing white decontamination suits advanced towards the platform accompanied by soldiers carrying silver cases and large green bags.

He returned to his position of control on the overbridge, typed 'complete' into the message box he had open with Frank. He knew that the whole operation had been observed from Si Radford's box of tricks in the control room but the message confirming a successful operation always gave him personal satisfaction, whatever the op may be. This one was no different to the many he had been part of, both for STAG and before that during his twenty years as a Special Forces Operator. He still carried the scars, both physical and mental, from those far off days but it gave him immense pride to see his team in action.

Below him a scene of efficient professionalism unfolded as the SAS team withdrew, Frank and the Director would complete the paperwork, and the Met's Tactical Firearms officers secured the station. The system would swing into place and very little, if any, of the detail of the mornings activities would make it into the press.

Any involvement by the Special Forces assault team would be met with a 'no comment' response and the Met Police would thank its officers for an efficient disruption of a potential terrorist attack in a carefully worded statement delivered by a Senior Officer outside New Scotland Yard at some point later that day.

On the target platforms the Ordnance teams were making sure there were no booby traps while white suited decontamination officers awaited any nasty discoveries. His surveillance team, another job well done, had now joined him and they would debrief before returning to the office, normally this would take place in a local pub but at this time of the morning it would have to be over a bacon roll and a coffee, and anyway Taggart felt this operation was not over by a long way. Special Branch officers had reported the train crew member was apparently spilling her guts during questioning, quite literally, but the other woman, so far, had only spat in the face of the arresting officers. The body of the second terrorist still remained where it had fallen, the pool of blood forming a halo around the head and shoulders and preventing any movement of the operators trains in or out of the station, much to the annoyance of the train company. At some point a forensic tent would be erected over the grisly scene but no one seemed in any great hurry although the station would need to be returned to normal working as soon as possible. There was already a sizeable crowd being held back by uniformed Police at the edge of the Station approach roads and inbound services were being held at red signals. The travelling public were used to such delays and not much fuss was yet being made.

=

In the STAG operations room Si turned to face Frank as they both watched the scene unfolding at the station. "Tell them they need to isolate the Internet capability of those devices. Yorkie can still trigger them if they can receive a signal." He hit a key on his laptop that brought up the tracking that was feeding in Yorkie's current whereabouts. "It looks like he is still in Grantham. Any idea what he might be up to?"

Frank turned to look over his shoulder at the display. "If you say he can trigger those devices from anywhere as long as he has an Internet signal then I suspect he is trying to get as far away as possible." He turned back to his communications with Taggart's team at the station and asked how many devices had been found in the bags.

Samantha walked back to the centre of the room from her desk. "I have just had an update from the SB team. The staff member is singing like a canary, in between blubbering something about not being a terrorist and needing the money for her husband's new Land Rover." She rolled her eyes and continued. "It appears that the three of them, including the staff member, were planning on concealing the devices on the first trains leaving the station for Bristol, Taunton and Swansea. SB have so far been unable to get her to say why. Of course she may not know and might just have been a highly paid pawn in all this."

Frank glanced away to read the message coming in from Taggart. "Confirmation from the station says three devices." He went back to the tracking device on Si's laptop as Samantha was called back to her desk by one of her analysts. "I have no idea why he has gone to Grantham. As far as I am aware he has no connections there."He paused and pursed his lips. "Unless he is making for the coast to leave the way he came in?"

Samantha rejoined them before either could speak. "I have just had an in depth report from Dylan Jasper in JTAC." Frank smiled, he had no idea how she managed to have the right contacts in the right places. "He has been doing some deep digging for me via the CIA. It turns out the Americans have been watching the development of remote triggers for some time and have a lot of historical data on Cold War developments and later. Yorkie, although they only knew him as Yvgeney Antonov and had no idea of his UK connection, has been of particular interest. He and Gregorio had only been able to secure enough Radio Active material for one prototype device. Which they appeared to have been hawking around to any rogue state and terror group that would listen to them. They are sending me over what they have but the gist of it is that they, the CIA, believe they were planning to detonate this device somewhere as a demonstration to the some of the more ugly regimes around the World in the hope of drumming up business." Frank took the offered piece of paper from her and read the few lines of information the JTAC contact had provided.

He stood and leaned on the back of his chair staring at the relayed CCTV pictures from Paddington. "So if our American cousins are right only one of those devices could have a nuclear capability."

Si cut in before he could continue. "Or, Frank, those three devices do not have Radio Active material in them and your friend Yorkie is planning something else spectacular. Don't forget he does not have to be anywhere near the device, if there is a fourth somewhere, he only needs to be able to access it via the Internet."

TWELVE

Yorkie pulled his bag from the small bed in the comfortable but very cosy room he had spent the night in. The small hotel in the centre of

Grantham overlooked the open air market that was now starting to bustle with traders as they set up for the day ahead. He had arrived late the evening before on the train from London. He had taken the necessary detour from Leeds and made sure he had used his phone at King Cross and made himself visible to the CCTV cameras on the Station. He had then immediately boarded a return train and alighted at Grantham. On the short taxi ride to the hotel he had received the confirmation message that all was going to plan. By now the devices should have been planted on the three trains heading for the West Country and Wales. He knew Frank Martin would be heavily involved in whatever hunt was under way for him.

He had made sure MI5 and Special Branch had picked him up as soon as he had arrived on the boat. He had also known that Frank would not have been able to ignore his message to meet him. Frank Martin had gone on to become a respected operator and later a highly regarded and professional intelligence officer after he had left for Russia all those years ago. The KGB, and later the FSB, had quizzed him about his colleagues, especially the closest, in the intervening years and had updated him on the progress of his once close friend. In return for the work he had done for them they had agreed to supply him with periodic reports on the career of his once close friend.

That he now despised and hated Frank Martin gnawed away at him on a daily basis. He hated him for his successful career and standing in the Intelligence community in the same way he hated his 'family' for their duplicity in keeping his genuine origins from him. The technology he had built, developed and perfected would now be used to exact revenge on Frank Martin and the country that had killed his father. Involving Martin in his flight from the Special Branch watchmen had been a stroke of genius that had ensured the hornets nest had been stirred. He knew Martin was clever and would eventually piece the disparate parts together but he hoped to stay one step ahead until he drew him into the web he was spinning. Martin would be there when he pressed the button, that would show the World how good Yvgeny Antanov was. It would also expose Martin to the public as a fraud. A failure unable to prevent an attack even when he had been given all the information from the horses mouth.

His chest heaved and rasped as he made his way down the narrow staircase to the small lobby. He pushed his room key through the slot in the box for departing guests, he had paid upfront and settled his meal bill the night before. The cold air hitting his lungs made him cough and gag as he stepped out from the hotel and by the time he had crossed the ten paces to the waiting taxi his eyes were streaming down his face. The driver took his large bag from him and he hugged the laptop case to his chest as he eased himself into the rear seat.

As the cab weaved its way through the narrow streets around the market square he leaned back in the seat and wiped the spittle from his lips. He pulled his phone from his pocket, one of three he carried, he checked for any incoming messages. He knew there wouldn't be any as the two operatives would have by now placed their devices and guided the hired help in placing the third. He expected to see at least one of the location icons flashing on the tracker but suspected they had already discarded their phones as they had been instructed. Making sure the phone still had a full battery, he had charged it overnight, he lowered the window and tossed it into the back of an open van as the driver negotiated the market stalls. Settling back against the seat he let his thoughts drift as the car headed towards the Railway Station. He remembered making this journey out to the coast by train once before, on the day he had left. He remembered the way the line had meandered its way through the Lincolnshire countryside and on through Sleaford where he had many memories of drinking in the pubs with Frank and his other 'mates'. He remembered that journey well. He remembered how he knew Frank would come for him. He had managed to smuggle a note out from the camp he had been held in with one of the Civilian catering staff who had promised to deliver it. When he walked out of the camp he knew Frank would come.

Landing in Russia from the cargo vessel all those years ago he had been scared, bewildered and feeling very, very alone. He had never thought he would actually board the ship, even when he waited at the dockside with his Russian minder he knew Frank would come for him. He knew he would come and take him back, back to face the music that he would have willingly done, it was after all not his fault. He had been tricked, conned, coerced into all the things he had done, Frank would understand that, Frank would come. But he never came and they moved him on from place to place, never aggressive, always welcoming from the beginning.

Their questioning, brisk and intrusive at first, had peeled back the layers of who he really was. The welcome intensified, lovers provided, home comforts much greater than would have been expected. In a matter of months he had been housed in a grand apartment and offered education and work, at first not realising who he was and what that meant to his new comrades. They fed his background to him slowly, in small bites, until the dynasty in which he belonged had been revealed. No longer was he Kevin, Yorkie, from a working class family in Barnsley but he was the son of a respected military diplomat and the Grandson of a National hero.

The work he had a natural ability for became respected and revered. The Soviet machine was embracing all aspects of computer technology and delivering it to their military leaders as fast as they could. The days of stealing and copying Western arms was in the distant past and they strove to produce their own and he was at the forefront of it all.

Meeting Gregorio had been the final sweet brick in his new existence. They had become lovers almost instantly and collaborators almost as quickly. When the Soviet Union started to break up and the State no longer required the technology they provided Gregorio had made the contacts, used his negotiating skills, provided them with a whole new market. And then he had gone. Gregorio had nursed him as his health had begun to deteriorate, they knew why. The years he had toiled to perfect the Nuclear triggers, the years he had lived next to its production, the day he was too close when the accident happened. Gregorio had been there for him until one day he did not return home. The official message had been immediate, killed in an accident just like his Father, and by coincidence on foreign soil.

Gregorio's legacy had been the engagement they both had with the Crimean groups and their struggle. Now working for a new leader, he was the leader, he continued the exploitation and development of his ultimate gift to his real home. His health became more and more of an issue but they encouraged and supported him to deliver and now he would. Gregorio's network were in place, all selected and vetted by him. They were trusted and trained, all now supporting him as he carried out the ultimate payback. The three target trains would now be on their way to the West, the high explosives they were packed with would be detonated by him at the point of his choosing. When all three had found their mark and the chaos and attention had been diverted his message to the world would go out, his revenge for his Father and his lover would be absolute. It was time to bring Frank Martin back onto the stage.

Even the clever Frank Martin would not realise the significance of the chosen target trains. It would be obvious that Taunton was the scene of his father's unlawful, in his eyes, death. But, he would never comprehend the reasons for choosing Bristol and Swansea. It was important to Yvgene that retribution was felt by all perpetrators.

The inquest cover-up was held in Bristol, the train driver who killed him was from Swansea.

He pulled the laptop from the bag he cradled on his lap. He turned the machine on and waited as it went through its boot sequence. The screen flashed and a green icon appeared in the top right hand corner. Yorkie opened the icon and three symbols appeared in the middle of the screen representing the three trains that were en-route to their destinations, all three symbols showing the trains were running to schedule. They would now be nearing the end of their routes and closing on the locations he had selected that would cause the most disruption due to the difficulty of reaching the explosion sites. The icons changed colour to yellow as he hovered over each in turn, then changed to red as he double clicked to activate each in turn. All three devices, secreted on board the trains, were now live and all that was needed was a strong Internet signal to allow the commands to be transmitted.

As he travelled East towards the coast on the rattling old train Yorkie constantly monitored WI-FI signals generated from businesses and households along the route. Most of the signals that appeared strong enough to transmit the commands were secured, and he did not have time to break the security, but he knew that he would encounter one in time that was an open network. Within a couple of miles the train entered a large built up area on the edge of a coastal town and the strength of the signals appearing on the laptop reached maximum. As they turned to follow the coast North they passed a large leisure centre that showed a public access Internet signal. Yorkie clicked open the icon on his control panel and the machine connected to the signal, the commands to the three devices transmitted automatically, without any further input.

Yorkie closed the laptop and replaced it back into the case. Stage one of his final act was now under way. Nothing could now stop the three devices from wreaking havoc. All that he needed to do now was summon Frank Martin to witness his finest achievement.

=

Frank had confirmed the actions that had taken place at Paddington with Taggart before he had recovered his team and made his way back to the office. Under Frank's directions the station had been reopened, apart from the one platform, and the three trains had been dispatched on time. Taggart sat opposite Frank as they both reviewed the latest material that had been provided by Special Branch via Avril at MI5.

Celebrations could wait as it now appeared the focus had moved to Yorkie somewhere in Lincolnshire, again. Neither Toby Gadsby nor Paul Whittle could be raised at MI5, the one on his way to a conference and the other conveniently on leave, so Frank had brought Avril up to speed on what had happened at the Station. The team was now preparing its equipment and weapons in the STAG armoury in the basement. The Director was now aware of the direction things were turning and the recovery of the three devices from the station and he in turn had briefed the Home Secretary. A further COBRA meeting had been arranged for midday. The operation had now risen to the level that required the Directors of all the involved agencies to attend, the meeting would be chaired by the Home Secretary. Operational control of the whole operation had been passed to Frank and all agencies would be under his direction for the duration of the operation.

CIA reports analysed by Samantha and two analysts indicated that a further device was likely to be the one that carried the nuclear capability. The three devices from the trains at Paddington had been found to carry non-nuclear high explosives, enough to wreck the trains and cause multiple casualties, but not to obliterate the City and surrounding area. The whereabouts of the fourth device was still unknown but Yorkie's visit to Kings Cross station had indicated that this was as good a place to start looking as any. The ordnance and special branch search teams had now been redirected from Paddington to Kings Cross and the station cleared. A finger tip search of the vast station was now under way.

Si Radford and two of his technicians had been able to provide an electronic shield to the three devices from Paddington that would prevent them from being triggered and a fourth shield was being prepared in anticipation of the device being located. Si had now rejoined Frank and Taggart in the STAG ops room.

"The tracker is showing Yorkie's phone location as heading West now towards Nottingham." He turned the screen to face Frank. "It doesn't really make sense. Does he have any connection with Nottingham?" he updated the location on the screen and the icon blinked on and off to show it was updating in real time. Before he could continue Frank's mobile interrupted them.

"Hello Avril." he put the phone on to speaker so they could all hear her rapid download of the latest from the two potential bombers arrested at Paddington.

"It would appear." She continued in her quick fire dialogue. "The crew member was nothing more than the hired help. She had been approached a week or so ago and offered a large amount of money to act as the contact, and a bigger amount to stash the third device."

Si interrupted her as she could be heard flicking pages."I thought railway staff were well enough paid not to require bribing?"

144

Avril continued her report. "They are, but this one and her train driver husband have a penchant for exotic cars and even more exotic holidays. They are, it would appear, up to their necks in debt and she was glad of the bung." Avril turned more pages. "The other female has been identified as Magda Svetlova and is well known by European Counter Terrorism teams for her involvement in Ukranian attacks, amongst others. The one the SAS dropped." Taggart raised his eyebrows at her description. "Has been identified as Petrov Labrov an ex-spetsnatz hero who just happens to be related to a certain Major Gregorio Alexayev."

Si whistled through his teeth but Frank beat him to the comment. "It is all beginning to become very incestuous!"

Avril proceeded with an evident increase in her voice cadence. "That's not all Frank. Today is the anniversary of the death of Yorkie's Russian Father." All the analysts and techies in the ops room were now listening to the narrative coming from the speaker. "The Met have now put all Special Branch and Counter Terrorism teams on full alert and they have deployed all their Tactical Firearms Teams, Sir Anthony is having a melt down! The county teams have been alerted and are awaiting instructions on where to deploy."She paused for breath before almost screeching. "Oh, and the SAS have two Sabre teams on standby, but I am sure your man will confirm that." Taggart nodded in Frank's direction. Frank thanked her for the update and closed the call.

Frankturned towards the monitor. "Si, do we have an accurate location for him?"

Si update the real time icon and turned to face him. "Unfortunately, all we have is the location of the phone he was using. He may or may not be with it."

Taggart was about to speak when Frank's mobile alerted him to an incoming text. He opened and read the message.

"It looks like he wants me to join him. I guess we don't need the tracker for this." The message read: "Frank. Come and meet me at the café. I will be there at four o'clock. Cheers. Your mate Yorkie."

"I think I've just found him Si." he tossed the phone cross the desk, and for once Si caught it. "Yorkie has been playing games with us, or at least me, all along. I don't know what his plan is but it obviously involves me. Have you had any results back from the Paddington devices yet?" Si turned to check his incoming messages as Frank continued. "I am guessing but I think you will find they do not contain any radio active material and the reports Samantha has been getting from the yanks are probably accurate. But that doesn't mean the fourth device will be the same." Samantha joined them from the corner of the room where she had been called to receive an incoming message.

"More from the CIA." She handed Frank the printed A4 page. "They have dug up some test data from a source in the Middle East that was known to be doing deals with Yvgeny Antanov for remote triggers. Apparently they were the middle-men and their clients had asked for some details on possible nuclear delivery."

Frank read the report pages that gave the CIA's take on what the capability was of the offered device. "Do we know who the end user of this might have been?"

Samantha answered quickly. "You won't like it, but the CIA are pretty sure the buyers were trying to procure weapons for onward sale to ISIS in Syria. The Americans have been monitoring and trying to disrupt any transactions, but they thought they were dealing with a couple of Russian Mafia types."

Frank whistled through his teeth and passed the report to Si in a swap for the update from the weapons analysts that were examining the Paddington devices.

"It is only a preliminary look Frank, but they are happy the devices contained only high explosives and there are no booby traps. My electronic shields, on the other hand, have taken multiple hits in the last thirty minutes. It would appear Yorkie is unaware we have intercepted them and he is still trying to detonate all three."

Frank grimaced at him. "Is there any way he can get through your shield?"

Si chuckled and shook his head. "Not now I have managed to disconnect them, or should I say my guys have, I am just collecting his data now for future use."

Taggart turned to Frank from the conversation he had been having on the secure phone at his desk in the corner of the ops room. "Two Sabre teams active Frank and at your disposal, transport ready when you are." Frank nodded and turned to Si. "You had better get your gear ready, looks like we are going on a trip."

Frank spent the next fifteen minutes in the secure cell, known as the 'Citadel', on the floor above giving the Director the latest developments on an encrypted line to the COBRA meeting. In turn he spoke to Avril and Sir Anthony Baxter with the instructions from the Home Secretary that they were now very much under the control of STAG, much to their distaste. But that was much better than either of their organisations having to answer to public scrutiny if it all went tits up. STAG was never publicly acknowledged, or praised, as the other mainline agencies were. In fact if it went to plan and succeeded, those same agencies would bask in the glory of their part in it. Alternatively, if it went belly up then a coverall 'security services' message would be sent out to the public that the security agencies were continuing to work hard to disrupt terrorism. STAG in the eyes of the public did not exist and that was how they all liked it.

Taggart appeared in the doorway as he finished his call to Avril in Thames House. "Our chariot awaits boss." There were no grades or ranks in STAG but old habits died hard with most of the ex-service guys. "Si and his opo are already aboard fiddling with some new fangled gadget or other." He had a very low tolerance of the geeky types, as he put it, but he knew, as did everyone else in the team, that without Si and his techies, and Samantha and her analysts STAG would not function.

He followed Taggart out of the door and down into the armoury in the basement. Two large black canvas holdalls were waiting on the floor next to an open locker against the wall. Frank waited as Taggart donned his black combat trousers and pulled his combat smock from the locker. He toyed with the idea of joining him as the adrenaline of potential action filled his body, but thought better of it. If he entered that café in combat gear Yorkie was likely to detonate the device immediately. He had to try and talk him out of whatever action he had planned. He instead pulled his outdoor jacket on, as he grabbed one of the holdalls and followed Taggart out of the building.

The blue liveried Dauphine helicopter sat with its rotas turning and burning in the middle of the parade square of Wellington Barracks. Frank and Taggart jogged the short distance from the back of the STAG building, down the alley way to Birdcage Walk and through the barracks main gate. Despite both being the wrong side of fifty they were hardly out of breath as they climbed aboard the bird as it lifted from the tarmac. Two of Taggart's operators were already aboard and Si and his technicians had plugged their toys into the aircraft's systems. High above them the lead helicopter carrying the two four man assault teams banked away over St James' Park and headed East. They both settled back into their seats and pushed the offered headsets on. Samantha would now act as the ground control and feed any updates to them as they headed North to Lincolnshire.

She would also liaise with the other Agencies and Special Branch on the ground.

Frank spoke briefly to Samantha in the STAG ops room to establish comms as they headed over the City of London going about its business far below. Did they realise how much danger they were in thought Frank as he shifted to look over Si's shoulder at the blinking lights of the tracker, now improved to seek and lock onto Yorkie's phone even if it was switched off. Frank had no idea how he managed these things but he was very glad he did. Patrols had been stepped up in London in the last hour and the search was still continuing in a cleared and deserted Kings Cross station, but the truth was they did not know where this last device, if it existed, was hidden.

Yorkie had to be planning some kind of grand finale to all this. Something spectacular that in his head would avenge all the wrongs and slights that he felt had been committed against him. For some reason it appeared that he felt Frank was one of the major perpetrators of these heinous offences. Yorkie my friend you are one seriously, warped and fucked up individual he thought as the drone of the rotas above him threatened to derail his thought process. As they headed North East the fading afternoon light and the low cloud that was forming, bounced the navigation lights of the helicopter back to them through the side windows. Up ahead the two pilots plotted a course for the East coast and pulled into a loose formation with the lead aircraft that Frank could just see slightly off to the left and slightly higher ahead of them.

Si's voice crackled into his headset. "Frank, we have just had a message through from the SB analysts looking at the Paddington CCTV. They have been viewing every angle and elevation from all the cameras for the last twenty-four hours. It would appear that our

Russian girl paid a visit to Paddington while our surveillance teams were trailing Rasputin through London. It took them a while but they have good images of her entering and leaving the station. They are sending them up to us via Samantha now."

Frank increased the volume on his headset so he could hear Si above the rota noise. "Do we know where she went at the station?"

Si nodded and turned his screen towards Frank to show him the grainy CCTV stills that had just come through.

"She tried to get lost in the crowd but they have managed to pull a couple of images of her heading to the far corner of the concourse. The only thing over there is the Lost Property office. Avril and a team from MI5 are on the way there now."

"If that last device is somewhere in that office what are the chances of them being able to find it?" He thought to himself probably not very high.

"It's not just that Frank. Even if we found it the chances of being able to mask it in time would be very slim. I got lucky with the other three devices but I suspect this one will be a lot more sophisticated, and I would expect an anti-tamper circuit at the very least. It would all take time and I'm not sure we have it. Two of my guys have joined Avril and they will report back as soon as they have found it, if they can."

Before he could answer Frank's attention was drawn to his comms panel and an incoming message from the ops room. Samantha had been monitoring his phone frequency, another one of Si's toys, and a message flashed on to the screen. "Hello Frank. Nice to see you are on the way to join me. I would expect nothing less. I guess by now my three little side shows have got you all excited, but I bet you still don't know why do you Frank?" So he didn't know that they had prevented detonation, you may have slipped up there Yorkie."I will

150

be in the usual place. Come alone Frank. I wouldn't want to have to start my final performance early. If I see any sign of the Police or even your tame Gorilla, I will have my revenge without you."

Frank closed the comms app and switched channels to speak to Taggart. "He is expecting us mob handed. You will have to drop me close and then come in on foot. Get on to Lincs Special Branch and arrange a landing spot."

Taggart pointed to the map on his knee. "Already done boss. You and I will de-bus outside town, they have cars waiting. How's your rope skills these days?" They both knew that if it came to it they would fast rope from the transport. Twice a year they went together on the 'Attached Others' course that the SAS ran for support personnel that may need to deploy, and twice a year they received the incredulous looks from the youngsters as they achieved the highest scores in all disciplines.

"It's OK boss, we are landing on the car park." His laughter was obvious but drowned by the throttling back of the aircraft as it descended through the cloud.

The chopper banked over the railway station, eased to the hover and landed with a compression of its wheels in the large car park built on the old goods yard and sidings. Two unmarked police cars stood a short distance away with their grill mounted lights flashing alternatively blue and red. Taggart slid the side door open and stepped down, pulling one of the large black holdalls behind him. Frank joined him as he made his way towards the cars, beckoned by a black clad police officer holding a short barrelled machine gun. The officer took the holdalls and placed them in the boot of the vehicle, holding the lid open long enough to show a glimpse of the racked arsenal it contained. Frank turned to give a thumbs up to Si who had moved forward in the helicopter to sit directly behind the pilot. He would now keep in direct contact with them both, Taggart would have comms with the assault teams who had now moved off to land closer to the beach. The two STAG men slid into the back seats and the car moved off at speed along the High Street towards the seafront.

The unmarked car manoeuvred through the crowd of retreating shoppers being evacuated by uniformed officers on the pretext of a gas leak. At least at this time of year there were not that many around at this late afternoon hour, the height of summer would have been another deal altogether. Frank remembered his last visit up this High Street and could not believe it was only two days ago. He could not believe that this whole sorry event had only been in train for that long. You really have got us dancing to your tune Yorkie.

The Police vehicle drew to a stop, its lights now extinguished, close to the beach car park approach road long enough for Frank to leave the back seat. As his feet touched the damp and sandy morass at the side of the road he squinted through the gloom to the lights of the beachside building where he knew Yorkie was now waiting. The car then turned right and headed away towards the far Southern end of the promenade. The light was beginning to fade and Frank could make out only a small number of cars and a few stragglers left on the beachfront footpath. The Police had taken the decision not to evacuate this far, allowing Frank at least some element of surprise, although he had no doubt that Yorkie was watching every inch of his approach.

Thecafé he had been in only a matter of hours ago, now seemed even less appealing as he quickened his pace along the sand strewn surface. The familiar, but long forgotten, feel of the covert earpiece brought memories back to him of distant operations. At least the modern kit was much smaller and less obtrusive, the microphone was taped behind the zip of his light outdoor jacket. Si would have a constant commentary of anything that went on once he had reached the café. He felt underneath his jacket to the comforting touch of the Glock pistol resting in the kidney holster at his back. He was not exactly sure what his plan was, but Taggart had insisted on him being armed and he was grateful he had done so.

Frank pushed open the door and the warmth and bright interior of the coffee shop rushed out to meet him. The interior was deserted apart from the barista. Sat tucked away in the far corner the dishevelled, hunkered and crouching figure of Yorkie. "Hello Frank. Nice ride in the helicopter? You always did like the warmongering part of the job, always relished the opportunity to get tooled up. Carrying some kind of lethal toy now are we? I'm sure that tosser Taggart wouldn't have let you come without. Yes Frank, I know it all. There is nothing I don't know about you or that pile of bollocks you work for." The spittle flew from his lips as he spat the words out.

Frank pulled the chair out from the table opposite and sat directly facing his old friend, or was it new adversary? "I'm here Yorkie, or is it Yvgeney?" There was not a flicker from the lined face. "You can't tell me that this whole thing has been about me and some self pitying idea that I should have saved you from yourself all those years ago? You went bad all on your own mate, you didn't need any help or encouragement from any of us. I had some small element of sympathy for you when it all kicked off, when you were coerced and trapped, but it turns out you were rotten from the beginning, it was in your blood."

What colour remained started to drain from Yorkie's face and spittle ran down his chin as he coughed the words back. "Not about you Frank? You think you are something big, war hero, celebrated spy. You know nothing about what happened to me. I've watched you Frank, watched you climb up the pole, what is it you run these days,

STAG? Is that what you think you are Frank some kind of rutting STAG?" The venom was real and Frank could see it had eaten into Yorkie like some kind of canker, but the self-pity was ever present, and despite the bullshit coming from his mouth he let him continue his rant.

"This isn't about you pal. This is about my family, my real family. Not those fuckers up in Yorkshire, not that bitch that lied to me for all those years. This is about my dynasty, my belonging. My belonging that was taken from me." A bout of haggard and raucous spittle strewn coughing racked his frail frame. Unlike the previous time Frank did nothing to assist his former friend, he was beyond help in many ways and it was obvious he knew it and was determined to have his glory day.

"My Father was killed here in England, but you already know that. Killed by your sort Frank. He was executed by one of your type. That's what you are Frank a murderer and so were they. It was hushed up, killed in an accident they said but I know different Frank. Just like my Gregorio, murdered Frank, far from home." The hacking and retching continued. "This is about them Frank not you. I will avenge them. Have already avenged them, did you like my show of strength Frank? I can do anything I want and when I want."

He stared back at the wizened, maggot of a man that he had once called a friend. Somehow the quiet, diffident guy he had known all that time ago had become twisted and poisoned, or had it been there all along and they had re-awakened the loathing and the spite? It was obvious that he did not know his devices had been compromised, intercepted and made useless. Si's toys had once again proved their worth, should he tell him or let him continue in the belief that part of the job was done? He noticed that he continuously glanced down at the open laptop on the table in front of him and could only guess that he was checking the status of his fourth device and could detonate it at any time. Si had been feeding him updates into his ear the whole time he had been sat in the café, but so far it had not been located in the Paddington Lost Property office. MI5 were re-interviewing Magda but she was refusing to make any comments and the rail employee knew nothing and pissed herself every time they took her to an interview room.

If the detonation of the fourth device was to be prevented then it had to be done here, it had to be done by him. He edged his chair closer to the table, but Yorkie was alert to him. "Yes Frank, it is here on my laptop. As your clever trained chimp Si Radford will have told you all I need is a strong Internet signal, and at the moment pal I am connected to at least five at full strength. All I needed Frank was you to be here to witness my success. I built all this, I designed it, built it and now I will demonstrate it to the whole world. Don't move any closer Frank, you have seen how good the other three have been but this one will eclipse them all. This is the big bloomer Frank. London will remember this day for a long time."

Frank edged his chair another few inches closer. "The others failed Yorkie. They were duds, just like you. I have served this country, you have just disgraced it. You are no more Russian than I am." Across the table the laptop was pulled closer. "Your family loved you and your Mother still does. Do you know I went to see her? I suppose you do, she wanted me to pass on her best wishes and hoped you were well."

The blood was draining quicker now and the spittle was soaking the already stained and yellowed shirt front. "None of the fuckers wanted me. I belonged with my own. I am Russian through and through mate. I have served my real country better than you ever served this one, you failed your comrades Frank on that hillside, you couldn't even save your leader." The putrid barbs hurt Frank as they spewed from the twisted and empty vessel that remained across the table. This vile excuse for a human could not be allowed to execute his deranged programme.

As the coughing hit a new crescendo Frank launched himself across the table. Despite the short distance between them for once his timing deserted him and he landed on the hard surface as the laptop was pulled away by a surprisingly agile hand. The other wizened and shrivelled limb managed to scoop the cup from the surface and launch the remains of his coffee into Frank's face as Yorkie made for the door dragging the adjoining table over as a barricade as he went. The door swung and slapped into Frank's face as he scrambled to his feet and extricated himself from the tangle of furniture. Out in the colder evening air he glimpsed the back of the huddled figure attempting a high-speed shuffle along the beachside path in the direction of the dissected pier, disappearing into the gathering gloom.

Pulling the handgun from its position nestled in the small of his back, Frank closed the distance between them at full stride and almost careered headlong into the side of the beachside shelter as Yorkie ducked into it. Turning to face his pursuer he held the laptop at arms length as he dropped on to the wooden bench. "Drop the gun Frank." He waved the machine towards the beach. "And tell the goons to back off." The four black shapes were only just visible in the folds of the sandy beach, silhouetted against the frothing surf. "We will have our day Frank." He coughed again and spat phlegm onto the path. "Gregorio and I have toiled for this Frank." The machine was thrust towards Frank again. "We have friends waiting to see this mate. When I get my revenge they will all see, they will all want one. You and your STAG bollocks can do nothing about it Frank."

Frank eased towards the bench and raised the gun towards the wizened face. "It's over Yorkie. The three bombs on the trains were duds and we have just found the fourth." Would the bluff work. "Si Radford's men have found it mate and they have disabled it." The laptop was raised again and the bony fingers reached out for the keys.

"It's impossible Frank. I will show you! I will fucking show them all!"

As the laptop was raised like a weapon the fingers seemed to loose all control and the machine slid away from the bony, outstretched hands. A loud, hacking, cackling like whistle emitted from Yorkie's mouth and his eyes rolled upward in his head. Frank dived forward and managed to intercept the laptop before it crashed onto the coastal path. He rolled onto his shoulder to absorb the impact of the collision with the ground and was only just aware of the wizened, shrivelled body falling backwards onto the shelter's bench. There was a muffled slap and an oily, slurping, gurgle as the breath continued to exit the body.

Black clad figures converged on the shelter as Frank scrambled to his feet, cradling the laptop in his arms. Weapons were drawn and pointed at the now very obviously lifeless figure hanging half on and half off the bench. The head of his one-time friend lolled to one side and there was no further breathing or rise and fall of the chest. One of the figures declared 'trap free' to indicate there were no hidden booby traps and withdrew to the side of the shelter alongside the others now protecting the scene. Taggart joined him just as he was easing the lifeless body down to the ground, amazed at how little it weighed. "I guess he almost did what he came to do." He looked down at the wasted shell at his feet. Yes mate, I think you have definitely come home as he turned away towards the sea.

The earpiece crackled with Si's voice. "We've found the fourth package Frank."

He responded in a quiet and measured voice, fighting to hold back the emotion. "Thank you Si. I think we are all done here."

=

Si Radford had seized upon the laptop as soon as Frank had made it the short distance to the waiting cars. Inserting his own toys into the USB drive he had declared the system inert and safe to transport for further analysis, that he was relishing carrying out. The system had been live at the point Yorkie had finally succumbed to the radiation that had been eating him all those years. The rucksack had been found in the lost property office but no one yet knew what it contained. Si was happy, after a cursory check of the laptop that no signal had been delivered or queued for sending, and had given instructions for the rucksack to be shielded and secured.

By the time they had returned to the awaiting helicopters the local Police had taken over preserving the scene to await the investigation into a 'tragic suspected heart attack of an elderly gentleman at the seaside.' Special branch would now tie up the loose ends and COBRA had been informed of a successful conclusion and all surge Policing had been stood down in London. The assault teams were already airborne and on their way home as the STAG team lifted away from the car park.

Updates coming in from the STAG ops room had confirmed the finding of the device at Paddington. They could not, however, confirm at this stage if it was a viable device. Si had issued instructions for the deployment of his electronic shield, the device had been made safe and was on its way to be forensically examined. Frank eased himself into the folds of the seat, removed his headset and tried to find some much needed sleep. Unfortunately his mind would not settle, nagging doubts were starting to eat into what should have been the satisfaction of a completed case. Things did not seem to add up, or was he just reading too much into the last few days and had Yorkie really been the mastermind of all this mayhem? As the beat of the rotas above his head induced heavy eyelids the smoke began to drift once again across the peat bogs, and the sweat formed in rivers across his brow.

=

In the two weeks following, the device found in the Paddington lost property office along with the three other devices had been examined and dismantled by a forensic team at Farnborough with regular interventions from Si Radford. The technology they contained was found to be very old school and much of the component parts, it appeared, had been lifted from an old Soviet era ballistic missile warhead, but missing much of its radioactive component. Had it detonated in the lost property office at Paddington a large area would have been contaminated but probably not as much as Yorkie had anticipated. The Internet trigger, on the other hand, had been cutting edge and state of the art, and according to Si, many years ahead of the protocols currently being used in the UK. Its signal agile abilities meant the circuitry within the device, once commanded, would continuously seek out a strong Internet path from whatever source was available. The neatest trick, according to Si, was that the signal did not have to come from a base station WI-FI LAN but could piggy back off a mobile roaming signal or several combined to create a strong stream to the device. Even if the signal was switched off or blocked once re-established the command would be actioned. Si and his team had spent endless days playing with the data and re-engineering the trigger until they knew exactly how it worked. When shared with some of Si's geeky contacts in the NSA in America a firestorm of interest erupted. None of their high-level scientists could believe the technology would work and Si had been invited to brief them in person as soon as he could make the trip.

Samantha and her research analyst colleagues had continued to dig the background of Yorkie's association with Gregorio and the details surrounding his demise while away seeking sales for their burgeoning illicit arms empire. Reportedly he had been killed while meeting an ISIS warlord in Somalia in the attempted sale of one of Yorkie's remote devices, having seemingly spread his wings from the struggle for a future Crimea back with Mother Russia. Despite the best efforts of Samantha and the CIA no real confirmation of his death could be found. This fact alone, along with his own nagging doubts, left Frank with a feeling that the demise of Yorkie would not be the end of this particular episode. He was keen to get to the bottom of the relationship Yorkie had had with this Gregorio, and also to shed light on what exactly the family connection had been that had rated him so highly in Russian eyes. He had agreed to accompany Si on his forthcoming trip and elicit the help of his own contacts within the US Intelligence family.

The investigation into the killings in the South of England and the subsequent thwarting of the operation in London had been wrapped up by MI5 and the Metropolitan Counter Terrorism Command. Magda had still refused to talk to anyone and a date at the Old Bailey was on the cards until the Russian Ambassador to London had paid a visit to the Home Secretary the previous Friday. A deal had been struck and Magda, along with the late departed Petrov, would be returned to Moscow, and the body of Yorkie Biddle would be returned to his family in Yorkshire. All connection by him to the Antanov dynasty would be quietly erased from the history books, in both countries. Although Frank and his STAG colleagues would be taking a much closer and very covert look at those connections.

The only person to have been dealt with in a disciplinary or legal way was the female rail employee who had been investigated by her company. MI5 had decided not to proceed against her and had left it to the railway authorities to deal with. British Transport Police, after a cursory investigation, had quickly handed it back to the company. The company had carried out a thorough investigation for gross misconduct, sacked her, but re-instated her on appeal.

Frank had travelled to Yorkshire to give his condolences to Yorkie's Mother, and he and Samantha had returned to attend the funeral. Frank had felt for the families sake he should attend, though he now felt nothing for his late friend. He had politely declined the invitation to speak at the funeral. As the small gathering of friends and family left the graveside outside the small parish church, they both stopped to read the messages on the small number of wreaths and bouquets that were laid on the manicured grass. Frank raised his gaze to see the back of a black suited man who had crouched to lay a simple wreath and was now striding away through the distant tombstones.

Frank glanced back to Samantha and when he turned again the man had disappeared from view at the side of the church. He knelt on the grass and turned the card attached to the flowers over, quickly straightened and showed her the hand written message in Cyrillic that was on the card. Samantha translated for him. "The fight continues. Sleep well my love. Gregorio."

THIRTEEN

Major Gregorio Alexayev joined the line that snaked between the roped barriers towards the immigration booths in the passport hall. To his left the queue for the European passport holders appeared, much to his annoyance, to be moving much more quickly. In his hand he held a green diplomatic passport in the name of Vitaly Popov. In Moscow he would have been escorted to the front of the line, in London you queued with the crowds of holiday makers and returning businessmen. His frustration had a very short fuse and he hated waiting in line to be dealt with by those beneath his status. Status was everything to Gregorio, he had worked hard both within and outside the system to raise himself above the ordinary Russian who he looked upon as peasants.

As the line inched forward he remembered the last time he had made the journey. It had been well over six months since he had watched the dry run operation unfold before him. He had never shown his hand, had stayed well in the background, but had been more than satisfied with the way his hand-picked team had given the stupid British authorities the run around. His directions had been carried out to the letter and the sacrifice of his lover Yvgene had been both painful and necessary. Yvgene Antonov, he hated the name Yorkie and he had never used it, had provided him with the ideal circumstances in which to impress his demanding pay masters. These days they were many and varied, who had less patience than he did but had very large cheque books. Yvgene's festering hatred for the country and his personal bile directed at Frank Martin allowed him to be manipulated, and ultimately forfeited in the pursuit of greater riches. Sentiment had never featured in Gregorio's life, from the grim existence and killing on the battlefield to the cut-throat business of underworld arms dealing that he now inhabited, and excelled at.

His only regret, if he had any, was the loss of two of the best operatives he had ever worked with. Petrov had been at his side throughout the grisly and gruesome butchery he had ordered in many disparate conflicts and to lose such an accomplished assassin was a difficulty he would have to overcome. To also lose the intelligent and resourceful Magda, was difficult but the loss of his lover for all those years was something he would not dwell on. The truth was one of manipulation and enforcement rather than love on Gregorio's part even if Yvgene had felt there was something more celestial, to him it was just business. Their meeting had been fortuitous, but engineered, and in the beginning very enjoyable for him. The Russian machine had manipulated the young British serviceman from the beginning, trapping him in their seedy cold war espionage game and then bleeding him dry once his talents had been identified. That they had engineered, and falsely created, a legend Yvgene could believe in, made him all the more malleable once Gregorio had come on the scene. As state control eased and big business, often Mafia led, took over Gregorio, had worked harder to keep the lies about his poor lovers lineage even more real.

The inching line finally brought him in front of the uniformed Immigration Officer and he handed over the passport. Without acknowledging him the officer gestured for him to stand in front of the camera mounted on the side of the booth. His passport was scanned and handed back to him, again without any word or acknowledgement. He took the offered passport. "Spasibo. Thank you." The miserable fuckers had no manners as well as being pig ignorant. He walked away to join the throng heading for the baggage claim area. Something else he despised, in Moscow his bags would have been carried for him.

Once reviled and rejected by the military elite that he had served for so long his stock had re-risen with the emergence once again of an anti-western feeling within Government circles. Still operating outside official channels, he was now trusted enough, by some in the hierarchy, to be travelling on an official alias diplomatic passport. That the Russian elite still operated under the guise of openness rankled with the Western countries that were forced to treat them as equals. Deep within the Moscow leadership a very close group still had influence and it was this group that were now sponsoring his crusade. His business associations with the most extreme terrorist groups was serving that element within the Russian government well, allowing them to influence strikes against their life-long enemies without having the blood on their hands. A small group of hard-liners still existed in Moscow and they had the ear of the President when it mattered. Seizing on the opportunity the Maverick Alexayev had provided they were only too happy to bypass the official routes and hand him the alias and passport he required, although he was not stupid enough to believe their support would continue if things went wrong. His new found diplomatic status would shield him from prying eyes and afford him at least some short-term protection. He was happy to take their patronage, but his own motives remained as always altruistic, he was also fully aware the unofficial regime were using him, but cared nothing as long as his status and bank balance grew. When Yvgene had first developed the technology for the remote trigger he was already planning the process of selling it on the open market. He had convinced Yvgene that his motivations were connected to the struggle for Crimea, another useful tool to be used to Gregorio's advantage, and gone along with the idea of combining a strike for the separatists with Yvgene's quest for revenge.

Poor Yvgene had not had the wit to understand he was being manipulated, both by officialdom and by Gregorio, worked almost to death in a deadly environment and then pushed to finish the trigger development before the long festering illness finally claimed him. To the Russian regime he was nothing more than a defector to be milked for his information and, in Yvgene's case, used for the considerable talents he possessed. It was true that his 'father' had connections to the Antanov dynasty but they were tenuous, a second cousin, and he had been sold a legend to keep him interested and keen to keep working. His father had been a junior Intelligence officer attached to the London Embassy in the late 1950s, carrying out menial collection tasks, but this had been embellished, as was often the case when necessary, by party officials. Their meeting had been far from an accident but had been orchestrated by the hierarchy. Gregorio's sexual proclivities, although still illegal in Russia and had been ignored, had suited their aims and he had been selected for the role. He had been a willing conduit for the false information that they were continually feeding to Yvgene and had continued to bolster his need for revenge when they had both left the government arena. The truth was that Gregorio had never left the influence of a small group of devoted men who still harboured hatred towards the West and his contacts amongst the Worlds warlords and terrorists served them well. There was also something very personal to Gregorio that Yvgene had never been told and it was this that would ultimately give him his revenge.

Yvgene had died in that remote, stagnant Lincolnshire shithole of a town, finally succumbing to the ravages of radiation inflicted on him over the years. He had died not knowing that he had been controlled and manipulated from the very first day he had set foot on Russian soil. The regime had seized the opportunity presented to them and had invented a false lineage to create a monster, a monster that they and Gregorio could exploit.

The baggage hall was a seething mass of bodies waiting for the carousels to regurgitate their belongings, something else that would have been taken care of for someone of his status at a Russian airport. He managed to identify his bag through the melee and snatched it through the flying elbows before it departed on another circuit. He detested this country, and all other western shitholes, but the lure of the money he had been offered by his clients had made him overcome the loathing and he was also satisfied that this time it was no dry run. This time Yvgene would have his revenge, and he, Gregorio, would have a massive pay day. Despite going against all his instincts of always staying as far removed from the operation as possible this time he would have to be at the point of impact, this time he would be delivering the strike. Much of his network still remained and they had been primed ready for this final attack. His clients had been happy with the results of the dry run and happy that he had lured the Security Agencies into believing they had produced a shield that could prevent the deployment of the trigger. When he finally delivered the weapon they would still believe they could disable the targeting pulse from the Internet, the reason he had encouraged Yvgene to demonstrate the tool so openly, but his own effort would be delivered covertly and timed to allow him to witness the devastation from afar.

The regime he was now working for would pay him well for the work he was about to do in their name. That they were the most dangerous of men to deal with did not worry Gregorio. He had dealt with the most murderous and vile regimes around the World and knew as long as results were delivered they always paid up, and on time. This time he would produce the biggest results they had seen. This time Major GregorioAlexayev would make the whole World sit up and take notice.

=

High above the floor level of Heathrow's Terminal 4 Gregorio's image was currently displayed in high definition detail on a computer screen in the Joint Liaison office. The office was home to a security team made up of officers from the Metropolitan Police, The Border Agency, Her Majesty's Revenue and Customs and MI5. The team was another example, envied around the World, of the way the UK had embraced joined up working since the devastation of New York during the 9/11 attacks. Their role was to scrutinise all arrivals with the aid of a complex array of technology linked to the immigration passport scanners and supported by remote and very discrete high-level cameras distributed around the terminal buildings. The jewel in the crown of this arsenal of computer wizardry was the recent addition of the state-of-the-art facial recognition system. This could compare library images of known personalities, even from many years previous, with the real time feed coming off the cameras. It not only compared the full face appearance but could focus in and compare minute portions of the face, even if a disguise was being used.

It was this suite of applications that was now being applied to the images of Gregorio streaming in from the baggage claim area. The presentation of the Diplomatic passport by Vitaly Popov, had alerted the operator as was normal practice when such passports were presented, particularly from Russia and other countries of interest. The operator entered the search criteria to the displayed images and the system went to work accessing the millions of facial photographs held in the computer linked vaults of Western Intelligence Agencies. The system automatically ran detailed visual analysis algorithms against the image, it could do in seconds what a team of analysts would take months attempting to do. In less than a minute a library photograph held by the CIA flashed on to the screen alongside the real time image. The screen also flashed up a detailed description and instructions for further actions. *Image Identity: Gregorio Alexayev. Reason for File: Known Russian arms dealer.* The operator scrolled down to the bottom of the screen where an instruction for further actions was outlined dated four months ago. *Of interest. Alert MI5 immediately.*

The operator immediately copied the image and the adjoining message, created a covering alert message, selected MI5 from the drop down destination box and hit send. The image and its annotation from the operator would be on the desk of the European section in Thames House within fractions of a second, the automatic routing system would have analysed the content and selected a recipient without any human intervention. Satisfied that the system would deal with the information correctly the operator picked up the phone on the desk and spoke briefly to the MI5 diplomatic surveillance team located in Terminal 1 alerting them to the arrival of a known Russian diplomat, or at least his passport.

=

Gregorio walked briskly through the Customs Hall and out through the throng of awaiting relatives and drivers waiting to meet arriving families and business travellers. Parked on double yellow lines with the door open was a black Mercedes saloon with Diplomatic plates, always use the best available Western cars. Ignoring the approach of a female armed Police officer he slid his bag into the boot, being held open by the driver, and climbed into the back seat before the officer that was paying them increased attention got too close. The driver started the engine, dropped his sunglasses onto his nose, and pulled away from the kerb and into the flow of black cabs and buses amid a cacophony of blasting horns.

Tucked behind two black cabs the nondescript and very battered looking Ford Focus followed the Mercedes as it made its way around the Heathrow inner ring road and out towards the M4. The car was being driven by one of Heathrow's resident MI5 Diplomatic watchers, it was their job to follow all Diplomatic arrivals and confirm their destinations. In the passenger seat was Avril Wentworth-Smythe.

Avril had been visiting the resident team at the airport as part of her new role as Diplomatic Liaison. Following the post-mortem after the 'Yorkie' affair, she had been moved sideways, in her eyes a demotion, by Paul Whittle for her poor handling of the surveillance on Magda and Petrov. Whittle's explanation being that a couple of years overseeing a real surveillance team would help her with any application for a desk head job in the future. Once again she had taken the rap, as she knew she would, and the desk head had been protected by the 'old boys' network. Whittle was now being touted as the next head of counter terrorism following the imminent retirement of, soon to be, Sir Toby Gadsby. Avril had been gutted, and had almost approached Frank Martin at STAG to ask if his offer of a job was still available, but her pride and determination to prove the Service wrong had prevailed and she had reluctantly moved to Diplo.

She had been about to leave the surveillance office at Terminal 1 when the message had come in from the watchers in Terminal 4. The name Gregorio Alexayev had meant nothing to the teams in the office and they had only reacted to the request to follow the Diplomat Vitaly Popov. Avril had been gob smacked when the name and photo match had flashed on to the screen. Until that point in time she had only the name, but the CIA had now provided a face, not only that but they had matched it to an alias. For once the new technology, which she was struggling to understand, was working in her favour. Sending her car and driver, one perk of the new role, back to London she had joined one of the two trail officers as he had identified and then followed the Mercedes from the underground terminal exit. Now four cars ahead of them, they watched as the car left the airport exit road and joined the roundabout below the M4 motorway. The Mercedes took the third exit and headed East on the M4 towards London as the second trail car overtook them and took up station ahead of the target car.

Avril toyed with the idea of alerting Paul Whittle in the European section that she was on the tail of Gregorio but very quickly dismissed the idea. One of the conclusions that Whittle had made from the débâcle of the previous operation was the non-existence of Alexayev, being happy to accept the dubious report of his demise on an arms dealing quest. She knew that raising the name with only a flimsy identification she would be ridiculed by Whittle and his umbrella protection of cronies. No, this time she would not be alerting the old boys network, this time, and for now anyway, this was a purely Diplomatic surveillance responsibility.

The driver of the Focus accelerated to close the gap on the Mercedes as it joined the A4 towards Hammersmith, the second trail car that had been ahead of the Embassy car for the last three or four miles dropped back. Not much of a driver herself Avril, in the short time in the role, had marvelled at how the surveillance officers could instantly react to any situation unfolding in front of them and stay anonymous in busy traffic without losing sight of the target vehicle. They very rarely lost a target, helped in some part by the cars, that although they looked battered, were highly tuned and extremely quick when required. The Ford dropped back to three cars behind the Merc in a queue of traffic as they passed the Earls Court Exhibition Centre and headed towards the river.

They followed the river on the North Bank as it headed towards Central London but to Avril's surprise the Mercedes took the right turn filter at a set of traffic lights and turned across Battersea Bridge to the South Bank. The Russian Embassy was situated at Kensington Palace Gardens, much further up the road and where the Diplomatic car should have been heading. The driver of the trail car cursed as a black cab cut him up as he attempted to follow and had to brake sharply to avoid running the red light. By the time the junction had cleared the Mercedes had disappeared off the far end of the bridge and Avril could see the second trail car close behind them as they crossed the bridge. "Bollocks!" The loud expletive caught the driver off guard and he whispered an apology as he negotiated the traffic on the bridge. Avril shook her head. "Not your fault. I just wonder where he is heading? He is nowhere near the embassy."She reached for her mobile from the door pocket. "OK. Call it in as a loss. I know someone who will be very interested in this arrival."

=

Gregorio sat back against the rear seat headrest and smiled ruefully as he saw the old blue car that had been following them from the airport abruptly stop at the red light as his driver crossed the river. He had been expecting a tail, it was routine for all Diplomatic arrivals to be followed, and had picked the Ford up almost immediately as they left the terminal. Gregorio had been in the business a long time and was well versed in surveillance methods and all the tricks used to counter them. He knew he, or at least Vitaly Popov, would attract attention from the Diplomatic team as soon as the passport was scanned at immigration control. He also knew that they would be expecting to follow him to the embassy as all official arrivals were expected to check in before going about their business. The difference in this visit was that his embassy had no idea he was coming and would definitely not be expecting, or happy, to see him. His Diplomatic status had been hard won and expensive to obtain by greasing the right palms at the right times and he was very definitely not on the official invitation list of any Russian overseas mission.

The driver of the Mercedes, the right model but wearing false diplomatic number plates, checked the rear view mirror was clear of a tail and turned the car off the main road into a small industrial estate located behind Battersea Park. Gregorio had picked his overseas team well and was impressed with the abilities of the driver in losing the tail. The car negotiated the numerous speed humps and chicane narrows and headed deeper into the estate. Turning down a side road the driver pointed the car towards an open set of double doors in the side of a nondescript and grubby looking industrial unit.

As the driver brought the car to a stand in the cavernous interior the electronically operated double doors closed silently behind them.

The inside of the warehouse was brightly lit by high intensity strip lighting positioned high up in the ceiling alongside large metal ventilation units that ran the whole length of the building. Half of the floor space was given over to metal racking that reached almost as high as the light units that was piled high with wooded packing cases to one side and cardboard containers to the other. Parked alongside one of the concrete walls were two large white Mercedes transporters carrying the painted logo of a well known London delivery company.

Gregorio left the back of the car through the door being held open for him and followed the unknown person through a door set in the concrete wall and into a double story building at the side of the warehouse. He followed the back of the figure up two sets of metal stairs and out through a further door into a long white walled corridor. At the far end he was shown into a large office with wood panelling to the walls and a large, highly polished, conference table filling the middle of the room. Seated behind a large leather topped desk at the far end was a stocky, bald headed and bespectacled man dressed in a dark three-piece suit with a Guards Regimental tie knotted neatly at his throat. "Welcome to Glamdon's Mr Popov." He offered an extended hand but quickly swept an invitation to sit down when Gregorio ignored the invite to shake the man's hand.

Gregorio lowered himself into the leather armchair that was positioned to the side of the desk. "Has my merchandise arrived yet." He spat the question at the seated figure who almost recoiled with the venom, but managed a controlled reply.

"The ship is due into Southampton this evening. We should have possession of the container by tomorrow morning."

Gregorio cut across the reply and spat a further question. "When can I expect my items in London?"

Again the venom surprised the man behind the desk but he managed to keep his cool despite his anger rising at the rude and arrogant man seated opposite him. He had taken over the family transport business from his father after he had followed him with service in the Coldstream Guards, the family regiment. He dealt with customers from all over the World, but he rarely came across any that were as rude as this.

"The items will be here by tomorrow evening for your inspection."

Gregorio rose from his seat and tossed an embossed business card onto the desk before turning abruptly and heading for the door.

"Call me the moment they arrive." he stopped briefly in the frame of the door. "If your business is important to you Mr Glamdon you will make sure my items are treated well. I have influence in many places and I am sure a recommendation from the Russian Embassy would sit well on your letter heads." Without waiting for a reply Gregorio headed down the steps to his waiting car.

Robin Glamdon watched the Mercedes leave the warehouse and head out of the estate from his office window. He had reluctantly taken over the reigns of Glamdon Professional Transport when his father had retired after serving fifteen years in the Guards. He had risen to the rank of Major and was destined for higher things when his father had surprised the family by taking early retirement and moving to Cyprus where he had himself served in the Guards. At first reluctant to become involved, Robin had eventually bowed to the inevitable and pushed himself wholeheartedly into making the business more successful than it already was. He had increased the services they provided and offered a very high-end and professional service to the well off in and around London. One of the areas he had expanded into, and was proving very lucrative, was offering a bespoke service, the reason for this warehouse, to high-end art collectors and dealers. Glamdon's was now the most respected delivery and storage business in London and its reputation was now growing internationally as well, hence his dealings with a member of the Russian embassy.

As he watched the embassy car turn back into the busy Battersea traffic he was puzzled as to why a foreign diplomat would behave in such a manner when dealing with a business in the host country. During his service he had spent five years in charge of an Intelligence cell offering support to Special Forces operations and the exchange, or rather the orders, he had just had in his office was beginning to sound alarm bells. He was used to reading the signs in behaviour that could point to other things. Maybe it was nothing, but it was still worth flagging it up to the authorities. Too much was happening in London at the moment, with terrorist activity and attacks, to ignore it. He reached inside his suit pocket for his wallet and pulled the still neatly folded piece of menu, he had scribbled the name and number on at his last retirement party at the Guards Club. He knew who might be interested in his hunch.

FOURTEEN

Frank Martin flicked the left turn indicator switch mounted on the handlebar with his gloved thumb and aimed the big Honda onto the slip road for the motorway services. He tapped Samantha, seated behind him, on the knee and said "Coffee time?" into the intercom lip mic mounted on the front of the helmet.

She squeezed both arms around him and replied. "Yes please. My bum's gone numb!" He accelerated the big machine past two cars on the slip road and turned into a vacant parking bay close to the services main building. The car park was full of families returning from holiday trips away, the 4X4s and estate cars packed high with cases. Samantha climbed from the rear seat, pulled her helmet off and shook her long blonde hair so it fell around her shoulders. "That's better. My knees have locked and I have lost all feeling in my buttocks." Frank removed his own lid and grabbed his wife around the waist.

"I will soon bring it back to life!" He thought she was getting sexier by the day. She pushed him away with a playful smile on her face.

"I think you have had enough of that over the last two days Mr Martin!" She wiggled her leather clad hips and moved away as he locked the helmets in the top case and they made their way, laughing, towards the entrance.

It had been Samantha's idea to spend the weekend riding around mid Wales. The six months since Yorkie, had been the most hectic period they had both worked since they had been involved with STAG. London and Manchester had suffered large terrorist attacks in the Spring, along with other European cities, and all of STAG's resources had been offered out to assist the other security agencies with the counter terrorism operation and investigation into the attacks. Samantha had taken her team to Thames House to assist with MI5 surge analysis while Frank had offered his services to Sir Anthony Baxter the head of the Metropolitan Police's Counter Terrorism Command. Even Si Radford had been farmed out and was currently living in a grotty bedsit in Cheltenham, much to his annoyance, while assisting GCHQ. He had managed a short trip to the US to follow up the Yorkie affair with his contacts in the CIA and National Security Agency, the American equivalent of GCHQ. Events had overtaken any follow-up work and the technical analysis of the trigger devices had been put on hold. His small team had accompanied him to GCHQ and were now fully occupied assisting with the masses of Internet data that the agency was trying to deal with. In addition there had been a major cyber attack on major European institutions, including banks and government offices, that was taxing their resources to the limit.

Both Frank and Samantha had been working long hours, often seven days a week, and had had very little opportunity too spend time with each other. Samantha had also seen a return of the nightmares and the troubled sleep that haunted her husband. Despite his denials she knew he was still troubled by the guilt he felt, after all these years, that he could have done more to save his Commanding Officer on that horrific hillside. Despite his outward strength and ability to take things in his stride she knew it was this one incident in his early career that caused him so much pain. She also knew the extra workload and the responsibility of keeping STAG operations running was having an effect on Frank. The Yorkie affair also had some loose ends that did not add up and this was continuing to trouble him, so as the workload had eased and the opportunity for a few days off had presented itself she had suggested they take off and head for their favourite bends in Wales. They had spent the past two days riding round the picturesque Elan Valley above Rhayader, making time for some circuits of grim reaper bends, and enjoying each others company in a 5 star farmhouse bed and breakfast near Builth Wells. It was over far too soon. Now as they made their way back down the M4 towards London, Samantha was determined that their plan to ease back and possibly retire early would became a reality sooner rather than later.

As they entered the services Frank reached into the pocket of his leathers for his phone. He had deliberately not had it connected to the intercom on the bike and had not checked it since they had started the journey back towards London. He switched it on and immediately a text message flashed onto the screen. It was from Avril Wentworth-Smyth who he had not heard from since the Yorkie affair had died down. He had been made aware through the grapevine that she had moved on, or had apparently been moved on, to pastures new. She had unfortunately been another victim to the old boys network that still existed within the walls of Thames House.

He opened the message. "I have something you might be interested in. Give me a call when you get this message." Before he could push the call button another message popped up on the screen. This time from Si Radford. "Sorry to break up your weekend boss. But Avril has some info that might interest you. See you soon. I'm on my way back."

Since Frank had assumed temporary responsibility for STAG in the absence of the Director, Si had insisted on calling him boss, much to his disgust. The Director had been moved across, on the request of the Prime Minister, to lead a high level working group. Their remit to look at the sources of the recent attacks, with the heads of the other agencies reporting to him on a daily basis. Not universally popular with the other heads it meant that Frank now had full control of the office as well as assisting Sir Anthony. Retirement was looking to be an increasingly good idea he thought as he dialled Si's number.

"Hello boss." Frank grimaced to himself as he heard Si's excited voice through the phone speaker. He nodded at Samantha as she waved a plastic wrapped sandwich at him from the cold counter.

"What's happening Si? I haven't heard from Avril in months. What has got her all excited?" He followed Samantha to the coffee counter and carried the tray to a table as he listened to Si recount the information he had got from Avril.

"She has been calling you all weekend boss, but your phone was off." Frank didn't think it was worth at this point to explain that he was carrying the office alert system that Si had invented and the shift officers had known exactly how to get hold of him if it had been deemed necessary.

"Are the Americans sure this is Gregorio?" It wouldn't be the first time the CIA had got overexcited and reported something before checking the facts. Si continued to update him on the reports from the Americans who it appeared had quite a dossier on his arms dealing, but had only ever treated him as yet another supplier in an industry of many. They were now, though, getting a little hot under the collar as recent indications were that the greedy Russian was starting to cosy up to some of the more repugnant of extremist reptiles including, it was thought, leading ISIS players. "OK Si. I will come into the office when we get back. Let Avril know." He could probably do without her high-pitched squeak for at least another couple of hours. He replaced his phone in his leathers and took a sip of his hot latte.

He brought Samantha up to speed on the conversation while they finished their drinks. She didn't seem surprised that he had reappeared, and if he was honest neither was he. He was sure the figure they had glimpsed at Yorkie's funeral had been the Russian and he fully expected him to make a return. Something in that whole affair had made him feel that it was part of something much bigger, and that perhaps Yorkie had not been the kingpin that they all thought he was, and he had led them to believe. One thing was for sure, if the Yanks had got their ducks properly in a row on this one then Gregorio Alexayev was alive and kicking and it looked a distinct possibility that he was now in London.

=

Si Radford tapped the keys on his laptop and the image displayed on the large monitor suspended from the office ceiling came into sharp, enlarged, focus before the four of them seated at the central meeting table. On arrival back in London Frank and Samantha had immediately gone into the office, still in their leathers from the bike journey. Si had beaten them to it, made four cups of coffee, and had already started analysing the images captured by the recognition software at the airport by the time they had arrived, and for once it was not his software that was being used. Avril had joined them a few minutes later, after Samantha had met her at the security entrance to sign her in, and she now sat fiddling with the visitors badge around her neck. The large black V on the badge not only, in her eyes, denoted she was a visitor to STAG but was somehow no longer in the know as far as high-level operations were concerned. Before being moved to the Diplomatic team her universal clearance and badge would have allowed her instance access to any of the agencies, and she was determined to win that privilege back and quickly.

Frank stood and looked more closely at the image displayed above them. "At least we now have an idea of what the mysterious Gregorio looks like, even if we have no idea why he is back in London." Avril turned and stood next to him.

"The second tail driver had a good look around the area near Battersea Bridge but could find no trace of the Merc. We have alerted the Met to keep a look out for the car and I have asked the Foreign Office to raise the issue of why we were not informed of the imminent arrival of the diplomat Vitaly Popov. The Americans have no further information and were surprised the match was made. They had no idea of the connection and believe Gregorio Alexayev to be a lone arms dealer who always travels on his own identity." She turned back to face the other two. "This could, of course, be a one off use of this identity or maybe this visit is something other than a business meeting."

Frank sipped his now cold coffee and indicated towards the second suspended screen that displayed the report from the CIA. "They seem to have been watching him for some time, but had not made any connection between him and Yorkie." He pursed his lips and asked Si to scroll the report down. "They also seem to have lost his movements in the last six months. Does this mean he has just kept

179

his head down or are we all missing something? The Yanks seem to think, according to Si, that he might be starting to offer his services to some extremely nasty people." His words were interrupted by one of the duty officers coming into the room.

"Sorry to interrupt Frank, but we have just had a message from Taggart on the alert system for you from Hereford." Frank knew he was away on his annual update course, he had meant to be with him but had not been able to find the time, and would have normally been out of contact. "He wants you to give him a call Frank. Something about receiving information from an old colleague. He was very vague, but then he always is." The duty officer left the office, chuckling to himself as Frank turned back to the other three.

"Not more work I hope? Things are getting bloody silly."

=

Frank shook the offered hand of Robin Glamdon and introduced Si as they both sat down in the leather armchairs in the plush office. Taggart had given Frank the details of the conversation he had had with the former Intelligence officer. Although he had only briefly worked with him prior to his Afghanistan tour he had remembered the stocky, thick set Major from the night in the Guards Club. Frank had started to note the information ready to pass onto one of the team to follow up until Taggart had used the name Vitaly Popov. It might have been a huge coincidence, but Frank had learned very early on in his career that sometimes coincidences were the best way to gain Intelligence. Taggart had passed him the contact details for Robin Glamdon and a meeting in his office had been quickly organised for the morning.

They both declined the offer of coffee and Frank, keen to keep the meeting short, came straight to the point. "Thank you Mr Glamdon for passing your suspicions on to us. Could you explain your relationship with Mr Popov, and why you feel things might not be as they seem." Frank did not want to give any indication that they also had a very keen interest in Mr Popov. He had introduced himself and Si as members of the Foreign Office Trade and Industry Team with a particular interest in any contact with Foreign Diplomats. He was sure that Robin Glamdon did not believe that and knew exactly who they were, but he was not about to reveal their reasons for showing an interest. Robin Glamdon shuffled some papers nervously on his desk.

"It just seemed odd to me that an accredited diplomat would act so aggressively towards a businessman in the host country. He made the approach to us, our name had been passed to him from a client we worked with recently. This is the first time we have had dealings with the Embassy, I am trying to take the business in a different direction and expand into international arenas." Frank let him continue explaining his reasons for the meeting he had had with Popov. It appeared that Glamdon's, being a new entry into the high-end art transport market had offered the Russian very favourable terms and a discrete service. Not that discrete thought Frank, or you would not have involved us.

"Do you know the nature of the items you are transporting?"

Glamdon continued. "No. That is one of the discrete parts of the service. Mr Popov used his own packing and shipping company, we just collect from the port and store the items here until the client is ready for them to be delivered. As you saw when you came through the warehouse we also offer a storage facility."

Glamdon went on to outline the process of storage and delivery. In this case the items would be collected from the port, held for a number of hours before being delivered to, an as yet, unspecified address. The consignment would consist of three wooden packing cases that were currently part of a larger container load awaiting unloading at Southampton docks. Glamdon himself was overseeing the collection and was waiting for confirmation of the unloading before joining his collection team.

Frank thanked Glamdon for his time, and promised that the trade team would look into Mr Popov. Before they left the office Si had asked for any contact details the company held. They made their way back through the warehouse and Frank noted that the pieces stored on the racking ranged from quite small boxes and packages to large crates. He had asked before leaving the office if Glamdon had any idea where delivery might be made, he did not, but promised to inform them as soon as he had received the details. He had explained that most of the art they dealt with was destined for private collections, usually in large houses in and around London, but that they also dealt with auction houses and art galleries. If Gregorio was planning on bringing arms into the UK then Frank supposed hiding them in a delivery of exotic art was as good a way as any. Si had taken the liberty of asking for a photocopy of the business card the Russian had given to Glamdon and had entered the details into his system as they had walked back through the warehouse.

As Si drove them out of the industrial estate Frank's mobile rang. It was Avril. Her high pitched excited voice made him wince and he turned the volume down. Ending the call he turned to Si. "Well, wherever that art, if it is art, is destined for it isn't the Russian Embassy. They have no record of an accredited diplomatic passport in the name of Vitaly Popov. They are checking with Moscow for new issues, but are not happy that they were not informed."

Si came to a stop at the traffic lights. "Maybe he knows someone they don't. Might be worth getting Samantha to nudge her contacts."

Frank smiled. "I am already on it." He hit send on the text box and closed the phone. "The Russians also have no record of that diplomatic number plate. It would seem that our friend is very definitely freelancing and not here in any official capacity."

Si turned off the bridge into the London bound traffic. "I think our workload just got bigger boss!"

FIFTEEN

Roger Biddle steered the Bentley down the gravel driveway away from the retirement home. The car had been a present to himself when his football career had ended. He also owned a Ferrari and a Maserati but the Bentley gave him an air of status and authority. His Mother stood in the entrance still waving as he turned out of the leafy gateway and onto the lane leading to the city ring road. He had been visiting her more often since the incident with his half-brother. He had refused to call Kevin his brother since the full story had emerged despite knowing that it saddened his Mother that he would not acknowledge him.

He had been seventeen years old and just breaking into the first team at Barnsley Football Club when Yorkie, as they now called him, had done his bunk. It had devastated his parents but he had been so engrossed in his blossoming football career that he had not paid much attention, they had never really been that close anyway. Even growing up they had never really had much to do with each other, he had been out playing football at any opportunity while Kevin had occupied himself with models and diagrams. Family life had gradually calmed down when they realised that Kevin had gone for good and his Father, in particular, had got behind him as he made a name for himself and was over the moon when he made the big time with Leeds United at the age of nineteen.

He had spent ten good seasons at Leeds until his pace had started to desert him and he finished his career moving from club to club further down the league structure. Finally forced to retire from a series of injuries he tried his hand at coaching, but could not put the same effort into others careers as he had in his own. His only regret had been the lack of an International call-up, even though he played for England at youth level. Two failed marriages proved that he was very much centred on his own life and didn't really have much time for others. That was still eminently true now and he resented any time he had to spend away from his beloved art business.

Throughout his time in football he had become interested in the fine art scene, at first buying for his own pleasure and later dabbling in the dealing world and had made some decent acquisitions along the way. Finally opening a gallery in Harrogate he had over the years become a well known figure in the Northern art world and appearances on a number of the burgeoning antiques TV programmes had further raised his reputation. He was now excited to be embarking on a new venture by opening a gallery in the centre of London. Recent appearances as a football pundit on a satellite TV sports channel had increased his popularity and he felt now the time was right to explore the southern arts market. His current girlfriend was a Ukranian model and it had been her idea to highlight some Russian artists at the gallery launch. He was now finalising the details for the opening night, leaving her to deal with the Russian dealer that had acquired the pieces they would display.

Although appearing pleased by the news that he had just given her, he could not help thinking his Mother had not recovered from the affair with his half-Brother. He felt she was somehow blaming herself for the whole thing, but he also felt she could not bring herself to actually believe that her 'Yorkie' could have had that amount of venom in him. Nevertheless, she had agreed to accompany him at the opening night, due in part to the Russian exhibit, and he had promised to put her up in The Dorchester and take her for a tour of the London sights the next day. She had never left Yorkshire after her return, in disgrace as she put it, not even to watch him play football. As much as he knew she loved him he also knew that she still kept a special place in her heart for her first born, and if he was honest a special place in her heart for his Russian father.

=

Robin Glamdon sat in the passenger seat of the transporter and watched his two man team supervise the removal of two large crates from the container. The dockyard had been extremely busy with a number of container vessels racing to unload their cargo and reload in order to leave on the evening high tide. They had waited and watched as container after container had been winched from the deck of the ship, placed on the overhead railway, that ran the length of the dockyard, and delivered to the reception yard. Having then negotiated the myriad of paperwork checks they had been allowed into the yard to take possession of the goods they were expecting. Two large crates were carried one at a time from the container and deposited by forklift into the rear of the truck. Signing, again, for the crates the driver and his mate secured the rear of the truck and climbed into the cab alongside him. "I thought we had three elements to this consignment. Have we something missing?" The driver turned to face his boss. He hated it when he decided to come along, but he was the owner of the company now and perfectly entitled to.

"One is marked 'special handling' boss and has to be collected from the fragile store. More bloody paperwork I expect!"

Glamdon nodded to the driver and pulled his mobile from his jacket. He opened the text function and hit send on the draft text he had written earlier. Almost immediately the phone beeped with a reply. "Return and await instructions." He clicked the phone off and threw it onto the dashboard. "That fucking Russian can be obnoxious even by text." The driver shrugged and headed for the fragile store. Robin Glamdon was seething. He knew his teams did not really respect or trust him yet. His father had treated his workforce like lifelong friends, most of them were, but he did not seem to have the same effect on them. He thought it was probably his military approach to everything, he had certainly tightened things up and made the process more efficient since taking over. His father had been happy to keep the company ticking over in the later years of his tenure and had never been one to chase new business. He, on the other hand, was determined to take the company onto new things. This was one of the reasons he was now courting this fucking prick of a Russian.

The driver negotiated the booking in booth at the fragile store, brought the truck to a halt as directed and parked up. "I will go."

The driver shrugged and handed the paperwork over as Glamdon climbed across the drivers mate and out through the cab door. The reception at the front of the store was congested with jostling drivers awaiting attention so he joined the back of the queue. His conversation with Taggart, he had never known his real name even when he knew him at Hereford, had been slightly awkward. Even as he was talking he felt like maybe he was making something out of nothing. He was so determined to make a success of the business and he really was not used to people talking to him the way the Russian had. Taggart had assured him that there was no such thing as a bad tip-off and the meeting with Martin and Radford had gone OK. He knew they were from one of the agencies and had assumed it would have been MI5. He had agreed to contact them as soon as he had any idea where the delivery would be made, the reason why he had joined his crew.

The queue in front of him cleared and he handed the delivery note to a very harassed middle-aged woman behind the counter. She disappeared into the back of the store, reappearing a few minutes later through a door at the side of the counter. She was pushing a small hand truck with a solid looking wooden crate on it the size of a small table. "It's bloody heavy love."She said, handing the truck over. "Take the trolley and leave it by the door. One of the lads will collect it." Glamdon thanked her and took the handles from her. He made his way back to the parking area where the driver was waiting with the tailgate open. They, together, manhandled the crate onto the tail lift and the driver elevated it and slid the crate aboard. She had been right, it was bloody heavy!

=

Frank juggled the cardboard tray of coffees in his left hand as he swiped his security pass on the reader with his right, leaned his shoulder against the door as it clicked open and entered the STAG building. He crossed the entrance hallway, still covered in the pre-war tiles, and through the inner security door as it swung open. The building they now occupied had housed one of the many departments associated with the clandestine work of the Special Operations Executive, or SOE, during the war and later occupied by a branch of the Treasury. It had lain empty for many years following their departure but kept in a good 'mothballed' state, as many such buildings were, until STAG had moved in. Many of the wartime features still remained, like the highly polished floors and banister rails. It was somehow fitting, Frank thought as he passed through the already open door, that the original interior should remain alongside today's high-tech toys. He never managed to beat the security guards to it, despite many attempts, as he knew they could see anyone approaching the building from 200 metres away via the high wall mounted cameras. Nevertheless, it was a game he liked to play. He climbed the ornamental staircase to the STAG operations room trying to remember which order the various coffees were arranged in, pushed the door open and deposited the tray on the central meeting table.

He had left Si and Samantha scrutinising the latest information from the Americans while he had attended an urgent meeting called by Sir Anthony Baxter. The number of potential threats and planned attacks was stretching resources to the limit and Sir Anthony was calling for even more assistance from the Security agencies, MI5 had already commandeered as many of his analysts as possible under the orders of Paul Whittle. Although Frank had agreed to offer as much help as he could he was not sure where he was going to get the bodies from. STAG, by its very nature, was a reasonably small organisation and was already beginning to operate well outside its remit. Given Sir Anthony's predicament he had felt it was not an appropriate moment to mention the reappearance of a potential threat from Gregorio. For the time being STAG would have to add it to the ever increasing workload and go it alone.

Frank handed out the coffees from the tray, then they all played 'swapsies' until they had the drink they had ordered. Samantha took a sip of her coffee and then moved her laptop closer to where Frank had taken a seat. "Some very interesting stuff has been coming in while you have been at Scotland Yard." She turned the screen so he could see it and Si joined them, looking over Frank's shoulder. "The CIA did some more digging after the recognition software made the match. It would appear that our Gregorio has more than one identity. In fact he has quite a few, but until the software started doing its stuff the Americans were treating each one as a separate person."

Frank watched as the image of the Russian started matching with different passport details, all in different names. Samantha continued as the two men read the information on the screen. "The FBI, apparently, have also had one or two of the names on their watch lists but also did not make the connection, until now that is. Our Gregorio has been quite prolific in his dealings with the dodgier end of the arms world it would appear." She turned the laptop back towards her and bought up another file. "This one is getting them overexcited." Frank and Si looked over to the screen as it flashed up a list of contacts. Samantha highlighted one name halfway down the list. "Mustafa El Gabo" Was the name that appeared and both Frank and Si spoke together.

"Shit!" Frank continued. "The Egyptian former Al Qaida warlord now believed to be number two in ISIS in Iraq but calling himself Mohamed Al Streti."

Samantha slid the machine back towards Frank. "The very same and the Americans are now going ape shit. Someone has decided to read the whole Yorkie report and they are starting to put twoand two together. El Gabo, or Al Streti has been trying to get his hand on a dirty bomb for a while and the Yanks now think our friends Yorkie and Gregorio were in the process of getting him one."

Frank let out a long breath. "Si, you need to start talking to your techie friends, and I think we need to get this to COBRA. If what we witnessed with Yorkie was a practice run for this then we could be on the verge of a potential attack that would put the recent events in the shade. Paul Whittle might just have the Middle East connection he craves. Well done Avril."

=

Gregorio heaved the body of the driver into the boot of the Mercedes and slammed it shut. It had been a long time since he had used his lethal, hard won, skills but he had found it easy dragging the sharpened blade across the driver's throat as he parked the car. The hardest bit had been pulling the body from the front seat and back to

189

the boot. He had deliberately made the driver park in the dark recesses of the underground car park, well away from the busy entrance. He had made sure none of the blood had seeped onto his hands as he had drawn the blade across the artery. To be sure he pulled a folded handkerchief from his trouser pocket and quickly wiped his hands before tossing it into the waste bin as he walked towards the exit.

With his own blood coursing through his body, a post kill reaction he loved, he made his way back to street level and walked towards the Underground sign he could see in the distance. Buying a ticket from the machine at the entrance he descended the moving staircase to the platform level just as the train arrived. The carriage was crowded with homeward bound commuters so he grabbed a swinging handle and stood in the doorway for the two stop journey to Soho.

SIXTEEN

Frank took a sip of his iced latte and unfolded the sheets of printed paper that lay on the table in front of him. He gazed out over the lake that formed the middle of St James' Park, the sun was gleaming off its surface and causing reflections off the bankside foliage. London was warm this time of year but at least it had not yet turned humid and sticky. The muted rumble of traffic on The Mall carried across to him as he sat in the shade outside the park café. This was his favourite spot to come and find some quiet when he needed thinking time. It was a short walk from the STAG building and he liked to take at least one solitary coffee a day, particularly with the workload that now confronted them. Frank often wondered how the Intelligence world would operate without coffee, he and the STAG team seemed to consume an awful lot!

Following the revelations by the CIA, that the character they knew as Gregorio was far from the small-time arms dealer they thought he was, the team had been frantically digging into every angle they could. Si Radford and his small technical team were busy resurrecting and analysing every little detail of the system they had extracted from Yorkie's devices. Samantha had spent her time mapping Yorkie's entire life, his connections and relationships, and that detail now formed the eight page report that he now had before him.

As always, Samantha had produced a report that lacked nothing and had missed not even the smallest detail. But despite reading it three times Frank felt they were still missing something about Yorkie. Something that might just shed some light on who Gregorio really was, and what he was now doing back in the UK. The potential connections drawn between him and a senior figure in ISIS, once highlighted to COBRA, had brought MI5 and the other agencies back into the game. Paul Whittle was currently creating a high-level operation, along with major input from Sir Anthony, into tracking down the Russian. All Robin Glamdon's communications, including Internet and mobile phones, were on twenty-four hour tapping watch and there was a three shift observation team outside his premises. Despite all this hubbub and activity no sign had been found and the Russian had very definitely gone to ground.

Frank was happy that Whittle was creating enough of a stampede to drown out any real progress being made. Frank and his small team could now go about tracking down the clues that might point to the answers quietly, covertly and without fanfare. This was what STAG did well and they were now free to get on with it. He had, following intervention from the Director, had Avril Wentworth-Smyth attached to them for the duration of the operation. She and Samantha were now in the bowels of the Foreign Office going through the archives with a fine tooth comb.

He finished the icy dregs from the cup and started to read the report again. One particular paragraph was grabbing his attention each time he read it:

TOP SECRET DENIM

REPORT EXTRACT

SUBJECT: KGB OFFICERS DEMISE

The two officers attached to the Russian Embassy In London were both observed at (location redacted) by MI5 Officers (names redacted) attempting to gain entry into secure storage facility Alpha. When challenged Officer Dmitry Sokolov opened fire with a pistol and was immediately killed by return of fire from the MI5 Officers. Officer Sergei Antanov fled the scene and attempted to cross the adjacent rail manoeuvring yard. Despite warnings issued by the MI5 officers Antanov continued and was struck by a locomotive pulling missile cannisters. Despite efforts by the MI5 Officers Antanov died at the scene.

EXTRACT ENDS

This time the significance of the small paragraph was not lost on him. All along they had believed, because Yorkie had told them so, his father had been alone when he died all those years ago. But this report, extracted from deeply hidden archives, appeared to be saying that there had been two KGB men at the depot that day. But what was the relevance of that to what was now happening in London almost sixty years later? Frank pulled his mobile from his pocket and dialled Samantha's number. She answered after two rings.

"Hi Frank." They were never more familiar than first names when in work, they always remained professional at all times. Frank gave her the name Dmitry Sokolov from the report and asked her to run a trace on his professional and private life. There was something in this small extract that was the key but at the moment they all seemed to be missing it. Before he could return his phone to his pocket it buzzed in his hand.

"Hello Si. Are you getting anywhere?" There was an excited tone to Si's voice as he replied.

"We have re-run the data we captured during the Yorkie observations and it would appear there was a hidden branch." Frank turned away from the lake to shield his conversation.

"What does that mean Si? In plain English please." Frank was normally lost after two minutes of techno babble from his opo. This time Si did as he was asked.

"Well basically Frank it means there was a spare channel on the feed into the devices that wasn't set up to receive commands from the Internet. The protocols are the same but it would appear the connection is for some kind of closed network. That's the good news, but the bad news is we have no idea what that network is."

Frank guessed it wasn't going to be that simple. "OK Si. Keep trying." He finished the call and called Paul Whittle and brought him up to speed, but omitted to impart his thoughts and Samantha's research on the report extract. Whittle could have that information when it was worth giving.

Frank ordered another iced latte from the waitress as she passed. All these loose ends had to eventually tie together. Eventually the real reason for all this, for Yorkie's re-appearance, for Gregorio, it all had to mean something. That moment that 'something' could only mean potential disaster.

He had been thinking a lot about the past, about those early days of his military career, over the last few weeks. Yorkie's words that night in the café had been burning into him. "You couldn't even save your leader". He had been going over and over that night on that shithole of a mountain amidst the carnage. Why didn't he save him? What should he have done differently? The sweat started to bubble on his brow as the images swam before his eyes. Maybe Yorkie had been right, despite the career he had carved out maybe he was a fraud, a failure at the first hurdle.

The thoughts had been turning increasingly negative in his mind since that evening on the Lincolnshire coast. He had started questioning his own motives for even being in the business he was in. The nightmares had not receded as they usually did, far from receding they had increased in intensity and horror. He knew he had to do something about it. He had to come to terms with his actions that night. He knew deep down that he had done all that he could. Why was he letting the words of a traitor make him question his own actions. No mate, I will get to the bottom of what you were doing. No mate, you will not destroy my career or my reputation.

The nightmare was shattered by the buzzing of his phone in his pocket. Samantha's voice brought him out of his thoughts as he answered. "We were missing a connection all along Frank. Alexayev was the name of Gregorio's mother after she re-married and he was given that name, and I might add used it to great effect." Frank was listening closely now, his head completely clear. "His birth name was Sokolov His biological father was Dmitry Sokolov, the KGB Officer who was with Yorkie's father that night." Frank was dumbstruck. Now it was falling into place. Samantha continued from the phones speaker. "You can thank Avril for that one, she put pressure on the Foreign Office until they cracked and gave us the connection." Avril was definitely proving her worth. He dialled Si's number as he paid the waitress and headed back across the park.

The web of intrigue that had started with the apparent chance contact from the past via Facebook was now beginning to make some sense. While he had bought into the notion that Yorkie was somehow taking some perverted revenge for the death of a father he had never known. Frank, until now, had been unable to reconcile the softly spoken, quiet and introverted Yorkie with the apparent monster that had confronted him on the Lincolnshire seafront. His years in the Intelligence business had taught him that things were very seldom what they appeared at first glance and there was often a hidden energy pushing things in a particular direction. It would appear that the hidden energy in all this was Gregorio. Could it really be that his friend from all those years ago had been manipulated right from the beginning, fed a story that fuelled a false anger and allowed him to be used, at first by the cold war Russian regime and later by the mutant freak that was Gregorio Alexayev?

Si answered after two rings. "Frank. I have been onto Robin Glamdon. He has the packages in his secure warehouse but has had no contact from our Russian friend. And all the numbers we have on watch for him are dead." There was a pause and shuffling of paper from the other end. "He has had a contact from an art dealer who is apparently, Glamdon says, the recipient of the two large crates." There was more shuffling and cursing from Si. "Sorry Frank, I've got that much info coming in on this guy from various sources we are struggling to keep up." Frank cut him off before he could continue with his diatribe.

"Do we know who this art dealer is Si?"

The cursing continued. "No. Glamdon won't release the name as he says all his contacts are kept confidential for business reasons. He did tell me the guy is well known and apparently from the North of England. The crates contain two signature pieces of Russian art that are supposed to form the centrepiece for the opening of the dealer's new gallery in London."

Frank had now reached the STAG building, took the stairs at a run and pushed the door open with his shoulder as Si paused for breath. "It's time we paid Mr Glamdon another visit I think."

Si spun round towards the voice. "Jesus Frank! I nearly crapped myself. I wish you wouldn't do that! Taggart is already on his way to have a chat, as they seem to know each other."

Frank grabbed a seat alongside him. "Bring me up to speed on what your contacts are saying about Gregorio."

Si and his team spent the next fifteen minutes outlining all the information that was coming in from the multi agencies, from nearly all then Western Intelligence services. It appeared that they had all had some kind of lead on him as a supplier of arms, of the increasingly nasty variety, to the most hated and wanted warlords and dictators in the World. The problem had been that he had been operating under so many different guises that until the MI5 recognition software had joined the dots they all thought they were dealing with multiple suppliers.

Si pulled all the information together in a conclusion. "The CIA have now narrowed his activity down to a potential plot involving the sale of several former Russian military battlefield nukes, Yorkie's 'duds' must have been replicas to test the system. Gregorio's deep historic contacts with his former paymasters have allowed him to obtain a number of low yield devices that he is now hawking to the highest bidder." He pulled a sheet of A4 from a pile of papers in front of him. "The Yanks have identified a potential sale to a Somalian terrorist with some very evil intents and it would seem they are demanding a demonstration. They believe the Yorkie thing showed them the trigger works. Now they want proof the nukes are real." Frank tapped his fingers on the desk in front of him.

"And by providing a demonstration Gregorio will exact revenge on Yorkie, or his father at least, and also satisfy his twisted Russian ideology with a strike against the West. He is one very dangerous, very screwed up fucker. We need to catch this guy, quickly."

The door to the office swung open and Taggart appeared in the doorway. "The art dealer is someone you may know Frank." He joined them at the desk. "A new gallery is opening on The Strand tomorrow. A grand affair with a lot of VIP guests. The owner is Roger Biddle."

=

Gregorio fidgeted with the plastic coffee cup as he sat in the hubbub of the Costa coffee shop in Covent Garden. He hated Western coffee, like he hated everything else about every Western shithole he had ever been to. Outside overexcited Japanese tourists ebbed and flowed like a shoal of gaudy electric fish. He looked at his Omega watch on his left wrist. Time to go. He swilled the last of the disgusting liquid and pushed his way to the door.

His visit to Soho had sated his sexual appetite. The young and pliable rent boy had attended to his every whim and need. Such a pity that someone so young, beautiful and useful should now be lying in a pool of his own cloying blood. He had thought the tender stroking of his neck were the afterglow responses of a satisfied and grateful punter. The blade Gregorio had dragged across his throat had brought an abrupt end to those thoughts.

On the far side of the cobbled courtyard the mime artist was climbing from his pedestal as the departing crowd dropped coins into the upturned hat at his feet. His performance over, he stretched his shoulders and arms to ease the ache from standing motionless for thirty minutes. Gregorio joined the tail of the thinning throng and edged close enough to claim the thin package as it was held for a fraction of a second by an outstretched arm from the artists coat. A perfectly executed brush contact, some trade craft never died. Another of his deeply embedded network. He quickly pocketed the package and turned towards the opera house on the edge of Covent Garden and headed for the taxi rank. He climbed into the rear of the leading cab on the rank as the driver turned off his 'for hire' sign. "Where to Guv?"

"Glamdon's Transport, Battersea." He passed a crumpled piece of paper with the address to the driver, another of his network, and settled back against the seat. Time to get this over with.

SEVENTEEN

Frank and Taggart tried to look comfortable and as though they belonged in the exalted company bedecked in ball gowns and tiaras. Unfortunately they were failing badly. Black tie and dinner suit was neither of their preferred dress style. Roger Biddle had been reluctant to allow them to be present at the opening of his new gallery, despite Frank outlining the very real possibility that his latest project was potentially the venue for a terrorist spectacular. It had taken the intervention of Mrs Biddle, Yorkie's Mother, before an invitation for them both had been produced. Frank's initial thoughts had been to close the whole thing down and send disposal teams to the gallery to rip it apart. The last minute intervention of Robin Glamdon and the news that he had delivered two large stone centrepieces, currently covered in two large red sheets, to the gallery that morning had persuaded him to use a different approach. A forensic search team had already been all over the two stone figures with a battery of electronic and scientific devices and were happy that both were inert and did not pose any danger. The question for Frank and his team was did this mean the device was already here? A sweep of the gallery had revealed nothing. If it was not here, how was it to be delivered? The other thought causing Frank some issues was that this may not be the chosen target and the device was about to be detonated in a different location.

Si Radford and his team now sat in a large white van further down The Strand monitoring an array of cutting edge equipment designed, by Si, to pick up any active signal that matched the protocols of the devices Yorkie had used. They were confident that their reverse engineering of the equipment they had recovered now put them one step ahead of anything using the Internet as a command network. As an added precaution Frank had got Roger Biddle, again reluctantly, to ask his guests to turn off their electronic devices. Si had also, in an attempt at belt and braces, deployed his shield at various points inside the gallery, including at the base of each stone statue.

Frank fiddled with the stem of his champagne glass and glanced across at Robin Glamdon, who looked at ease in this company. Always the Guards Officer I suppose thought Frank to himself. He had alerted them as soon as Gregorio had appeared at his offices that morning but the Russian had disappeared by the time a Special Branch team had arrived. According to Glamdon the Russian had paid for his services in cash and handed over the delivery address and detailed delivery instructions before heading for a waiting taxi.

Glamdon had allowed them full access to check out the ornaments, supervised the placement of the stone pieces himself and had returned later as an invited guest. He now stood about ten feet away sipping champagne and chatting to a tall, elegant blonde woman in a shimmering dress, who was wearing enough gold to replicate the crown jewels. Frank had asked him how they had arranged the delivery of two such large pieces in such a short time and Glamdon had been in his element telling him about the state of the art system he had on board his delivery fleet. It appeared that he already had the delivery date but not the destination, so the items had been loaded and dispatched that morning. Once Gregorio had provided the delivery location, it was just a matter of communicating it to the items. As Glamdon described the innate details of the system, Frank's mind was already turning to more pressing operational and urgent matters.

A black limousine pulled up at the kerb outside the gallery, squashing the two plastic cones that had reserved the space. Frank could only imagine the high-level contacts that had allowed Roger Biddle to reserve a parking slot in Central London. No doubt some palms had been greased somewhere. The general hubbub of conversation quietened as Biddle and his mother emerged from the rear of the car, the door held open for them by a liveried chauffeur, and they made a grand entrance into the gallery to be met by rapturous applause. As they made their way through the crowd to the centre of the room a quick movement on the edge of the throng caught Frank's eye and he turned to see Robin Glamdon heading out of the gallery with his mobile phone at his ear. At least one guest had not followed instructions.

Frank made for the door only to see Taggart beating him to it. He had obviously been watching Glamdon as closely as he had. By the time Frank had made it to the pair, Glamdon was already explaining his hurried exit. "That's my alarm company." He said, waving the phone in Frank's direction. "Someone has broken into the warehouse, they have sent a mobile patrol but they have now lost contact with them. One of my men is on the way there now."

Taggart turned to Frank. "I will go with Robin. Not sure what we might find." He called for the car on his concealed radio and turned back. "I think you had better alert young Si to be on his toes." They both headed for the car as it pulled up at the kerb. Frank called Si Radford on his radio then switched channels to alert the Special Branch team that were stationed around Covent Garden and The Strand. No sign had been seen or heard about Gregorio since he had disappeared from Glamdon's offices but Frank had a feeling they were about to witness his re-appearance and it was not going to be a positive meeting.

From someone that was supposed to be only a business and sexual partner of Yorkie's, Gregorio had now taken centre stage in Frank's ever increasing black thoughts. He was now beginning to think that maybe Yorkie had actually been an unwilling victim in all this. But could it really have been a plan all those years ago to manipulate him from the off with the aim to deliver some kind of final blow to the West? Somehow he doubted there had been such a strategic objective, and the regime had changed, but something was not ringing true in all of this. The revelation that Gregorio's father had been killed during the same operation as Yorkie's in Frank's mind very definitely meant that he held a long festering grudge. Maybe his engineered meeting of Yorkie by the Moscow hierarchy all those years ago had not only served the regime well, but also had given Gregorio the opportunity he sought to exact revenge. He had absolutely used his old friends skills and talent to feather his own nest and enhance his criminal reputation. Frank was sure that his feelings for Yorkie had been nothing but pecuniary.

A black BMW pulled up at the kerb and Sir Anthony Baxter climbed from the rear seat. His face was ashen and the worry lines looked like deeply carved craters in his face. Frank thought he looked like a man who could not really take any more. His counter terrorism command had been stretched to the limit and beyond this Spring, and now Frank was going to make his life a whole lot worse.

=

Gregorio steered the Glamdon transporter through the heavy traffic on The Embankment and cursed as he stopped at yet another red traffic signal. Breaking into the warehouse had been easy, despite triggering the alarm on his way out he was satisfied things had gone to plan. It had taken less than a minute to download the code from the flash drive he had inserted into the computer in Glamdon's office. Now the panel of the integrated communications system in the van blinked a dark blue to confirm he now had access to the closed Intranet that the system, and most of London's black cabs, operated on. The vehicle he was driving had now effectively become a command vehicle and the third of his packages, that now sat in the rear of the van, was about to cause devastation.

The only negative in the whole episode was the intervention of the two security men as he climbed aboard the van. They had turned the corner into the Glamdon warehouse yard just as he was about to drive away and parked alongside the transport vehicle. Both men had walked towards him as he sat in the drivers seat, one shining a torch at his face through the open window. He had fired two well aimed shots into the chest of the first as he approached him, then climbed out of the van and shot the other in the back as he ran for cover behind his vehicle. Making sure they were both dead, he had fired two more shots from his silenced handgun into both their heads before climbing back into the drivers seat.

The light changed to green and he pulled away in a slow moving snake as it headed through Parliament Square and down Whitehall. As he approached Trafalgar Square the connection icon on the control panel on the van's dashboard blinked green to indicate he had entered the next zone. Yvgene had shown his genius in designing the intricate code that controlled the devices via the Internet protocols but it had been he, Gregorio, who had identified the secure system being used in London. It had been introduced to make life easier for black cab drivers operating within the M25 motorway and operated on its own set of transmitters, most of them secreted into street lamps and traffic signals. The system allowed black cabs operating in Central London the ability to share information, take bookings and communicate electronically much quicker than using the open Internet. It had been such a success that other business users, such as Robin Glamdon, had been quick to exploit its effectiveness. Gregorio could have used any one of the hundreds of transport companies operating in the city to deliver his hardware but Glamdon's was the only one that offered him this unique way of striking. Keen to drive his company forward and exploit new markets Robin Glamdon had invested in the new technology when it had been offered by the networks owners. They had viewed him as a pioneer for furthering the commercial uses of the system. Gregorio had viewed him as the means of delivering devastation.

Poor Yvgene, he thought, as he negotiated another set of traffic signals. Your energy and talent had been focused on striking back at the very people who had welcomed you and nurtured you. But you fell ultimately for a story that suited your twisted romantic ideals. Your father was a small time loser and you would have been treated the same if you had not brought the skills the regime had craved all those years ago. And for me, he thought, I just fucked your brains out because you suited my plans. Bad luck Yvgene, I win. The codes he had acquired from his contact in Covent Garden had allowed him to override Glamdon's security and penetrate the firewall of the Intranet system the company was using. Courtesy of a disgruntled employee not happy with Robin Glamdon's drive and energy, who now lay in his dingy bedsit with two bullet wounds in his lifeless head, he now had the final piece in his deadly armoury. He would now exact his revenge and propel his reputation amongst the big players in the rare atmosphere he desired.

He steered the transporter into the rear loading yard behind the gallery, waved through by the security guard at the flash of his stolen Glamdon pass. He opened the sliding side door and extracted his rucksack before removing the Glamdon jacket he was wearing and tossing it into the van. From his pocket he took a small grey device that looked like a TV remote control and clicked a button. There was a feint hum as the device contained in the small crate activated and an audible beep as he set the controls to 'arm'. Slamming the door he picked up his rucksack and made his way out of the yard and across the cobbles towards Covent Garden at a half trot and into the back of a waiting black cab.

=

Inside the gallery Frank was talking to Sir Anthony when his mobile rang. "Yes mate?" The unmistakable deep Glasgow voice of Taggart boomed out of the speaker. "Frank it looks like this job here was our man." Frank turned the phone so Baxter could hear the exchange. "There are two dead security guards and one of Glamdon's vehicles is missing. Robin also says the comms system has been tampered with." Frank interrupted him before he could go on. "What comms system?"

Taggart quickly explained the basics of the system that Glamdon was using and how it operated on the secure cab net. "So Frank." He continued. "The vehicle he has taken can effectively control any items delivered by Robin's company by small electronic tabs attached to each item. It is how they can offer a faster service than their rivals." Frank turned to Baxter and told him to clear the building and get his officers to check the statues for tabs, but Taggart cut him off. "It isn't the statues Frank. Glamdon didn't install them on those items as he supervised the delivery himself. Anyway the ordnance team would have picked anything up when they checked the statues."

Keeping the call open to Taggart, Frank called Si on the secure radio and brought him up to speed. One of Baxter's SB men came through from the rear of the gallery, avoiding the surging crowd as they made for the door despite Roger Biddle's protestations. Alongside him was one of the uniformed security men that Biddle had employed. The SB officer spoke directly to Frank. "This guy admitted a Glamdon van to the loading yard about fifteen minutes ago Frank. He says the driver has now disappeared."

Frank turned and ran to the rear of the building while talking into his radio. "Si, get over here now." He switched to the mobile in his other hand and spoke sharply to Taggart. "Is there anything else missing from Glamdon's?" Sirens could now be heard in the area as the response teams, alerted by Baxter, started to converge on the gallery. Si Radford burst through the back of the yard with two of his team, all out of breath from the short run from their van.

"Frank, I can't block the cab Intranet."Si gasped as he arrived at the now open van door. "I don't have the access codes and it will take too long to smash them electronically and the shield won't work without those codes."

Frank turned back to his call to Taggart. "Ask Glamdon for the codes." The reply was quick.

"I have, Glamdon says the flash drive that Gregorio used to gain access has now corrupted the codes."

The gallery was now empty apart from Roger Biddle and his mother. Two Special Branch officers were attempting to move them outside to a waiting car. A road block had been hastily erected on The Strand, London was used to emergencies, and uniformed Police officers were ushering the crowds down into basements below the adjoining buildings. Frank emerged into the street in an attempt to locate Sir Anthony who was trying to bring some kind of structure back to the chaos. He quickly handed the operation back to Gold Command at Scotland Yard, they would coordinate the greater evacuation while he, as the highest rank on the ground, attempted to deal with the immediate threat.

Frank spotted the Commander on the edge of the square but before he could reach him Si Radford joined him. "Frank, our only option is to get the cab net turned off. I have requested it through the borough but I'm not sure how urgently they are treating it." Before either of them could continue one of the Special Branch guys who had been with the Biddle's appeared. "Could you not turn it off yourself?" He spoke directly to Si.

"I could but the server hub is in Uxbridge." The officer nodded but continued.

"Yes, but there is a repeater station for this area at the back of one of the platforms at Covent Garden tube station. I was assigned to guard it during its installation as a PC." Baxter had now joined them and overheard the last part of the conversation.

"We need to do something Frank. This thing may not have long to run." The four of them turned and headed north across the cobbled square, Baxter started shouting commands into his radio as they broke into a jog and Frank re-started the conversation with Taggart.

"Baxter's SB guys are on the way to you. Tell Glamdon to give them anything they ask for. Take the car and go mobile, I might need you somewhere quickly."

As they arrived at the tube station entrance Frank stopped to call Samantha before they descended. Covent Garden was one of the deepest stations on the network and he knew he would have no signal at platform level. The call took several seconds to connect and it was obvious Samantha was talking hands-free when she replied. "Hi Frank. I am with Avril on our way back to STAG."Frank brought them both up to speed on developments at the gallery.

"Stay mobile in case I need you." He killed the call and followed the trio down into the depths. I hope to hell you known how to turn this thing off Si, he thought as he took the steps four at a time.

=

Gregorio sat with his laptop on his knees as the cab negotiated the traffic on the outer reaches of Hammersmith as they headed towards the motorway. The signal from the secure cab net was strong here due to the high-rise buildings and the high number of aerials required as a result. He tapped the icon that blinked on the screen and typed in two short codes as a prompt box opened. He hit the send button and allowed himself a brief inner smile as the screen reported 'Command Accepted', in large Cyrillic text, and turned a bright green colour. Nothing could stop that command now it was on its way to the device in the back of Glamdon's van parked at the gallery. The secure cab system would ensure nothing could stop the signal getting through. Even Si Radford could not stop it now.

As the driver slowed the cab in the traffic as it approached the Hammersmith flyover Gregorio started to cough and tapped the drivers screen for attention. "Could you please pull over for a minute, I feel unwell." The driver, concerned that the Russian was about to throw up in his cab pulled over to the kerb as they entered the roundabout under the motorway. Gregorio climbed from the rear seat and doubled over at the roadside gasping for air as though he was about to be sick. He hated having too use a non-network driver but it was one element he had been unable to arrange. As the concerned driver approached him he pulled his silenced weapon from his jacket and fired two aimed shots into his temple, knocking him back against the cab and covering the side window in a crimson spray.

Gregorio dragged the body off the cab and dumped it heavily into the overgrowing bushes at the side of the road. He slid into the driver's seat and pulled away sharply into the oncoming traffic amid a cacophony of vehicle horns and raised shouts from the busy roundabout. Jumping the red light at the exit of the roundabout he pointed the cab towards the motorway and joined the taxi lane on the M4 with his foot flat to the floor.

The traffic was heavy in the two inside lanes but much lighter in the steady stream of black cabs and chauffeur driven vehicles in the taxi lane and Gregorio made swift progress away from the flyover. He glanced at his wrist watch as he headed West. His plan was working and he was on schedule. By now the device would have detonated and sent the centre of London into a frenzy. The blast was designed to cause complete devastation to all buildings within two square miles, battlefield specific, and the fallout would inflict further destruction much wider. Every cop in Greater London would now be heading towards the scene of the blast, no one was going to investigate a shooting at the roadside for a long time.

In the middle lane of the M4 heading back towards Heathrow the driver of the shabby and run down looking Ford noticed the large smear of red liquid on the black cab as it passed in the outside lane. To the untrained eye it would have appeared as a paint mark, but to the driver who was a highly trained observer it started to become interesting. He had just received a call from his control at Heathrow to look out for anything suspicious on his ride back and this was very definitely suspicious. Waiting for two more black cabs to pass him he manoeuvred out into the taxi lane. The smear on the window and door of the cab had looked very much like blood and had it been any other substance he was sure the driver would have cleaned the cab immediately. No self respecting London cab driver would drive a vehicle that was not in pristine condition at all times.

As he followed the cabs Westward the diver switched the in-car Police radio to the traffic channels. Almost immediately he picked up reports of a shooting under the Hammersmith flyover and the possible involvement of a black London taxi. Ignoring the Police traffic he called his sighting into his control, they would inform the Police if deemed necessary. He was told to follow but not intercept, the job he was paid to do.

=

In Central London Frank and Sir Anthony climbed into the back of a waiting Special Branch car and it immediately pulled away towards a now deserted Leicester Square. Behind two black Range Rovers each containing four black clad figures, Sir Anthony's tactical SB team, pulled into convoy behind it. Frank was satisfied that Si had disabled the cab signal system and had left him and his team dealing with the device that sat in the van at the gallery. Covent Garden, The Strand and the surrounding area was now in the hands of armed Police units and the public were being escorted to designated safe areas.

On emerging from the Underground station Frank had received a call from Samantha informing her of the possible sighting of Gregorio on the M4. The driver of the Diplomatic surveillance vehicle had called Avril on her mobile to report his suspicious observation, she was still nominally his boss and highly respected by the Diplo teams. They were now en-route to Heathrow as it seemed the only logical place he could be making for. What Frank could not fathom was how Gregorio thought he would get through the heavily Policed airport, even if he resorted to disguise. Baxter had immediately deployed two units of his Counter Terrorism Command to supplement the armed units already at the airport and tasked the Met traffic teams to broadcast an 'all ports' to its drivers. The SF teams had already been summoned and were on their way to Heathrow by helicopter. MI5 had alerted its watching teams and they were already in contact with the following Diplo driver, the net was closing.

As their car sped West, both Frank and Sir Anthony were busy coordinating the response of their respective assets. Taggart was closing fast behind the black cab as it made its way towards the M25 junction and Heathrow, and Frank's hardest job was trying to keep the communications to a minimum from all the interested parties. As they joined the M4, passing the Police vehicles responding to the shooting at the flyover, Baxter told the driver to put his foot down. Traffic had been diverted down the A40 and prevented from joining the motorway, giving the small convoy a clear run. As they accelerated down the middle lane Frank's mobile alerted him to an incoming call from Taggart. "Frank, its not Heathrow." The call faded and then boomed as the signal strength ebbed and flowed. "He has turned up the M25 Northbound." The call cut off abruptly.

"Where the fuck can he be going?" Frank enquired of Baxter. "The only airfield that way is Northolt and he won't be getting in there, the RAF will stop him." The SB passenger in the front of the vehicle turned towards them.

"If he turns back down the A40 he can get to Elstree. They fly private charters out of there."

=

Gregorio steered the cab through the entrance of the private airfield. Along the fence line stood a number of small turbo prop aircraft used for flying lessons. In front of him as he drove down the narrow road was a large hanger and a number of smaller buildings. The airfield was deserted apart from a number of small aircraft parked near to the hanger. In the distance he could see a single engined aircraft attempting to land at the far end of the runway, and a couple of overalled figures working on the engine of an aircraft in the hanger doorway. He brought the cab to a stop at the grass edge of the taxiway and climbed from the front seat, reaching back to claim his rucksack.

The noise of a racing engine alerted him and he turned his head to see a fast approaching car as it sped through the entrance. The battered Ford sped towards him and he could see the only occupant in the front seat waving his arm at him through the opened window. He moved to the front of the cab, pulled a folding stock rifle from the rucksack and slammed on a magazine. As the car came towards him he dropped to one knee at the side of the car, pulled the stock of the rifle into his shoulder and loosed off a pair of aimed shots. Both shots impacted on the front of the car shattering the windscreen, he fired again and two further rounds hit the car sending it veering towards the first of the parked aircraft.

Alerted by the sounds of the gunshots the two overalled figures working on the aircraft dropped from the wing and turned towards him. He fired off two more shots that had them scurrying for cover behind the heavy hanger doors. Gripping the rifle he made his way across the grass fringe of the taxiway just as the sound of a jet engine could be heard from the far end of the airfield. Gregorio watched as the Gulfstream G550 private jet cleared the threshold and gently touched down on the runway. He watched it as it slowed and then turn back to face towards him. The sound of the approaching convoy of Police vehicles had been drowned in the jet wash as it had passed him but he was now aware of shouted warnings from behind.

The lead SB car entered the airfield and turned to come to a stand just short of the first of the small buildings. Frank and Sir Anthony climbed from the car as the two Range Rovers turned in opposite directions and headed in a wide arc to take up positions on the taxiway. The Gulfstream had taxied back down the runway and was now stationary about two hundred metres away on the far side of the wide expanse of tarmac. Gregorio could be seen making his way across to the aircraft steps that had now been lowered. At the foot of the steps crouched two figures aiming what from that distance looked like automatic assault weapons towards the car. A third figure stood in the doorway with an RPG pulled into his shoulder. As Frank and Baxter exited the vehicle the two automatic weapons opened up in their direction making them both hit the ground and roll away from the front wheels as the driver spun the car into reverse. Rounds chewed up the ground in front of them and they both crawled then ran the few metres to take cover near the buildings.

As Frank reached the cover of the first small building he heard an explosion to his right and looked up to see one of the Range Rovers erupt in a ball of bright orange flame as an RPG round impacted. Out near the Gulfstream Gregorio was about a hundred metres from reaching the steps but he seemed to stumble and go down on one knee. The figures from the second Range Rover had started returning fire and were now fanned out on the edge of the runway and their sustained fire was starting to cause damage. The figure holding the RPG seemed to bend at the waist and then crumple down the steps as round after round slammed into him. Gregorio attempted to drag himself to an upright position but one of the SB men had a bead on him and he had to dive back to the ground as the rounds sought him out.

Alerted by a vehicle engine and a shout from his rear Frank stood, shielded by the brickwork of the building, and accepted the Heckler and Koch MP5 offered from Taggart's outstretched hand as he pulled his vehicle in close. He turned to talk to Sir Anthony but had to duck back in to cover as fresh rounds arced towards him and Taggart's car. As the incoming fire ceased he turned back to find Sir Anthony laying spread eagled on the grass with a large wound to his chest. He rolled across the grass to his side but he could see from the size of the wound and the spread of fresh blood there was nothing he could do for him.

Ahead of him the remains of the first Range Rover still burned and there appeared to be no sign of life from that vicinity. Two more figures had emerged from the aircraft and were contributing to the heavy barrage now attempting to suppress the fire coming from the second SB group. Gregorio had managed to raise himself again and was limping towards the steps until another fusillade of hot rounds sent him back to the ground. Taggart appeared at his side tapped him on the shoulder and pointed towards the smouldering remains in front of them. "If we can get behind that lot we can draw their fire and the SB boys will be more effective." He set off at a low scamper, firing from the shoulder as he ran, and Frank quickly joined him, pulling the MP5 into his shoulder. Together they covered the short distance to the vehicle and took up positions in the scrub grass a short way to its rear, shielded from view by its still burning carcass. Taggart pointed to the far side of the runway and then took off at a crouched sprint as Frank covered him from his position. The MP5 felt like an old friend in his hands as he fired short, aimed bursts towards the aircraft steps. The figure furthest from the aircraft buckled and fell backwards as Frank's tight grouping slammed into his torso. In front of Frank, the firefight to the left was beginning to go in the favour of the SB guys as two more figures dropped at the steps. Taggart was now lying in the middle of the runway pumping round after round back towards the crouching figures.

As Gregorio attempted to close on the steps the Gulfstream started to move forward, the steps were pulled up and the door closed. The one remaining shooter on the tarmac dropped his weapon and raised his hands but Gregorio immediately shot him in the chest. As the figure fell forward Gregorio dropped his rifle and pulled the bigger calibre weapon from the fallen man's hand. He then turned towards Frank as he raised himself from the grass and started aiming rounds back towards him. Frank pulled back into cover behind the now smouldering vehicle, checked the magazine and rolled back out into the open with the weapon firmly in his shoulder. Gregorio raised the assault rifle but before he could loose off a shot Frank squeezed the trigger on the MP5 and put two well aimed rounds into the Russian's forehead. Gregorio's eyes bulged as the shots took the back of his head away and he dropped on to his face.

From the far end of the runway the Gulfstream's engines could be heard screaming as they searched for the lift that would take the jet beyond the perimeter of the airfield. When it seemed as though their cries would be in vain the fleeing aircraft managed to claw itself into the air and turn away into the wispy low running cloud. As the sound of the jet faded the bellowing sounds of sirens could be heard in the distance as the cavalry in the form of the SF teams raced to the scene. Sorry boys, Frank thought, we don't need you this time.

The whole exchange had taken no more than five minutes but the airfield was now littered with the carnage of the firefight. Frank made his way slowly to the middle of the runway where the Police Tactical Teams were now securing the scene. A number of ambulances were arriving and paramedics were attempting to deal with the casualties. Only one of the attackers remained alive and he was being guarded by two heavily armed Police officers. Away to his right a team of Police and Paramedics were searching the wreckage of the SB Range Rover for survivors, but sadly there were none. At the edge of the taxiway another team were attending to Sir Anthony but Frank knew their efforts would be in vain.

As he approached Gregorio's inert body Taggart joined him and showed him his mobile. "Si has just reported from Covent Garden Frank." He flipped the message on to the screen. "The device in the back of Glamdon's van was very definitely a battlefield nuke." Frank took the phone from him. "It would have taken out half of London then." He looked down at the prone and lifeless figure of the Russian.

"He almost got his family revenge on us all then." As he finished speaking he turned to watch a black BMW make its way across the runway and come to a halt fifty metres away. The director of STAG left the rear of the vehicle and walked the short distance to stand next to Taggart and Frank.

"The Prime Minister has called an urgent COBRA meeting Frank. I think we had all better be there." He turned to look at Gregorio's dead form and then turned back to address them both. "Now we need to find out who was actually behind all this." He started to walk back to the car, stopped and turned back. "But well done."

=

The COBRA meeting lasted a very short forty five minutes and did nothing more than confirm that another lethal attack on London had been thwarted. The City was getting used to clearing up after terrorist action and it was nothing more than going through the motions, the investigation as to motive and authorisation would take much longer. The Chief Constable of the Metropolitan Police had closed the meeting with a sombre tribute to the five officers, including Sir Anthony Baxter, that had perished in the action at the airfield. The Prime Minister had thanked every one for their swift responses and then left to brief the waiting press.

Frank had sat next to the director of STAG throughout the meeting and had made very little contribution other than to brief in an update on the state of the device at the gallery. Part way through the meeting the MI5 representative, Paul Whittle, had been called away by an urgent call telling him that the Gulfstream had been intercepted by two RAF Typhoon jets and had made a forced landing at Stansted Airport. There was now an ongoing operation at the airport to apprehend the remaining occupants of the aircraft. MI5 had assumed control of any follow up investigation and Frank was happy to leave Whittle to bask in the glory.

As the meeting broke up Frank was joined by Taggart, who had taken up his customary seat at the back of the meeting, and they walked back to the STAG office. They walked in silence through St James' Park, stopping to pick up coffee for the team that had now all reconvened. Taggart broke the silence as they climbed the stairs. "I'm getting too old for this boss." Frank paused and turned to face him.

"I think you might be right. Maybe it's time to let someone else chase the bad guys."

EIGHTEEN

Frank Martin leaned back against the first class seat and took a sip of his coffee. The new inter-city train bringing him back from the West Country was certainly a big improvement on the trains he had used as a young serviceman. He could remember vividly the late night journeys back to camp in the cramped, cold and smelly coaches. Public transport was obviously heading in the right direction at last.

The six months that had passed since the thwarted attack on London had been both frenetic and revealing in a number of different ways. The days in the immediate aftermath had been filled with meetings at the highest level as STAG, and the intelligence community in general, tried to unravel the whole Yorkie and Gregorio affair. Si Radford had accompanied Frank the week following the attack to the USA for discussions with the American agencies. Si had spent three days with the geeks at the National Security Agency, better known as NSA, investigating the finer details of the trigger mechanism. Frank had toured the offices of the CIA and Homeland Defence gathering every disparate detail of worldwide trading of the pair under various guises.

Back in London, along with Samantha and her team, Frank had dug further into the disappearance of Yorkie all those years ago and his recent reappearance. A contact of Samantha's in the FCO had introduced them to a Russian diplomat who was more than willing to spill the beans on what he felt was a dark period of his countries history. One of the rare Western leaning few still remaining, he helped them piece together what Frank believed was now the true story about his old friend.

It had indeed been true that Yorkie's mother had conducted a very brief affair with a low level KGB operator, but Mrs Biddle had not been very good with her dates it would appear. Although she had been somewhat indiscreet the father of Yorkie was very much the man that had brought him up. DNA samples taken from Yorkie following his demise in Skegness had revealed that all along he was the son of Mr and Mrs Biddle. Unfortunately following Yorkie's flight to Russia the KGB had exploited the brief liaison between their resident and Mrs Biddle and created a whole new persona and ancestry for him. Even after the collapse of the Soviet machine he had continued to be manipulated and used. Gregorio had come on to the scene and very quickly established there was a connection between his own late father and that of Yorkie.

Once Gregorio had learned that Yorkie had technical skills that could enrich both his wealth and his standing in the torrid world he lived in he manipulated him even more. Frank took another sip of his coffee. If there was one thing that the Yorkie he knew had as a weakness it was his innate trust in people and this had been ruthlessly exploited by Gregorio. The Russian was a twisted, evil psychopath as evidenced by the number of bodies he had left around

London. He was also a twisted sexual predator and he had used Yorkie's proclivities in that area to his full advantage. The more Yorkie thought he was being loved the more Gregorio played on his emotions and drove him to greater technical achievements that would further his own twisted and perverted ideology.

Frank turned to look out of the window as the train sped through the green countryside. He and Samantha had made a trip up to Yorkshire to give the news to Yorkie's mother that, after all, he really was the natural son of her husband. There was no way of disguising the fact that he had been a traitor to his country, but at least she had the comfort of knowing that he had not been Russian after all. This trip that he was now returning from was, though, one he had to make alone.

One morning during the madness of digging into the past of his old pal, Frank had received an email from a high ranking Army officer at the Ministry of Defence. General Peter Mills was in fact the son of Frank's troop commander in the South Atlantic. Frank remembered that Mills had had a son who would have been about ten years old when his father had been killed. He had joined the Parachute Regiment in honour of his father and had risen to Command rank. In recent years the General had been researching his father's military career and now at a level where he could have influence he had been investigating the circumstances of how his father had died.

The email had invited Frank to the family home in the west country and to visit the grave of his old CO in the village churchyard. Frank had, at first, been reluctant to accept the invitation but, with persuasion from Samantha, Si and Taggart, he had made the trip. The General had been appalled by what he had discovered, the 'cover up' as he called it, and the fact that no recognition had ever been made of the efforts of the troop. He had told Frank that he had now raised it at ministerial level and he was hopeful recognition would be forthcoming, even after all this time.

He had told Frank that he believed there had been a cover up by some of the senior officers involved in their patrol's deployment. The repeated requests Frank had made for permission to engage the enemy that morning had never been passed on to the commanders on the island. Some perverse territorial pride and obstinate assumed superiority by the SAS hierarchy had resulted in the real intelligence picture unfolding before them had never been relayed to the people who really needed it.

Once the realisation had emerged that their actions may have contributed not only to the loss of his father but to the carnage that Frank and the rest had witnessed, a number had colluded in a false report that had put the blame squarely on to Mills. The report had also rubbished the contribution played by the patrol and had denied that any calls had ever been made from the hillside.

Frank took a last sip from his cup and looked again from the window. He felt that despite everything that had happened in the last year some of the things that he had locked away really did deserve to be remembered. Standing next to the grave in the churchyard and listening to the General tell him that he really had done his best that morning and maybe it was time to let them go.

He placed the cup back on the table, closed his eyes and let the smooth, gentle motion of the train assist him as he drifted into a contented sleep.

Printed in Great Britain
by Amazon